Weave Me a Rope

A Twist Upon a Regency Tale
Book 5

By Jude Knight

© Copyright 2024 by Jude Knight
Text by Jude Knight
Cover by Kim Killion Designs

Dragonblade Publishing, Inc. is an imprint of Kathryn Le Veque Novels, Inc.
P.O. Box 23
Moreno Valley, CA 92556
ceo@dragonbladepublishing.com

Produced in the United States of America

First Edition January 2024
Trade Paperback Edition

Reproduction of any kind except where it pertains to short quotes in relation to advertising or promotion is strictly prohibited.

All Rights Reserved.

The characters and events portrayed in this book are fictitious. Any similarity to real persons, living or dead, is purely coincidental and not intended by the author.

ARE YOU SIGNED UP FOR DRAGONBLADE'S BLOG?

You'll get the latest news and information on exclusive giveaways, exclusive excerpts, coming releases, sales, free books, cover reveals and more.

Check out our complete list of authors, too!

No spam, no junk. That's a promise!

Sign Up Here
www.dragonbladepublishing.com

Dearest Reader;

Thank you for your support of a small press. At Dragonblade Publishing, we strive to bring you the highest quality Historical Romance from some of the best authors in the business. Without your support, there is no 'us', so we sincerely hope you adore these stories and find some new favorite authors along the way.

Happy Reading!

CEO, Dragonblade Publishing

ADDITIONAL DRAGONBLADE BOOKS BY AUTHOR JUDE KNIGHT

A Twist Upon a Regency Tale, The Series
Lady Beast's Bridegroom (Book 1)
One Perfect Dance (Book 2)
Snowy and the Seven Doves (Book 3)
Perchance to Dream (Book 4)
Weave Me a Rope (Book 5)

The Lyon's Den Series
The Talons of a Lyon

ABOUT THE BOOK

When the Earl of Spenhurst declares his love for a merchant's niece, he is locked away in a tower. Spen won't get out, the marquess his father says, until he agrees to an arranged marriage.

After the marquess unceremoniously ejects Cordelia Milton from his country mansion, she is determined to rescue her beloved, but it all goes horribly wrong.

She needs time to recover from her injuries, and Spen has been moved across the country under heavy guard. It seems impossible for two young lovers to overcome the selfish plans of two powerful peers, but they won't give up.

Dedication

To the readers who loved Cordelia and Deerhaven in the first four books of A Twist Upon a Regency Tale and asked for their love story. Here it is.

Chapter One

A London garden, March 1802

THE LAMPS STRUNG through the garden cast pools of light that made the shadows even darker. Perfect cover for a beleaguered gentleman escaping the zealous marriage hunters who turned every entertainment into a labyrinth of mantraps.

The young man currently hiding in one particularly remote corner was a prime quarry for this Season. His father, the Marquess of Deerhaven, had made it known he wanted his heir married and breeding. Those hungry for a title were in a frenzy.

Paul Ambrose George Bedevere Forsythe, Earl of Spenhurst, had not yet reached his twenty-first birthday and had hoped to delay choosing a bride for another decade. Spen's observations of his father's three marriages had not endeared the institution to him. But the marquess had spoken and it was for his son to obey.

He wouldn't mind if he could find a wife he liked. Spen had seen marriages where the couple were friends and were faithful to one another. Spen wanted one of those, and a town chit just would not do.

His father dismissed his concerns as irrelevant. A man, he said, put babies in his wife's belly and took his pleasure elsewhere. Spen had seen how unhappy such a marriage had made his mother and his stepmothers. He could not bear the idea of being responsible for such misery.

Half the crop of females his aunt paraded in front of him left him cold, and the other half struck horror in his heart. Was that to be his fate? Married to an insipid female with nothing to recommend her beyond her bloodlines, or to one with a bit of gumption and a vicious character? Either choice was unacceptable.

The first group would lie down and let him walk all over them. Any one of them would bore him to tears inside of a week. The second would expect to walk all over him. They would go looking for a lover as soon as they were bored with him, which he didn't expect to take much longer than a week, for he had nothing much beyond his title to offer them. Or so his father had always given him to understand, and the diamonds of the ton certainly seemed to agree.

He was not much of a conversationalist, at least when it came to the flattery and trivial chatter that passed as conversation in the circles these ladies adored. Spen would far rather discuss wool yields, the Corn Laws, the ambitions of General Napoleon and what they might mean to England or even some of the subjects he had read at Oxford. Ancient Greek culture, perhaps. Or natural philosophy. Both had intrigued him and still did.

Spen liked some things about town living—the theatre, the museums, the lectures. But most of it left him cold.

He knew little about fashion. He couldn't care less what the knot in his cravat was called and knew nothing about what colors were fashionable, or what many of them were named. He left his own clothing decisions to his valet, who enjoyed turning Spen out to be, as the valet put it, a credit to his skills.

He hated gossip and scandal, which always struck him as cruel torment, and he could not see the point of the social maneuvering that named some diamonds and others wallflowers, some nonpareils, and others gudgeons.

All this meant most town entertainments bored him. Or

worse. Large numbers of strangers or mere acquaintances, all squashed into a small drawing room or ballroom, anxious to speak to him because he was the son of a marquess, made it hard for him to breathe. His head swam and his heart thumped in his chest.

He feared a repeat of the condition he had suffered when he was first sent away to school, shortly after his mother died. In his first six months at Eton, he had fainted eleven times when his chest stiffened, and his lungs refused to work.

Panaphobia Hysterica, the doctor had called his condition in the hearing of one of the servants. Panic terror caused by vapors. The servant had passed the diagnosis on to certain of the pupils. His years at school had been blighted by jeers and jokes about his delicate nature, though the persecution never turned physical again after an attack landed him in the infirmary with a broken leg and his father turned up at the school breathing fire at the risk to his heir and the assault to the marquess's own dignity.

As he pushed the memories away and concentrated on slowing his breathing, the clamoring in his mind slowly silenced enough for the noises of the night to register. Close at hand, water tinkled—that would be the fountain. Foliage stirred—the wind, perhaps, or the movement of man or beast. The whispering and giggles that reached his ears suggested the latter.

From beyond the garden, the sounds of the city penetrated, muted in this area of town and at this time of night, but still, people shouted, dogs barked, horses clopped, and wheels rumbled.

Even this far away from the house, the sound of the ball dominated. Not just the orchestra, but the buzz of hundreds of voices plus the occasional crash or bang, betokening clumsiness on someone's part.

He would have to go back in. But not yet. He sat on a stone seat in the shadow of a tree. When the orchestra took a break, he would take that as his signal to return.

They were still playing when a girl stepped into the paved

area around a fountain that lay beyond the edges of his shadow. By her white dress, he knew she was a debutante, slender and of medium height. He couldn't tell her hair color in the indifferent light, but it must be fair, for it looked almost white.

Astoundingly, she was alone. She sat on the edge of the fountain bowl and stretched out her fingers, so the water fell on them. She giggled, then lifted her face to the sky.

She didn't behave like a particularly audacious hunter, but why else would she be out here alone? Pretty girls of his class were never allowed to go into dark places without their dragon protectors. A mother or chaperone was probably waiting in the wings ready to pounce on anyone foolish enough to accost the damsel.

He did not see how he could be her prey, for no one knew he was here. Still, to be on the safe side, he should withdraw through the bushes, as silently as possible, trusting the sound of the water to disguise his passage.

Before he could move, though, three more ladies hurried through the trees to join the first. "Here she is," one called over her shoulder to the other two. She advanced on the first damsel, coming into a circle of light cast by one of the lamps. Spen tensed when he saw her cruel smile. He had been the target of such a smile many times until he learned how to fight back with fists and words.

He also knew the three ladies, by sight at least. Mainly because his aunt, whose ball this was, had pointed them out and warned him to avoid them. The leader was Miss Wharton, and with her, of course, were her two friends and supporters, Miss Fairchild, and Miss Plumfield. They were seldom apart and had a reputation for cruel tongues and sly tricks. His aunt thought them willing to use any means to trap a husband.

"I have to invite them, Spenhurst," she told him. "For I promised Miss Fairchild's aunt. However, you would be a far better husband than any of them could hope to win on their own merits," she had told him. "Be very careful."

Spen hoped the first girl was able to stick up for herself, for if he had to intervene, those three would be sure to make a scandal out of the pair of them being discovered together. Or perhaps just threaten it to pressure him into showing one or more of them some sign of favor.

Miss Wharton cooed, "Whatever are you doing, Lady Daffy?"

The lady she had addressed, who surely could not really be named *Daffy*, smiled in answer, though her gaze did not leave the fountain. "The water is so pretty. Look how it sparkles."

"No one cares about the water, you idiot," Miss Fairchild jeered. "You have got your glove wet. Look, ladies, Daffy's glove is all ruined. She hasn't even enough sense to take it off before she puts her hand in water."

"Such a fool," sneered Miss Wharton, and Miss Plumfield snickered.

The lady they addressed as Daffy looked bewildered.

"You want water?" asked Miss Wharton.

It took Spen a split second to realize what she was about to do. Before he could react, it was too late. Miss Wharton had given Lady Daffy a shove, toppling her off the edge. The poor lady shrieked as she fell sideways into the pool of the fountain.

As the three tormentors roared with laughter, Spen worked his way through the shrubbery until he could step onto the path behind them, saying, "What is going on here?"

Someone pushed past him and hurried to the side of the fountain, holding out her hands to the lady in the pool. "Lady Daphne! Here. Let me help you." In the half-light, he could not tell her hair or eye color, but he could see that she was lovely. Not fashionably slender, like a half-starved boy. But curved in all the right places, and most pleasing to the eye and less decorous parts of his anatomy.

"You are not needed here, mill girl," sneered Miss Wharton.

The newcomer ignored her, helping Lady Daphne to stand and clamber over the pool edge and onto the paving, where she wrapped the poor girl in a quick hug, ignoring the dripping gown.

"There now, Lady Daphne," she crooned. "You are safe now."

Spen removed his coat and offered it to the unnamed lady, who said a distracted thank you, all her attention on Lady Daphne. She wrapped the coat around Lady Daphne, ignoring her own wet dress. Together like this, the two ladies were much of a height, and similar in their coloring, except that Lady Daphne's hair was almost white and her eyes a blue so pale as to be nearly silver, whereas the unnamed lady was more vivid in every way.

He could not be certain until he saw her in a better light, but he was prepared to bet her hair would be a golden blond and her eyes that kind of blue that begged comparison to the sky. The vividness extended to her expression, which had all the intelligence and humor missing from the first girl's.

"I have an ouchie," Lady Daphne announced, holding up her hand for the other to inspect.

The new lady cradled it gently. "Poor little hand. Did you scrape it when you fell in?"

Lady Daphne untangled her other arm to point at Miss Wharton. "She pushed Daphne. Daphne has an ouchie."

Miss Wharton blatantly lied. "I never did. She was sitting on the edge, and she lost her balance. You cannot believe a word she says. Everyone knows she is a moon baby."

"You pushed her," Spen said. He didn't raise his voice, but he had been taught to speak with authority since he was able to toddle. The ladies turned towards him.

Miss Wharton sneered. It seemed to be her preferred expression. "I did nothing of the sort. Did I, girls?"

Miss Plumfield echoed her leader. "Of course not, Miss Wharton."

Miss Fairchild, on the other hand, frowned and said nothing.

Spen was still seething at the sheer meanness of the three of them, but the most important thing was to look after Lady Daphne. "If you come with me, Miss," he said to the unidentified angel of mercy who had come to the wet lady's aid, "I will show you a way into the house without attracting attention."

He couldn't just let the three nasties off without putting a little fear into them. "As for the three of you, make your excuses and go home. As soon as I have seen Lady Daphne inside, I shall be speaking to our hostess about having you sent home. The way you picked on Lady Daphne was despicable."

"I will have you know," Miss Wharton declared, "I was invited to this ball by Lady Corven herself. I am staying until I have been introduced to Lord Spenhurst, Lady Corven's nephew. Furthermore…"

She broke off when Miss Fairchild tugged at her arm, and whispered, loudly enough for Spen to hear, "Eloise, I believe this man *is* Lord Spenhurst."

Miss Wharton's mouth dropped open and Miss Plumfield whimpered.

Spen's angel of mercy, her arm around Lady Daphne, had given the three a wide berth and was on her way down the path back towards the house.

"You are correct, Miss Fairchild. I advise the three of you to be gone before I speak with my aunt. Miss Fairchild, Miss Plumfield. Miss Wharton." Leaving them to worry about the fact he knew their names as well as their faces, he hurried after the unknown angel and the damp damsel.

The pair had turned the corner onto the main path back to the house and had been met by an older lady, who was fussing over them both. The mother or chaperone of either the angel or Lady Daphne, he supposed.

"…fell into the pool," the angel was saying. "Lord Spenhurst is going to find us a quiet way into the house." She noticed him coming out of the hidden corner. "Aunt Eliza, this is Lord Spenhurst. My lord, my aunt, Mrs. Walters."

Mrs. Walters bobbed a curtsey, but otherwise showed little interest in Spen, being more concerned about the fact Lady Daphne was dripping so much she stood in a little pool of her own, and that the angel's gown was damp, clinging to her form, and nearly transparent down one side.

Spen was having trouble keeping his eyes from devouring the curves so displayed and was grateful when Mrs. Walters pulled off her own shawl and wrapped it around her niece. "Oh dear, Cordelia, you shall both catch your death of cold!"

The angel had a name. *Cordelia.* It was as lovely as she was. Unexpected and strong. Pretty, too. Cordelia raised her eyebrows at his searching look. "Come along, Lord Spenhurst. Get us safely to a place where we can dry Lady Daphne off, and then, if you would be so kind, I will send you to find Miss Faversham, Lady Daphne's companion."

His father the marquess would never stand for being sent off on an errand like a footman. Spen found it rather endearing. His angel of mercy was certainly not going to lie down and let him— or anyone else—walk all over her.

>>><<<

For Cordelia Milton and her aunt, the evening was finished. Aunt Eliza was inclined to grieve over their early departure, but relief was Cordelia's main emotion as she sat in their carriage considering the events of another evening foray into the black heart of London society.

Aunt Eliza had been delighted with the invitation to Lady Corven's ball, but it was clear from the first moment they saw their hostess that Cordelia's uncle had pulled strings to get them there. Uncle Josh was known not only for his wealth but also for his relentless search for information and other ways of gaining advantage. He was willing to use these ruthlessly, both in business and in seeing his brother's child established. It did not make her welcome. Lady Corven's demeanor said as clearly as words that she might be forced to have the merchant's niece and his sister in her house, but she did not have to like it.

Cordelia was used to the contempt of those who considered

their pristine family trees made them more worthy than an upstart merchant and his niece, however overeducated for her class she might be.

Uncle Josh had promised his mother on her deathbed that her granddaughter would marry into the gentry. Gran Milton had begun with a barrow in the square of a market town in Kent and worked tirelessly to establish a small chain of haberdasheries, which in turn became the foundation for Uncle Josh's commercial empire.

Gran had wed her own daughter to a country gentleman. He and Aunt Eliza had never had children, but Aunt Eliza had fond memories of Mr. Walters. When she was widowed, though her husband had made sure to provide well for her after his death, she returned to live with Uncle Joshua because he and Gran were raising their deceased brother's daughter, and Gran was getting old.

Gran was proud of Aunt Eliza's match, but she wanted even better for Cordelia.

Fortunately, Gran had also made Uncle Josh promise her only grandchild could choose her own husband. So far, Cordelia had not met anyone with whom she could bear to spend the rest of her life. Some of the ladies and gentlemen she met were not unpleasant. Perhaps some of them were even nice. Even so, Cordelia was inclined to think they were civil to her because her uncle could buy and sell them, and they knew it.

As much as she did not wish to disappoint Uncle Josh, marriage was for life. Her life. Cordelia was skeptical about the benefits of a love match, having seen marriages fade. But at the very least, she wanted to respect her husband and have his respect in return.

This evening, she had escaped to the garden from the heat of the ballroom—both the oppressive warmth of too many bodies in too small a space and the emotional scalding administered by many of the other guests. The retreat had been a response to one arrogant man who had announced, without preamble, that he was willing to marry her, for he could always refuse to acknowledge her uncle, and her own flaws were not bad enough to outweigh the size of her dowry.

No doubt she would find it funny in the morning.

She thanked him for his condescension and told him her answer was no, and then left while he was still gaping. The other option had been to take some action that would upset her hostess and embarrass her dear but ineffectual chaperone. Such as tipping her ratafia (that ghastly liquid) down the ornate waistcoat of the prat.

Cordelia had intended a short stroll, and then a dive back into the fray. She and her aunt had been enjoying the cool breeze and the night scents of the garden when they had heard the hateful tones of her most ardent persecutor in full torment mode, followed by a scream and then a splash.

She had known Miss Wharton was at the center of whatever happened before she recognized that the person sitting sobbing in the pool was Lady Daphne Ashburton. She was a sweet person with the body of a woman and the understanding of a child—a little timorous mouse to Miss Wharton's cat.

Like a mouse, Lady Daphne liked to creep into corners in the hope of being unnoticed. Since Cordelia was also relegated to the corners by virtue of her tainted bloodlines, they had met several times.

If the Earl of Yarverton, Lady Daphne's father, had to cast the poor girl on the non-existent mercies of Society, the least he could have done was provide her with more effective protection than a governess-turned-companion. Not that Miss Faversham didn't try, but those whose instincts tended toward cruelty were not deterred by the opinion of a servant.

Perhaps the Earl of Spenhurst might achieve more. If he *did* speak to Lady Corven, and if Lady Corven *did* take any notice, perhaps other hostesses might realize Miss Wharton and her friends, and others like them, needed to be curbed.

Cordelia had her doubts that any of them would do a thing.

Yes, these attacks concerned one of their own, a titled lady. But Lady Daphne embarrassed them. The fashionable world was nervous around those who were not like them. Uncle Josh said they demanded outward perfection of body and mind because they were so twisted in their characters and their morals, and the more rotten they were under the masks they wore, the more they rejected those whose infirmities frightened them by reminding them of their own. Which begged the question of why he was so determined she should join their ranks.

Still, Lord Spenhurst seemed sincere enough. Cordelia had been unsettled by her meeting with the elusive earl. Society had been buzzing with the news his father intended the young man to choose a bride this Season. It was, all agreed, unlikely he would look outside of the daughters of dukes, marquesses, or earls for candidates. Those who qualified were jostling for position.

The earl had been playing least in sight. Rumor had it he was reluctant to obey his father's edict, but whether that was merely a guess because he had not arrived in London in time for the first entertainments of the Season, Cordelia did not know.

In fact, this was the first time his and Cordelia's paths had crossed, and he was not what she expected. She had imagined an arrogant young man sure of his own consequence and disdainful of anyone whose birth did not match his high standards. The young lord had certainly sounded arrogant when he instructed the three hellcats to leave the property, but from then on, he was nothing but pleasant and helpful. He was also kind to Lady Daphne, which was a mark in his favor.

Why was she thinking about Lord Spenhurst? He was so far above her touch he might be the moon, and she was no moth to flutter hopelessly in his direction. He was unlikely to as much as acknowledge Cordelia when next they met, and the highest sticklers would praise him for it. After all, the pair of them had not been properly introduced. He had every excuse for ignoring her existence.

And Cordelia would not care if he did. What was the Earl of

Spenhurst to her, even if her stomach did flutter when he'd bowed over her hand after they introduced themselves to one another. Actually, the flutter had started earlier, when she'd brushed by him on the path. It had only gotten worse as his fingers touched hers when he gave her his coat to put around Lady Daphne.

Cordelia was an innocent, but she was not a fool. She had felt such flutters before. She had met other attractive men: a dancing teacher at her school, a handsome clerk in her uncle's London offices, a young officer who had danced with her at a local assembly in a town where she was on holiday.

A flutter, a heightened sense of awareness, a pleasant exchange of smiles, and they'd gone their separate ways. Two of them had proved a disappointment on further acquaintance, and no doubt the young officer would also have failed to live up to expectations, had she ever seen him again.

But after Lord Spenhurst found Miss Faversham and had seen her and Lady Daphne on their way, he'd offered Cordelia his arm to escort her to her coach and the flutters increased. And then he'd bowed over her hand. She had removed her wet gloves, so his lips touched her skin, sending a quiver all the way up her arm and down her torso into what had become a veritable storm of butterflies.

So, yes, she found Lord Spenhurst attractive, but there was nothing notable about that. He was tall, slender, and well-dressed. He had the straight carriage expected of a gentleman. In the better light of the terrace, she could see that his eyes were blue and his hair a light brown. His face was symmetrical and therefore pleasing, though what attracted her most was the warmth and concern in his expression. He spoke kindly to poor Lady Daphne and with respect to Cordelia.

The world was full of good-looking men who carried themselves well and spoke pleasantly. He was not for her, and she would soon forget him.

Chapter Two

WHEN SPEN VISITED his Aunt Corven the following afternoon and told her about the events in the garden, she refused to sanction the three termagants who had caused Lady Daphne's accident. "You should not have involved yourself, Spenhurst," she growled. "Dear heavens, young man, what were you doing in the garden alone? Do you want to be trapped into marriage by some ambitious young trollop? The girl Cordelia, for example? A title-hunting mushroom if ever I saw one."

That wasn't Spen's impression of the young lady. Unless, indeed, she was clever enough to know treating him with veiled disdain and largely ignoring him would attract his attention like nothing else.

Arguing with his aunt was pointless, but perhaps he could appeal to her sense of self-worth, which was as inflated as his father's. "Lady Daphne was your guest, Aunt Corven, and those three young women—for I shall not call them 'ladies'—insulted you when they tormented her."

Sure enough, his aunt was struck by the point. "True," she said. "I shall need to have a word with their sponsors. Lady Daphne might be simple, but she is the daughter of an earl, and those jumped-up young misses need to be reminded of what is due to her consequence. And mine!"

This gave Spen the result he wanted, and so he complimented his aunt on the cake she had served with his tea and said his farewells, pleading another engagement. As he left, however, she returned to the topic of his angel.

"That girl is a sort of relative of a mill owner or a merchant or some other kind of tradesman. She may catch herself a lesser title, for her dowry is obscenely large, but she shall never be accepted in Society. The best she can hope for is that her encroaching ways will not be held against any sons and daughters."

Some imp of mischief prompted Spen to comment, "She is pretty and has the manners of a lady." Both were true, but he should have had more sense. He had to endure a ten-minute lecture on his duty to the title and his family, which precluded him from ever choosing a bride whose breeding was not the equal of his own.

"Though an earl's daughter would also be acceptable, Spenhurst. We ought not to be too particular."

He was quietly seething as he descended the stairs of the Corven townhouse. Spen was not a person to his father or his aunt. He was a demmed stud for the Deerhaven bloodline.

It was partly out of pique over his aunt's attitude he decided he should visit Miss Cordelia, to see she had come to no harm. *Lady Daphne and Miss Cordelia*, he corrected himself. He should visit them both. He might be a pawn in his father's dynastic machinations, but he was also a gentleman.

He refused to think about the fact that Miss Cordelia was the lady he could not forget, and she was the one he wanted to see. She was low-born? So what? He wanted to check on her well-being, not propose to her.

All right. He could be honest, if only to himself. He wanted to kiss her. But she was a lady, no matter who her parents were, and he was a gentleman. Kissing was not an option, even if the thought of it filled his mind with images he had better banish before their impact on his anatomy became embarrassingly obvious.

He would call on Lady Daphne immediately, for Ashburton House was just around the corner. How did he discover where the other lady lived without word of it coming to his father's ears? And should he take flowers?

※

LADY DAPHNE HAD taken no harm, her companion assured him. He had had the happy thought of buying two bouquets of flowers, one for Lady Daphne and one for Miss Faversham, and the older lady, at least, was delighted. Lady Daphne bobbed a polite curtsey, but soon slid off the chair to the hearth rug, where a basket of kittens absorbed her attention. It was clearly her opinion they should stay in the basket, but they were of a different mind. She had no sooner retrieved one than another escaped.

Miss Faversham regarded her with benign affection and confided, "I know sitting on the floor is not quite the thing, Lord Spenhurst, but indeed, I do not have the heart to rebuke her."

"Certainly, do not do so on my account," Spen assured her. "I would not for the world spoil her pleasure. She is very gentle with the little beasts."

"The stable boy brought them inside this morning," Miss Faversham explained. "They are old enough to be handled and she will do them no harm. It is very kind of you to understand." She blushed. "We did not expect callers, or I would not have permitted them in the parlor."

"They are sweet," Spen said, as one daring feline sniffed at his boots and then reached to bat at the tassels. He picked the little creature up and tickled its tummy, to be rewarded by a strenuous effort to bite his fingers.

Lady Daphne retrieved the kitten, scolding it as she put it back in the basket. "No biting. Biting is naughty." She then abandoned it to chase after another runaway.

"May I offer you tea?" Miss Faversham asked. Somewhat reluctantly, if Spen was any judge.

"Thank you, but I must be on my way," Spen said. "I should also call on the other lady of last night. Her aunt was Mrs. Walters, and I heard the younger lady addressed as Cordelia. I do not suppose you know her direction."

He was in luck. Miss Faversham confirmed the lady was a Miss Cordelia Milton and gave him the address. She found it necessary to explain the circumstances as if there was something a little shameful about the fact, that she and Mrs. Walters had struck up a sort of friendship in the wallflowers' corner. "She is really a most gentile lady," Miss Faversham said, adding, "given her circumstances. And Miss Milton has had a most superior education."

Armed with the information he needed, Spen made his farewells and set off to buy two more bouquets.

Mr. Milton occupied a large townhouse in one of the newer squares in Mayfair. Spen wondered what the man's neighbors thought of his presence, but certainly, there was nothing in the house or its appointments to hint that the owner was an upstart. A very proper butler accepted his card, informed him that the ladies were receiving, and conducted him up a flight of stairs to the drawing room.

Unlike the parlor at Ashburton House, the room was full of callers. Not a large enough crowd to bring on his affliction; that would take thirty or forty, all strangers. He'd learned to tolerate and even enjoy smaller groups long ago.

But nine callers, all male, were a lot for a medium-sized parlor. Spen even recognized a few. If the rest were of the same ilk, Miss Cordelia Milton was being besieged by gazetted fortune hunters and rakes.

For a moment, he watched her unobserved. She was, he had noticed last night, quite similar in overall shape and size to Lady Daphne. Her curves were a little more pronounced. In daylight, he could see that her hair and eyes were not as pale in color—

Lady Daphne's hair was near white and her eyes the pale blue of a winter horizon, whereas Miss Milton's hair tended towards gold and the blue of her eyes echoed a summer sky.

Nonetheless, Miss Daphne was merely pretty, but the intelligence in Miss Milton's face as she chatted with her admirers made her lovely to him. She looked up when he was announced, smiled, and rose to her feet to come and meet him. "Lord Spenhurst, how nice of you to call."

"My first errand is done, Miss Milton," he said, "for I can see you are well after yesterday evening. As for the second..." he offered one of the bouquets. Pink and white roses, which the flower seller assured him meant friendship and innocence. He offered the other identical bouquet to Mrs. Walters, who accepted it with a blush and gushing thanks.

"Do you know these other gentlemen, Lord Spenhurst?" Miss Milton asked.

What was Miss Milton's aunt thinking, allowing such hawks and wolves into the house? Not that he could see Miss Milton as a lamb, but the competence he had already observed would be no protection against the experience these men—gentlemen only by birth—brought to the hunt.

The Duke of Richport could be up to no good, nor the Marquis of Aldridge, who had been a contemporary of Spen's at Oxford and was a womanizer from his cradle. Neither man would consider taking a common-born bride, so what were they doing here? Aldridge was not known as a seducer of innocents, but the same could not be said of Richport.

Three others of the most notable rakes of the ton were also here, along with a coterie of fortune hunters whom he either knew or had heard about. One of them was Stanley Wharton, brother of the infamous Miss Wharton.

Spen had intended to leave after presenting the flowers, but his feet would not take him. He could not leave Miss Milton in such company. Not because of the fierce proprietary need to protect surging within, but because it would not be the act of a gentleman.

Five minutes' observation, though, showed her holding her own. She dismissed a particularly florid compliment by providing two facts that made it ineligible. She held up a hand to stop a slyly erotic comment. "I do not understand what you said, Your Grace, but I suspect it was not suitable for my ears. Please do not make such remarks in my presence."

With courtesy, intelligence, and firmness, she controlled the room. What a magnificent marchioness she would make. Such a pity she was ineligible.

After a while, Aldridge took a seat next to him. "What are you doing here, Spen?" he asked. "You are not pockets to let, and your father would no more tolerate such a connection than mine."

"I could ask you the same question," Spen pointed out.

"I'm watching Death and the others," Aldridge replied. "Death" was the Duke of Richport. His baptismal name was pronounced to rhyme with *teeth*, but he had long since adopted the more macabre sound for his nickname. "There's a bet on in the clubs," Aldridge explained, "about who'll be the first to seduce the girl, and most of them are not concerned about lying to get what they want. I'm keeping an eye on them to make sure she knows that, to them, it is no more than a game."

Spen was surprised and must have let it show. However, it must be true. The man, for all of his tomcat morals, prided himself on always telling the truth and never breaking a promise.

"What?" Aldridge said. "I am not allowed to show concern for an innocent? For she is an innocent, though a bold one. The aunt is no protection at all. I have sisters, and I dread to think of them on the marriage mart, but few people would risk annoying either me or my mother." His mother was raising three girls whom she called her wards, but the whole world knew they were her husband's get. Aldridge was right. Many of the men of Society would think the circumstances of their birth made them fair game.

Aldridge continued, "Women like a bit of sport as much as men, though most would deny it. And I am, as you are too polite to say, happy to take advantage of that fact. But if it is marriage she is after, she won't find it with any of my crowd, and she needs someone to tell her."

"As for the rest of her callers," the young marquis said, "they are a sorry lot of gamblers and drinkers. Except for you, Spen, which brings me back to my question. What are you doing here?"

"Delivering flowers," Spen told him. "After being introduced yesterday at my Aunt Corven's ball."

Aldridge studied him with narrowed eyes. "Not by Lady Corven. She is higher in the instep than my father at his grandest. Well, keep your secrets. In fact, if you are in the lady's confidence, tell her what I just told you. Forewarned is forearmed."

Spen wasn't in the lady's confidence, of course. But more and more, he would like to be, and he certainly did not want to see her ruined by Death or his ilk.

THE USUAL ORDEAL of callers was lightened today by the presence of Lord Spenhurst, though Cordelia could not imagine what he meant by coming here. The rest she could account for. She had an obscenely large dowry and was therefore a magnet for fortune hunters. She was also well aware of the wager in the betting books at the clubs—little escaped her uncle's eye, and he had informed her as soon as he knew. Ignorance, in her uncle's words, was risk.

"Go nowhere without your aunt," he instructed her, "and give these rats no encouragement. Trust me to deal with the bets." More than that, he would not say, but Cordelia knew his methods. Undoubtedly, he was finding the weak points of each person in on the wager and was then applying pressure to that point. Already, three of the would-be seducers had dropped out of the race.

Meanwhile, she could be certain of a few dance partners at each ball. And if they were after her virtue, it made a nice change from those who were after her dowry. After all, what could they do in plain sight of an entire ballroom of people?

Nonetheless, she found them nearly as boring as the fortune hunters. Lord Spenhurst made a nice change, for his father was one of the richest men in England and she had never heard that Lord Spenhurst was a rake nor had Aunt Eliza. Mind you, he appeared very comfortable talking to Lord Aldridge, and that man was definitely a rake.

Or so rumor had it. Lord Aldridge did not whisper wicked things in her ear or suggest she might step into the garden with him or propose clandestine meetings in the park or any of the other things the others in his crowd did. Especially His Grace the Duke of Richport.

His Disgrace, the man should be called. She might have been charmed by some of the others without her uncle's warning, but the duke made little effort to endear himself to her. Indeed, he seemed to consider his rank sufficient incentive for her to throw away the training of a lifetime, her sense of modesty, any hope of being a wife and mother, her pride, and her purity. No. Not just for his rank. He offered, as he had told her during a dance one evening, "…to bring you to the heights of erotic pleasure, Miss Milton, for there is none more experienced and more skillful than I in inducting a virgin into carnal activities."

She should have pretended she had no idea what he was talking about. The lady her uncle had found to explain such matters to her had assured her such knowledge was kept secret from ladies of her age, and she must pretend ignorance. Cordelia scorned to dissemble with this oaf. "I will wait for my husband to do so, Your Grace," she had replied, "and he and I shall, I hope, discover such skills together. Certainly, I shall never know the difference, since I plan to go to the marriage bed a maid."

He had been amused. "We shall see, Miss Milton." His fingers slid over her own, his thumb stroking her palm, even as he swept her into the turn demanded by the dance. "I enjoy a challenge."

If only it was ladylike to slap a man's face when he insulted her. Or, better still, if Cordelia had a way to place a bet against each of her persecutors, and collect when they lost, as they inevitably would.

Almost inevitably. She would not put it past some of them, including the duke, to resort to foul play, though they would find it difficult to carry out a plot against her. She went everywhere accompanied by Aunt Eliza and protected by stout footmen and a maid. Her servants were armed and trained in combat. Cordelia herself carried both a knife and a gun and knew how to use them.

Yes, they would lose. But was Lord Spenhurst one of them? Or not?

It was an odd thing, but when she allowed her mind to consider the carnal activities His Grace of Richport spoke of with such authority, she found herself wondering how experienced and skillful Lord Spenhurst was.

Chapter Three

AFTER THAT AFTERNOON, Lord Spenhurst seemed to be everywhere Cordelia went. He took her walking at garden parties, visited her box at the theatre, and danced at least one set with her at each ball and assembly.

"Is Lord Spenhurst courting you?" Aunt Eliza wondered.

Cordelia was certain he was not. "Watch him, Aunt Eliza. He also spends similar amounts of time with Lady Daphne and three other young ladies. All we have in common is that none of us is a marriage prospect for the Earl of Spenhurst." Which was a pity, for the more Cordelia saw of Lord Spenhurst, the more she liked him.

His attention had consequences, both good and bad. On the good side, most of the fortune hunters saw his interest and moved on to other heiresses. The rakes, too, drifted off, one after another, though Cordelia did not know whether that was because she could not be tempted, or because Lord Spenhurst glowered at any who came near, or because her uncle found a lever he could use to chase them away.

The Duke of Richport was the last to give up, but eventually, even he moved on to other prey.

However, Cordelia's pool of partners did not reduce with the defection of those she was pleased to see disappear. Apparently,

Lord Spenhurst had brought her into fashion, and not just her but three other young ladies, too. While none of them could boast full dance cards and hordes of suitors, all of them had acquired a circle of interested gentlemen who were apparently eager to dance, make afternoon calls, and provide escorts for walks and carriage rides.

Further evidence showed that Lord Spenhurst was not courting Cordelia, for he did not visit again, nor did he ask her to walk or drive with him. What a pity he was the only one who sent the butterflies fluttering in her middle.

Then there were the negative consequences. At the top of Cordelia's list was the disapproval of some of Society's most eminent matrons. Lady Corven even visited one day to tell Cordelia bluntly that Lord Spenhurst would never marry her.

"Of course," Cordelia agreed. She had been receiving glares from the august lady for the past week, and had half-expected her call, so she had prepared a speech that was consoling without being obsequious. "I am grateful to him for sparing me a little of his attention, as he has for several of the other wallflowers. By being kind enough to do so, he has drawn us to the attention of several other gentlemen who are not so far above us."

Lady Corven made a considering noise. "Several others, you say?"

"Yes, my lady."

The lady was obviously not convinced. She glared, her voice challenging, as she asked, "What are your expectations, Miss Milton?"

Cordelia had an answer for that, too. "I promised my uncle I would complete one Season in London before I looked for a husband among my own kind. In two months, my promise will be fulfilled. I expect to end the Season as I began, as a maiden and unmarried."

"And your uncle will be satisfied with that?" asked Lady Corven, frowning in suspicion.

The lady had been blunt, so Cordelia would be blunt in return. "Lady Corven, in the end, my uncle wishes me to be happy. Marriage is for a lifetime, after all, whether happy or miserable. I know I will not be happy unless I find a husband who sees more to me than my dowry. One I can like and respect and who likes and respects me. One who is not ashamed of me because of my origins. Do *you* think I will find a husband to meet those conditions within the ton? Because I do not."

Lady Corven pursed her lips. "In my world, young people are guided by their parents. However, if you are satisfied, I have no complaints. Very well. We understand one another, Miss Milton. I will wish you a pleasant time until the end of the Season and will not expect to see you again after it ends."

She must have told her friends, for after her meeting with Lady Corven, the matrons thawed. It could not have been her aunt's growing friendship with Miss Faversham. The two older ladies gravitated towards one another whenever they were at the same event, which meant that Cordelia and Lady Daphne also spent quite a bit of time together. But Lady Daphne, though the daughter of an earl, was ignored by most of those who governed Society, and the other three were of no account at all.

Another bad outcome of Spen's attention was the increase in hostility from those ladies whom he had not so favored, particularly Miss Wharton and her two sycophants. That also led to something good, for they bailed Cordelia up in the ladies' retiring room one day, having sent the attending maid on a wild goose chase. When their attack turned physical, another young lady intervened and routed them with a few well-placed threats. She turned out to be a viscount's daughter, and much better connected than any of the three, even having a duchess for a godmother, so the harpies backed down and backed away.

After their introduction in the line of fire, as it were, Cordelia and her rescuer, Regina Kingsley, quickly became friends. So, her worst annoyances were gone or neutralized, and she had a friend at her side.

Cordelia set out to enjoy what remained of the Season, which would have been easier if she had not made the mistake of falling in love with Lord Spenhurst. She looked for him at every entertainment, waited for those moments he always spent with her, delighted in his presence, and floated through the rest of the event buoyed by the knowledge yet another memory had been stored away as a treasure to be examined at her leisure when the Season was over.

No other man came close to measuring up. She very much feared no man ever would. Her uncle would have to be satisfied with redeeming the promise he would not force her choice, for she was no longer willing to marry without love, and she could not have the man she loved.

As the summer warmed, people began to leave London. The pace of events increased as if those remaining were determined to wring every last drop of pleasure from Town society before they retired to the country. Many of those who had not made a match would enter another social round, perhaps at a regional center or a spa town, or perhaps at a succession of house parties.

For Cordelia, her time as a debutante was nearly over. She did not allow herself to think about the future. Somewhere hidden within her, a hollow void of grief waited to burst forth—a heart fractured, not by broken promises– for Lord Spenhurst had made none– but by the loss of a bright future that was never hers to grasp.

She threw herself into the last round of entertainments, for each was an opportunity to capture another memory for the lonely times ahead.

Perhaps her preoccupations made her careless, because one warm evening in early summer, she was walking in yet another garden with Aunt Eliza and a group of other young ladies and their chaperones. Regina was having an evening at home, and Lord Spenhurst had not yet arrived.

Cordelia was enjoying the scent of roses in the dusk when she realized she had let herself drop back behind the group. She could see the last two ladies ahead of her, just going out of sight around a turn in the path.

She hurried her steps but, just before she could follow them around the corner, someone reached out from the foliage and dragged her into its concealment. She struggled against the arm that held her tight against a large strong body, the hand that clasped her mouth so she could not scream. Her frantic efforts were to no avail. Her assailant ignored them, half-carrying and half-dragging her out of whatever tree he had hidden within, and down between two clipped hedges until the noises of the party became faint with distance.

"I am going to let go of your mouth," said the clipped tones of the Duke of Richport, not at all slurred, although the sound was carried on a cloud of brandy fumes. "If you scream, you will be ruined. My reputation will not suffer, for I am a duke, and you are a nobody. But be silent, and I will let you go in thirty minutes or so, with no one the wiser about our little assignation."

After that speech, he released her mouth and then let go of her entirely. Cordelia kept silent. For the moment. He was right about the consequences of screaming, but they wouldn't stop her if it became necessary.

"That's a good girl," the duke said, approvingly.

Cordelia ignored the provocation of the patronizing remark. "I suppose this is about your stupid wager."

The duke raised his eyebrows. "You know about the wager?"

"You won't win it this way, you know. The conditions called for a seduction. What you have in mind is a rape."

His eyebrows shot higher. "What sort of maiden are you?" he demanded. "You should not even know that word."

Stupid man. "An educated one, obviously. My point remains."

He shifted restlessly but rallied. "If I say it is a seduction, who will know any different? You are hardly going to talk, and the men at the clubs won't doubt the word of a duke."

It was Cordelia's turn to raise her eyebrows. "Why would I not talk? What have I to lose? I am leaving your circles anyway, and being ruined in the eyes of your world will not stop me from helping my uncle run his business and, if I choose, finding a husband in my own world. After all, money does much to paper over scandal."

The duke frowned in thought, narrowing his eyes, then shook his head as if to clear it. "Enough. I am going to swive you now. Relax and you might even enjoy it." He took a step forward and Cordelia stepped back, further into the shadows of a tree where, she hoped, she would not be noticed reaching through the slit in her side seam to the pocket she wore under her gown.

"Don't be foolish," the duke scolded, his diction still perfect though he wove slightly where he stood and the fumes of brandy were so strong, she fancied they, rather than her fear, accounted for her light-headedness.

He took another step, and she backed away again, fetching up against the trunk of a tree. The duke chuckled. "That will do nicely," he said, and pressed up against her, using his body to trap her as his hands grasped her face to hold it still for his mouth.

Cordelia brought her hand out from her skirt and stabbed the duke in his thigh.

He screamed and fell back, ripping the knife from her hand.

Chapter Four

IT WAS NO good. Spen had tried to follow his father's decree and find a wife among the suitable young ladies on offer this Season, but his heart had other ideas. His heart had it right. No one was more suitable for Spen the man than Cordelia. As for Spen the prospective marquess, Cordelia was clever, competent, and capable. She would be an excellent marchioness, whatever his father and aunt might think.

Somehow, he was going to have to persuade them to accept Cordelia as his bride, for Spen could marry no one else. That is, if Cordelia would have him.

He was late to tonight's ball, for he had rejected several cravats as insufficiently elegant for the occasion, changed his waistcoat at least three times and then reverted to the first one, and realized halfway to the ball that he had, after all his fussing, left the token he had purchased that day. He hurried home and collected it from his desk, where he had left it.

It was a ring featuring two clasped hands, one in gold and one in silver. He hoped to replace it with something more valuable when he had his father's permission and that of her uncle, but he wanted to give her something this evening when he declared his love and asked her to marry him. The friendship ring, as the jeweler called it, had been both within reach of his allowance and meaningful, for hers were the hands he wished to clasp for the rest of his life.

He could not see her anywhere in the ballroom. She must be out on the terrace in the garden with her aunt and her friend Regina. It was a large garden. When he did not see her on the terrace, he began methodically searching the paths.

He found her aunt in a like pursuit, very distressed and close to tears. "She was right behind me," she kept saying. "I cannot understand what happened. I was only a few paces further ahead, but Miss Faversham was explaining the pattern for her shawl, and I lost sight of her. Only for a moment. This is all my fault. She was right behind me. Oh dear, what can have happened to her?"

Spen's vague sense of concern sharpened and coalesced into fear. "This way," he said, leading Mrs. Walters into a path that struck off into the farther reaches of the garden.

Surely Richport would not attack her? It was only a bet, after all. That said, Richport's name was still showing in the betting books under the wager when everyone else had struck theirs off.

As the path turned to run beside the wall at the bottom of the garden, he heard voices and then a scream, followed by a man's voice, bellowing. At the first sound of the scream, Spen threw himself off the path and into the foliage, tracking straight in the direction of the commotion. He was almost upon the source of the noise before his brain had processed that the screamer was also male, and by then he could understand the words in the bellow.

Someone was accusing a woman, in the most vulgar of terms, of assaulting him. Spen hurled himself through the last bush in his way, bursting into a clearing where Cordelia stood at bay against a tree, a small lady's pistol in her hand. The Duke of Richport was struggling from the ground, bent over at an odd angle, and spewing invectively.

Spen rushed to Cordelia, and she moved into his sheltering arm but did not take her eyes off Richport or lower the gun.

"That hellion stabbed me and threatened to shoot me!" the

duke accused.

Sure enough, even in the half-light of dusk, Spen could see the handle of a knife protruding from Richport's thigh. "You'll need a doctor for that," he said.

"I'll have the bitch arrested," Richport threatened, his words slurring a little. He was obviously drunk, which might have helped with the pain, at that. "She'll hang for stabbing a duke."

"I understand your point," Spen said, tightening his arm around Cordelia. "Whoever did this should at least be thoroughly questioned, and then given a public trial to find out if there are any mitigating circumstances. I am sure the scandal sheets will be grateful to ferret out every detail of what led to your defeat at the hands of a woman. Once we get you some medical help, we will send out some servants to search the grounds and see if they can find any clues to show where the woman who knifed you has gone."

Richport glared at Cordelia. "She is standing right there."

Mrs. Walters came hurrying, almost running, around the curve of the path. Spen smiled at her and told the villain, "You are mistaken, Richport. Mrs. Walters and Miss Milton were strolling with me in the garden when we heard you scream. As if you were knifed. By an unknown woman. One smaller than you, to look at the position of the knife. I daresay people will be interested to know why you were back here, and fascinated at how this unknown woman was able to get close enough to you to stick a knife in your thigh. But, of course, with your reputation, I imagine they will find it easy to leap to a correct conclusion."

Richport went still as Spen's innuendos sank into his sodden brain. Cordelia shifted so one side of her face was hidden from Richport, and Spen saw that corner of her mouth tilt up.

"We were strolling in the garden?" Mrs. Walters wondered. "Yes. The three of us. All together. That is what happened, Lord Spenhurst. Certainly. We were strolling in the garden when we heard His Grace scream."

"His *Disgrace*," Cordelia muttered under her breath. Spen

suppressed a chuckle.

Voices heralded the arrival of other people. Cordelia did something to make the gun disappear. Spen suspected a pocket under her gown and admired her wisdom. He called out, "Over here! The Duke of Richport has been wounded!"

In moments, the clearing was full, with more people gathering all the time. Spen heard the duke explaining he had been about to enjoy a cigarillo in private when someone leapt out of the bushes and struck him. "A woman or a young boy," he said. "I could not see clearly. Now for God's sake, someone help me to my coach."

A buzz of contrary opinions suggested to Spen that someone was going to have to take charge to get the despicable man some medical attention. He sighed. "You," he said to one footman, "run and order His Grace's coach brought to the side garden." He ordered another to organize a search of the garden, and the third to fetch the duke's doctor to the duke's townhouse.

On Spen's direction, a couple of the gentlemen formed a chair with their arms to carry the duke, who had ceased bristling and had become alarmingly pale and quiet. "We need some light," Cordelia suggested quietly. "If he is losing too much blood, he cannot be sent home. The doctor must attend him here."

"I am used to battlefield medical emergencies," said a bluff fellow in a military uniform. "I'll take a look at it if someone has a knife to cut his pantaloons away from around the wound. Dear me. What is London coming to?"

Spen, content the duke would get the help he needed, stayed back with Cordelia and Mrs. Walters and then led them in the direction of the house by another path. "If it is all the same to you, ladies, may I order your carriage and conduct you home?"

"Please, Cordelia," begged Mrs. Walters. "I am quite shaken."

"Yes, Lord Spenhurst," Cordelia agreed. "Please do." She was clinging to his arm as if he was a fixed point in a string wind, and he could feel a shudder run through her.

Spen could sympathize, for he had only just managed to hold

back another of his panic attacks, as one doctor called them, when the crowd began to gather, all talking at once. He could not afford to flee as he normally did. He had to protect Cordelia. In desperation, he had donned the mask he usually wore and given orders. It had worked. People had done what they were told, and the panic had receded. Food for thought.

Nearly everyone must be following the duke, for the garden was deserted, but when they reached the better-lit area by the terrace, they were stopped again and again by guests who wanted to know what was happening. Spen repeated their story several times but was supplanted as others began drifting back from farther down the garden, which saved him from having to assert himself again to get himself and the ladies out of there.

The duke was injured, but not bleeding badly, they said. Major Petersham predicted the wound would gush when the knife was removed, so it had been left in place, and the duke had been loaded into his carriage with another gentleman to watch him until he was safely at home.

Wasn't it terrible what the world was coming to, all the bystanders agreed?

※

CORDELIA SAT BACK against her seat in the coach and began to shake. She couldn't forget the sensation of the knife going into the duke's flesh and the sound of his scream. *I had to defend myself. I had to.*

Lord Spenhurst showed how attuned he was to her feelings by saying, "You did the right thing, Miss Milton. You had every right to stop the fiend. I only wish we could see him further punished without causing any harm to your reputation."

Cordelia couldn't answer. Tears were running down her cheeks, and if she tried to speak, she would lose the battle to keep her sobs from becoming audible. Her effort to remain silent must have been a failure, for Aunt Eliza embraced her. "There, there, darling child. It has been a difficult evening."

A typical Aunt Eliza understatement. Cordelia gave a watery chuckle.

"It is a reaction," she explained to Spen, her voice quavering on another sob. "I am good in a crisis, Uncle says, but afterward..." she flapped a hand. He could see for himself what she was like afterward. She must have given him a complete disgust of her.

Yet it didn't seem so, for he came with them into the townhouse Uncle had taken for the Season, followed them into the drawing room, and suggested to Aunt Eliza, "I am certain Miss Milton could do with a cup of tea. Would you organize that? And perhaps something sweet to eat?"

Even upset as she was, Cordelia realized he had just masterfully removed Aunt Eliza from the room to leave them alone. She watched him, eyes wide, as he spread his arms.

"May I give you a hug?" he asked. "I have never felt so frightened in my life as when I guessed the duke had something to do with your disappearance. And when I heard that scream—!" He shuddered, shutting his eyes as an anguished expression moved over his face.

Cordelia walked into his arms, and he closed them around her.

They stood for a moment, each taking comfort in the other, for even as she relaxed and let go of her own fear, anger, and stress, she could feel the tension draining from him.

A touch on her head made her look up. His face was just above hers, his lips still forming the kiss he had just given her. She stretched so her own mouth met his, and the brush of his lips sent a shiver to her core. Then his mouth closed over hers, took possession and all her consciousness narrowed in on the sensations coursing through her body from the points where they touched—mouths, torsos, one of his hands cupping her head and the other cupping her behind, her hands doing their best to burrow under his waistcoat.

When the door opened, he pulled back. She let go, but not quite quickly enough.

Uncle Josh strode in already speaking. "Dee-Dee, what is this I hear about..." He broke off, his eyes blazed, and he took another two steps towards Spen, his face working, and his fists raised. Aunt Eliza, who had followed him into the room, gave an inarticulate cry of protest.

Cordelia stepped between them. "Stop, Uncle Josh. I kissed him first."

"This is not what you think, sir," Spen said, in almost the same breath.

Uncle Josh snorted. "Unless you plan to offer for my niece," he scoffed, "it is exactly what I think."

"Uncle Josh!" Cordelia scolded, while Spen tossed his hands in the air and groaned.

"I wanted to make it special. I rehearsed in front of the mirror and everything. And then that blackguard Richport spoilt it all," he said, looking up at the ceiling. Then he turned his gaze to Cordelia and dropped to one knee.

"Cordelia Milton, from the day I first met you, I have been unable to keep away from you. I treasure every moment I spend with you and think about you constantly when we are apart. I admire and esteem you more than I can say. I cannot imagine spending my life with anyone at my side except you. My heart is bound to yours, and if you can imagine the possibility of coming to care for me, then I beg you to honor me by agreeing to become my wife."

He added, in a conversational tone, "I did not plan to make my speech in the presence of your uncle, of course, and I thought we could ask your aunt to stand out of earshot. But there you have it."

He fell silent, gazing up at her hopefully, worry mounting in his expression as she floundered after a response. It was everything she wanted. Not the title and the appalling weight of history, but Spen himself. However, it couldn't be true he wanted her, too. He was proposing because of Richport's attack. She should have expected it. He was so wonderful he would sacrifice his own chance of an appropriate marriage because he thought she was ruined, and he wanted to help.

"You don't have to do that," she assured him. "I do not think the duke will admit he was bested by a woman and a commoner, and neither you nor Aunt Eliza will talk."

He blinked at her, then looked horrified. "You think I am proposing because of what happened with Richport?"

"What happened with Richport?" Uncle Josh roared.

Cordelia had no attention to spare him. "Of course, Lord Spenhurst. I know what your aunt thinks of me."

"My aunt is not proposing, my love. I am. Did you not listen to a word I said? Shall I repeat my little speech? I can, you know. I have been writing it for days. I learnt it by heart last night, and I have practiced it in the mirror at least a dozen times today."

Her heart stuttered. "You have?"

"I was afraid my words would dry up when I tried to tell you how I felt. You take my breath away, Cordelia, and muddle my brain. You have from the first, and I believe you will until we are old and grey."

"You do?" Her own ability to form more words than the most basic seemed to have evaporated.

"I can prove I planned this," he said, his eyes lighting up. He pulled a small box from his jacket pocket. He held it up and opened the lid. "Here. I had this made for you."

Cordelia could not resist. She reached out a hand and touched the ring—a gold hand and a silver hand, clasping. The wrist of each was carved into a cuff and the cuff was decorated with tiny gems. On one cuff, they formed the letter C, and on the other the letter S. She took it from the box to examine it more closely, smiling at the clever way the silver and gold twined together on the other side of the ring.

"Well, Dee-Dee?" Uncle Josh said. "Give the man his answer and let him up off of his knee."

"Cordelia Milton," Spen began again. "From the day I first—"

As if in a dream, Cordelia found herself fitting the ring to her finger and saying, "Yes."

"Yes?" Spen repeated, joy beaming from his face.

She gave him both hands and pulled him to his feet, laughing and crying at once. "Yes, Spen, I will marry you."

Spen hugged her, then Aunt Eliza hugged them both, and then Uncle Josh hugged her and shook Spen's hand. "You'll be asking for her, mind," he warned, "and agreeing to my conditions." When Uncle Josh was much moved, his tongue slipped back to the Kentish of his childhood.

"Of course, sir. May I call on you tomorrow afternoon? I intend to inform my father in the morning." Spen took Cordelia's hands. "If he will not give his consent, Cordelia, I cannot marry until after my birthday in October. Once I am twenty-one, I no longer need to have his permission."

"I do not wish to cause trouble between you," Cordelia fretted.

Spen's laugh had a bitter edge. He had not told her much about his father, but what he had said made the man sound most unappealing. "Any trouble will be of my father's making, not yours. Nor mine, for that matter."

"Well," said Uncle Josh. "We'll talk about all of that tomorrow, but tonight we'll sit down and have a drink, and the lot of ye'll tell me what happened with the Duke of Richport."

>>>*<<<

SPEN SPENT NEARLY as much time getting dressed and groomed for his meeting with his father as he had the evening before, for his proposal. He could not believe his father would take the news well. Spen could withstand one of the marquess's tirades without outwardly quailing—nearly two decades of being hit at the least sign of fear had seen to that. But the man's voice raised in anger still had the power to bring back all the emotions of a frightened child.

"I am taller and fitter than him," he reminded himself, as he strode through the streets from his bachelor apartments to the family townhouse. "What can he do? Refuse his permission? I will marry her anyway when I am of age. Stop my allowance? Remove the Hertfordshire property from me? I have savings enough to keep me until my birthday, and that will give me time to find a position."

He had been given full authority for a little estate in Herefordshire when he was seventeen. "Make your mistakes before you are marquess in my place," his father had said. "You can keep any income the place makes, but any losses come out of your allowance."

A retired solicitor had been hired as his tutor, and the estate's steward did the actual work, but all final decisions were his. He gloried in working with his advisers, the tenants, and other locals to learn about the people, the land, and the livestock, and to cautiously make improvements. Income was up in the past two years, but most of it had to go back into the neglected estate, of course.

If his father cut him off, could he perhaps get work as a land steward? Perhaps Mr. Milton could find him a job, though he did not fancy asking such a favor from the man whose niece he wanted to marry. Still, Spen's pride did not matter to him as much as Cordelia.

The townhouse loomed above him. He checked his watch. Ten minutes after ten. His father's reply acknowledging his message had said to call at half past ten. He could walk around the streets for a little longer, but instead, he forced his reluctant feet up the steps.

"I am meeting with my father this morning," he told the butler, handing the man his hat, coat, and walking stick.

"His lordship is not at home," the butler intoned. Which meant, Spen guessed, that the marquess was still in bed after a late night of socializing.

Spen shrugged. "I am a little early. Is Mr. Morris here? I will drop in on him."

Morris was the man who had helped train him in estate management. He worked one day a week in the marquess's estate office and was, as Spen expected, already at work and pleased to see his former pupil. They spent ten minutes discussing the latest reports from Herefordshire, before Morris said, "This has been delightful, my lord," which was a polite dismissal and Spen took the hint.

The butler was hovering in the hall, his face blank of expression except for a small hint of worry about the eyes. "Is the marquess up yet?" Spen asked.

The butler allowed himself to disclose a little more information this time. His lordship is not currently in the house."

Spen sighed. His lordship was not likely to have woken and gone out this early in the day, so he had probably been out all night, with his mistress or carousing with friends. Whether or not he turned up any time soon, and in what condition, depended on whether he remembered the meeting with Spen. "I will wait in the library," Spen told the butler. "Please have someone bring me tea."

He preferred coffee, but no one in this house brewed it correctly.

The daily newspapers, neatly ironed, had been laid out on a table by the window. Spen sat with his tea and scanned them, one after another. He may have read them, even, but he had no memory of the words. His mind was replaying memories of that kiss, rehearsing words that might convince the marquess in the coming interview, and enjoying pleasant daydreams about a future with Cordelia.

He could not see the clock on the mantlepiece from where he was sitting. It chimed the half-hour shortly after he sat down, and the three-quarters as he was pouring his first cup of tea. The tolling of eleven o'clock felt so much longer than fifteen minutes later that he got up to check whether the clock was still working. It seemed to be doing so, but Spen had never known time to creep so slowly.

He'd sent for and consumed a second cup before the door opened and the marquess erupted into the room. "Spenhurst!" His father strode towards him, weaving slightly, and threw himself down on one of the library sofas. His cravat was rumpled, and his clothing creased, as if he had slept in it, or tossed it on in a hurry.

Spen rose and bowed. "My lord."

The marquess indicated a chair. "Come and sit. Here, where I can see you," he ordered. A slight slurring of his consonants hinted at the level of his inebriation as much as the weaving. The marquess was in his cups, which—given the man's tolerance for alcohol—hinted at huge quantities consumed.

Spen did as he was told. Close at hand, the man stank of brandy, sweat, floral perfume, and a faint fishy smell that hinted at what he'd been doing with the owner of the perfume.

"You wanted to talk to me about your marriage," the marquess announced. "You've been paying attention to one young woman. M'sister keeps me informed."

Where was the thundering? The abuse? "Yes, my lord, and I seek your consent for our marriage."

"Not the choice I expected you to make," Lord Deerhaven commented.

The alcohol must have mellowed him. That or his copulative activities. "My aunt does not see the lady's strengths, and how she will benefit the family," he said.

The marquess responded with a snort. "Fortunately, it is my consent you need and not that of my sister." He hoisted himself to his feet and stood for a moment, looking dazed, before sharpening his gaze and turning it on Spen, who had also risen to his feet.

"I'm for my bed. Bring her to Deercroft, Spenhurst. I am not displeased, but I will meet her before I give my final consent.

Send a message to your stepmother and tell her I said to set up a house party and to invite your intended and her companion a day or two before."

Ignoring Spen's thanks, he left the room, and Spen could hear him calling for his valet, the voice fading into the distance.

Spen sat as if his strings had been cut. He had not expected it to be so easy.

Chapter Five

MINUTE BY MINUTE, the carriage carried Cordelia ever closer to Deercroft, the principal estate of the marquesses of Deerhaven. She was excited and anxious in equal measure.

Spen would be waiting for her. Spen wanted to make her his wife.

Spen's stepmother, father, and—Cordelia's wildest nightmares insisted—every one of his august ancestors in their frames on the wall would also be waiting. In her dreams, they cried out as she walked in the door. "Mill girl!" they shouted. "Doesn't belong here! Away with her! Off with her head!"

His father will not be home yet, she reminded herself. Spen had asked her to arrive a day or two before the other guests so that he had time to show her around the house and the estate. The marquess would not be there for several more days.

They entered the ornate gates, the outriders without whom her uncle would not allow her to travel arriving first and ensuring the gates were opened and the carriage was waved through.

"So considerate," Cordelia's aunt enthused, and then, as they turned a bend in the carriageway, "Oh, my word!"

For a few minutes, the park, and then the gardens, spread before them. On the far side of the gardens, an enormous house dominated the vista, the golden stone lit by the sun that sparkled

JUDE KNIGHT

off dozens, perhaps scores, of windows.

Cordelia barely had time to take in that much before the carriage turned another corner. Spen had told Cordelia the final approach to the great house ran in a straight line through the stately garden until it passed through an arch and terminated in a courtyard at the foot of stairs up to the main entrance.

Short of leaning out of the window, she would not see the house again until they arrived. Cordelia said a quick prayer that Spen would be waiting to welcome her. She could face his father if he was at her side. She could face anything with Spen beside her.

Aunt Eliza might almost have read her mind. "I imagine Lord Spenhurst will be waiting for you, Cordelia. Such a nice young man. Not at all proud, as I imagined an earl might be."

Aunt Eliza and Uncle Josh were thrilled Cordelia had attracted the attention of an earl. It was a courtesy title, Spen had said, modestly. He was not an actual peer, but merely the eldest son of one. The title Earl of Spenhurst was merely the next most senior title of the Marquesses of Deerhaven.

"Imagine," Uncle had said. "Our little DeeDee. A marchioness."

When Spen's stepmother had sent the invitation for Cordelia and Aunt Eliza to visit Deercroft, she had also invited Uncle Josh. "Nay, lass," Uncle Josh had said. "I know my place. I'll not be embarrassing thee in front of all of them fine folk. Nay, Lizzie'll be the ticket. Lizzie knows the gentry ways. Aye, thou'll be safe wi' Lizzie."

Aunt Eliza was nearly as much out of her depth in the rarified upper reaches of Society as Cordelia, but neither his sister nor his niece would tell him so. He would be most upset to know how Society had looked down their collective noses at the widow of an obscure country gentleman and the niece of a man in trade. At least until the Earl of Spenhurst began to pay Cordelia singular attention.

The bright sunlight was suddenly cut off as the carriage

passed under a long arch, almost a tunnel. In the stone walls on either side, shallow steps led up to a door. The arch of which Spenhurst had spoken passed through a building.

A moment later, they came out into the courtyard, turning left to pass beside the building they'd driven under, then continuing on in a circle past another long building to come to a stop before the third, the great house itself.

Then Cordelia lost all interest in architecture, for the Earl of Spenhurst was gesturing the footman out of the way and opening the door himself.

"Cordelia! You are here at last." He remembered his manners and looked past Cordelia to her aunt. "Welcome, Mrs. Walters. Thank you so much for coming."

Cordelia took Spen's hand, feeling the thrill of his touch even through her glove. He helped her down and turned to offer the same assistance to Aunt Eliza. Cordelia gazed up the stairs to the huge wooden doors, ornately carved with leaves, flowers, and even animals. She could make out a stag, or was it a unicorn? Above, between rows of pillars, stretched a leaded window at least another story high, and above that, a ledge holding more pillars.

Spen spoke from just behind her, his voice warm. "You'll get a crick in your neck, Miss Milton. The best view is from across the courtyard. There is a roof walk, and I look forward to showing it to you."

She turned with a smile, and he gestured to the building they'd driven under. She couldn't see the roofwalk of which he spoke, just a row of pilasters along the top of the wall, with glimpses of tiles behind.

The courtyard was surrounded by the house and its outbuildings, so that it was completely enclosed and could be entered only by the arched opening behind her and two other paved openings below the buildings to each side that allowed passage into the world beyond.

The great house made up the tallest wall, with four rows of

windows and dormers in the roof above. The three lesser buildings were half the height. Most impressive of all were the two towers placed one at each corner of the great house, stretching twice the height of the house. Surely from the windows at their highest level, one would be able to see far across the estate, and miles into the countryside beyond.

Spen offered her one arm, and Aunt Eliza the other. "Come," he said. "I am looking forward to introducing you to my stepmother." Lady Deerhaven had not been in London for the Season, as she was approaching her confinement.

The entrance hall soared the full height of the building to a magnificent cupola, the biggest Cordelia had ever seen. Cordelia promised herself she'd come back for a better look, but for now, she needed all her wits about her to make a good impression on the Marchioness of Deerhaven, to whom Spen was now presenting her and her aunt.

Aunt Eliza was overwhelmed, as evidenced by the court curtsey they had practiced together, but never yet had the opportunity to use. Cordelia fought the urge to do the same and succeeded. She had to present herself as a lady worthy to be Spen's countess. Proper respect, but not the obsequious humility the aristocrats expected from those beneath them. "Be yourself," Spen had said. "My stepmother will love you."

He said nothing about his father.

A bob of a curtsey. That is what her finishing governess would have decreed, and that is what Cordelia did.

Lady Deerhaven was a surprise—not the elegant matriarch Cordelia had expected, but a small, faded lady who could not have been more than a few years older than Cordelia herself. Her pregnancy was obvious, and she walked awkwardly.

"Welcome, welcome," she said. "I am so pleased you were able to come. Let me show you both up to your rooms. You will want to tidy up. Perhaps to rest? I always find travel so exhausting."

Cordelia glanced at Spen. Rest? When they had been separated for days and were only just together again?

Lady Deerhaven must have noticed, for she added, "If Miss Milton is not tired, perhaps Spenhurst would take her for a tour of the house?"

Aunt Eliza looked alarmed. "With her maid, of course," she insisted.

"Yes, of course," agreed Lady Deerhaven. "Please come this way, and I will show you to your rooms. Spenhurst, Miss Milton will be with you shortly."

She personally conducted her guests up to their rooms. They had been given a little suite—two bedchambers, each with a tiny dressing room, and a sitting room in the middle.

"How lovely," Cordelia said, sincerely. She washed as quickly as she could, and she and the maid left Aunt Eliza sitting next to the window with a rug over her lap and the promise of a cup of tea on its way.

Spen was waiting on the landing just outside of the door to the guest wing, and his eyes lit up when she joined him. "I thought of showing you the picture gallery," he said.

Cordelia, remembering her nightmare, shivered. Of course, Spen noticed. "Are you cold, Miss Milton? These halls can be chilly. Would you like a shawl?" Of course, he would address her formally in front of the maid.

She followed his example. "Thank you, Lord Spenhurst. I am warm enough."

He offered her his arm, and the maid fell into step behind. "First, would you mind if we went up to the children's floor? I would like to make you and John known to one another."

Cordelia resisted the urge to skip. From what Spen had said, he and his brother were very close, even though Spen was seven years older than John.

"I would like to meet Lord John," she said.

"He should be at Eton in Windsor," Spen explained, as he conducted her up the stairs. "But he had a fall and broke his arm, and they sent him home to recover since the summer holidays start in just two weeks."

"The poor boy. How did it happen?"

Spen grinned. "He must have been doing something he should not, for he is reluctant to talk about it. Lady Deerhaven had the physician, and he says it is just a simple fracture and should heal without any difficulty."

They crossed another elegant landing, went through a door, and arrived in a stairwell very different from the entrance hall. Left behind were marble steps wide enough for four people walking abreast, with ornately carved balusters, half-paneled walls, statues, and huge paintings—landscapes and heroic scenes.

They were now climbing narrower stairs in polished wood with a central runner of plain serviceable carpet. The watercolors and illustrations on the walls were more domestic and far less deftly painted. "Most of these were done by my aunt or great aunts," Spen said, "when they were children."

Cordelia was charmed at the idea. "And what of you and John, my lord? Are you represented here on the walls?"

Spen looked astounded at the very thought. "Only the girls. Painting is not an activity for boys." He frowned. "Though it is a pity some of John's drawings have not been framed. He is very good. The marquess would never permit it, though."

That was the opening for Cordelia to ask, "When may I expect to meet Lord Deerhaven?" To be presented for his disapproval, from all she had heard of the man. But he could not be as bad as people said if he had allowed his son to invite her here, despite her common birth.

She followed Spen along a long, narrow passage. He kept talking as if he was afraid to be silent lest she ask her question again. It was just Cordelia's imagination. He had no need to avoid her question. "The nursery has always been on this floor," he said, "with bedrooms and the schoolroom along the passage at this end and the playroom in the tower, and the same in the other direction, but for guests."

He stopped outside the door. "John has made the playroom

into a sitting room since he is the only inhabitant of the family side of the children's floor." He knocked and then opened the door into a round room that must occupy the entire top of the tower. The space was light and sunny, though the windows were barred.

The boy who stood at their entrance did not look much like Spen. His hair was a darker brown, and his skin was lightly tanned. His face was more oval than square, though that could be his age. He had hazel eyes, too, instead of Spen's blue. He was tall, though very thin. Cordelia guessed he had grown upwards, as boys did at his age, and had not yet had time to put on muscle and flesh to match his height.

Cordelia knew him to be thirteen, but his eyes were older—cautious and assessing. Perhaps it was just the pain from the bandaged arm she could see protruding from the sling he wore.

"Miss Milton, may I present my brother. John, this is Miss Cordelia Milton, my betrothed."

"I am very pleased to meet the lady my brother has been enthusing about in his letters this age," John offered, a smile lightening his solemn visage.

"And I am delighted to meet the brother Lord Spenhurst speaks of so often," Cordelia returned.

They talked for a few minutes more, and when Spen mentioned he was showing Cordelia around the house, John asked if he could come.

"I am tired of seeing the same rooms over and over," he said. "I won't be able to come down once the guests arrive, even if the marquess is not expected home until later in the week."

That was a curious thing to say. Did John mean he was not allowed from his rooms? Perhaps the marquess was an overprotective father, but nothing in the little Spen had said about him fitted that conclusion. Indeed, Cordelia had the impression Lord Deerhaven was harsh and demanding.

Eventually, no doubt, her curiosity about the man would be satisfied. She shivered again at the thought. "He is probably not happy about us, even though he did give his consent," Spen had said. "But what can he do? I shall reach my majority in a few months. He must realize I can marry you then if he does not give his consent now."

As they retreated down the stairs and out into the public rooms of the house, Cordelia put the marquess out of her mind and asked John about his schooling, and what activities he liked best. They arrived back on the floor where she and Spen had started, and this time turned away from the guest wing to go through a door and across what looked like a drawing room. "One of the parlors," Spen said, dismissively, as if multiple parlors were not a circumstance worth commenting on.

The other side of the room had a long row of doors. Spen opened one near the middle. "These fold back to join the two rooms together," he explained, as he led the way through yet another parlor.

John was explaining the relative roles of heavy and light cavalry—it was his ambition to be a cavalry officer. He stopped on the threshold. "Are you going to show Miss Milton the picture gallery, Spen?" he asked.

"I thought we'd start there," Spenhurst said. "I wanted her to see the portrait of Mama."

The enthusiasm drained from John's eyes.

"Wait for us here," Spen suggested, but John braced his shoulders and followed them through the door.

This room had two doors on the opposite wall, and Spen opened the one on the left. It led to a long gallery, with statues between narrow windows on one side, and portraits all the way along the wall on the other.

It was very like the room in Cordelia's dream and to her eyes, the unsmiling people in the paintings looked as unhappy with her presence as she had anticipated. *Do not be foolish*, she scolded herself. *You are an invited guest. Lady Deerhaven was welcoming, and John is a delight.*

John was eyeing the portraits with less enthusiasm than Cordelia felt—even with apprehension. If Spen noticed, he showed no sign of it. He led them two-thirds of the way along the room and stopped before a little portrait squeezed between two large ones. "Mama," he said.

The countess had a kind face, Cordelia decided. She was portrayed seated, on a stone bench, with a garden behind her, and a boy leaning against her knee. Cordelia didn't need to ask whether he was Spen or John. Cordelia knew the shape and color of the lady's eyes because she looked into their likeness whenever she was with Spen and dreamt of them when she and Spen were apart.

The little boy was dressed as a gentleman of the previous century, in breeches almost the color of his eyes, and a matching coat over a pale brown waistcoat. His shirt had a wide lace-trimmed collar, with a narrow, dark blue ribbon around the vee-shaped neckline under the collar and tied in a bow at the bottom.

"How old were you when this was painted?" she asked him.

"Six," he said. "Perhaps six and a half."

Cordelia moved closer, putting a hand on the frame as she examined the painting. "She died when you were ten," she commented, remembering what he had said. She looked away from the painting in time to see a frown exchanged between John and Spen.

"We lost her when I was ten and John was three," Spen confirmed.

A panel in the wall a few yards away swung open, and a woman in a maid's gown, cap, and apron poked her head out. "Master John!" she said in a loud whisper. "His lordship is coming. Quickly!"

Spen tensed and cast a glance down the gallery towards the door at the far end. "The marquess is home?" he questioned. The maid nodded.

John was already at the panel door. He stopped to look back at Spen. "Do you want me to stay?"

"No," Spen said. "Get back to your room before he sees you.

I'll come when I can and let you know what happened."

John climbed through the panel, and it closed. "Do not be afraid, Cordelia," Spen said. "He will probably shout, but I will not let him hurt you."

Cordelia's alarm was climbing. "Spen?" Her questions were tumbling over themselves, jamming up in her brain. Why did the maid come to fetch John? Would he be in trouble for being out of his chambers? Certainly, he had looked frightened, and then as determined as a knight errant when he offered to stay.

Why did Spen think she might be afraid? Why would the marquess shout? Would he try to hurt Cordelia, a guest in his house? Why, when he had told the marchioness to invite her? How could Spen stop his own father if the man was intent on violence?

She lifted her chin. Did Spen think she was a frail damsel who fainted at a harsh word? She wasn't.

At that moment, the door at the far end of the gallery was flung open so violently it crashed against the wall and a bulky shape loomed in the doorway.

"Spenhurst!" It was a roar. The man who now strode down the gallery was taller than Spen and much more heavy-set, with the broad shoulders of a man who had been athletic in his youth and the large torso of a person who had indulged his love of food long after he gave up regular exercise. Spen stepped between Cordelia and the man, who must be the marquess.

Was he a giant or was it just the anger rolling off him that made him seem so large? Four footmen scurried in his wake, but Cordelia merely noted their existence while keeping her eyes on the marquess, who had come to a halt in front of Spen.

"You invited that female to my house," he growled.

"My lord, this is Miss Milton, the lady I wish to marry," Spen insisted. "You gave me permission to invite her."

"I thought you were courting the Yarverton chit!" The marquess shrieked. My sister told me you were paying her particular attention!"

Yarverton? The Earl of Yarverton was Lady Daphne's father. Was Spen courting her? No. Spen had paid her no more attention than he did anyone else.

"I have been courting Miss Milton, my lord," Spen insisted. "I cannot imagine my aunt didn't notice my interest."

Cordelia could. Lady Corven had dismissed Cordelia as beneath her notice and therefore assumed Spen felt the same way.

Spen told his father, "I certainly did not spend any time with Lady Daphne beyond common courtesy. I intend to marry Miss Milton."

The marquess's dark eyes scanned Cordelia from head to toe. He then turned back to Spen and ignored her, as if she was of no account.

"Get rid of the chit," he ordered. "I have signed the marriage settlements. You are betrothed to Lady Daphne."

Cordelia couldn't help a squeak of protest. The marquess glared at her. Spen's swift look held contrition, despair, and defiance. He set his shoulders and said in a voice that tried to be firm but shook. "I have not agreed. I will *not* agree. I will marry Miss Milton. When I turn twenty-one, if not before."

"What is her breeding?" the marquess demanded. "What is her family?" He turned another scathing glare on Cordelia. Something shifted in his eyes, and she suddenly felt unclean, as if slugs crept over her skin. "She's comely enough. Is she hot in bed? Her sort knows how to lead a man around by his prick."

Spen protested. "Sir! Miss Milton is a lady! Be careful of your language."

The marquess's bark of harsh laughter was contemptuous. "Miss Milton is a common slut from a common family, with enough schooling in proper behavior to keep you panting at her feet rather than letting you have your way with her."

Spen said, hotly, "It is not true." The marquess ignored him. Instead, he focused his ice-blue eyes on Cordelia.

"Tell your uncle your tricks have failed, girl," he said to Cordelia. "Our sort have your sort as mistresses, but never as wives.

Not unless they are so badly pockets-to-let they're willing to dig in the mire for a bride, which will never be the case for the future Marquess of Deerhaven. Tell him to set his honey trap for some other fool. A baronet or a squire drowning in debt and not too particular, like that idiot Walters who married his sister. Someone without a father to protect his family name."

He gestured to the footmen with a jerk of his head. "Two of you escort *Miss* Milton," the emphasis he put on the honorific was an insult in itself, "and anyone she brought with her off the estate. If she won't move, throw the baggage out with her bags. I want them gone when I come down from dealing with my son."

"I am leaving with Miss Milton," Spen insisted, defiantly.

The marquess didn't spare him a glance as he turned on his heel and marched away, saying to the two other footmen, "Bring him."

Chapter Six

WHILE CORDELIA WATCHED, helpless to prevent it, the two footmen grabbed Spen by the arms and dragged him backward, easily ignoring his struggles.

Oh, Spen. She would cry later. The remaining footmen were moving on her, and she would not put it past them to drag her, too. Perhaps her uncle could do something to help the man she loved. "Gracie," she said to her maid, "let Aunt Eliza know we are leaving. I want you and her downstairs at the front door with our belongings as quickly as you can make it."

She fixed one of the footmen with a stare she had seen the Duchess of Haverford use on a gentleman who was in his cups and making a nuisance of himself. "You will go with my maid to carry our bags. You may need someone else to help." She applied the look to his companion. "You will conduct me to my coachman and other servants so I can order them to have my father's carriage brought around."

For a moment, she thought they would be difficult, but they must have concluded her instructions fitted within the commands of their marquess, for they nodded and obeyed.

She had to get Aunt Eliza out of here before that horrid man did something nastier still.

Oh, Spen.

No. She could not let herself break down. That evil monster could not hurt Spen too much. Her beloved was his heir. And in a few short months, Spen would be twenty-one. No wonder he had warned her they might have to marry in defiance of the marquess! She wished they had known the man had misunderstood who Spen planned to marry.

Again, fear and grief threatened to overwhelm her. Again, she thrust them away.

She could break down after she had safely removed her people from this house.

SPEN LAY ON his stomach while the housekeeper, who oversaw the estate's still room, slathered salve on the stripes where his father's whip had broken the surface. She said nothing, her lips pressed tightly together. Her eyes spoke for her, screaming her anger and disdain. For Spen? Or for the marquess?

Spen hoped it was the marquess, for he was desperate to know whether Cordelia and her aunt were safely away. When he had tried to ask, the brutal footman—one of the two who had held him for his father's beating—had threatened him. "Shut your lip, or I'll shut it for you. My lord."

The last two words were a sneer. *The marquess won't let them kill me.* They could make him even more uncomfortable, though. Many of his bruises had been his punishment for fighting them when they first seized him at his father's command. One had held him by his elbows pulled behind his back while the other applied a fist to his face, shoulders, and thighs.

Not the torso, the marquess had instructed. "I want him alive to sire an heir who isn't the brat."

Lord Deerhaven was too proud to repudiate John as someone else's get, but he was also determined the only other son born to a wife of his would not inherit. No, Spen's life was not in danger.

The beating had been designed to cause the maximum amount of pain possible without more than minor, and easily mended, damage.

The physicking was also a torture, but one to his benefit, and if the housekeeper was not sympathetic, she was at least as gentle as she could be. Spen ignored the pain as best he could, wracking his brain to figure out a way to ask his questions without the guard overhearing.

The man solved his problem for him, by hovering so close to the housekeeper's elbow that she turned on him. "Get out, William Fielder. You are in my way. Go and guard the door if you're afraid you haven't beaten his lordship enough to prevent him from trying to run away, or whatever it is you think you are doing."

"The marquess said I wasn't to let him out of my sight until the door is locked," the bully grumbled.

"Then stand in the doorway," she retorted. "Just don't stand so close you jog my elbow."

Fielder hesitated.

"What?" the housekeeper scoffed. "Do you think he is going to fly out the window? It is barred, you fool, and besides, we are on the sixth floor. Even if Lord Spenhurst was capable of moving, he is not leaving this room. Now move!"

Fielder did as he was told, but stopped short of the door, where he could still see Spen's face. Not the housekeeper's though. She whispered, "Your lady is safe, my lord. He didn't hurt her or her aunt. They and her servants are gone."

Spen managed to freeze his face so Fielder couldn't see his reaction. Inside, he was grieving his beloved already, even as he rejoiced she was not hurt. His hands were masked from Fielder by the housekeeper's body. He shifted one to touch her hand in thanks. She spared him a smile.

"Now lie you still, my lord. You'll do well enough but give my salve time to do its work. I'll come up tomorrow morning to check on you."

"Don't go pampering the little snot," Fielder said. "The marquess…"

"You're a fool, William Fielder," said the housekeeper. "Who do you think is going to be marquess when Lord Deerhaven is gone?" She looked back over her shoulder at Spen. "I trust you will remember my service, my lord, in years to come."

Spen accepted the opportunity she offered. "I will remember everything that has happened this day, and the roles played by all of those in service to my family," he promised, catching Fielder's eye and hoping the man could see his determination in his eyes.

Fielder had clearly been employed for his bulk and his strength, not for his brains. Spen was able to count to twenty as the man puzzled out the implications for him if he was still in service here when Deerhaven died.

It could not be much more than a decade away—probably less. His father was nearer to seventy than to sixty. He had not married until he was in his forties, and Spen's mother had lost several children before Spen was born, and more in between Spen and John. While the marquess had had two wives since, he had not fathered another live legitimate child. Furthermore, he had spent a lifetime indulging himself in the richest of food, alcohol, women, and other appurtenances of riotous living.

Fielder eventually reached the conclusion Spen might be able to take his revenge sooner rather than later. "I followed orders," he offered, hesitantly.

Spen lowered his voice. "It is your enthusiasm I will remember, William Fielder," he said.

Fielder backed away out the door, and the housekeeper gave Spen a broad smile. "You'll do, my lord," she said.

"Thank you," Spen told her. It raised his spirits to know he had at least some support in the house. Well, of course, he did. He glanced at the door to check Fielder was out of earshot, and whispered, "My brother?"

She did her own check on the doorway, and her voice was a mere thread as she told him, "No problem there, my lord. I think the marquess has forgotten he is at home, and we'll not remind him. Lady Deerhaven is having a tray in her room."

That sounded ominous. Spenhurst's mother used to eat in her room whenever she had bruises she did not want to display to the household, and so did the marquess's second wife. Spenhurst had felt guilty enough that the failure of his scheme had brought Cordelia such insult. But he'd never imagined the marquess would hurt his third wife, since she was with child. Indeed, the old man had been relatively doting, at least by comparison to his usual behavior.

"I am sorry," he murmured.

Sorry about it all, he reflected, as the housekeeper dipped a curtsey and left the room. Sorry he'd not thought to actually name Cordelia to his father. They could have fought it out there and then, where Spen had more allies and Cordelia would not have been involved. Sorry she had had to see his father in a rage. Sorry he had put his brother and his stepmother in danger. Sorry, above all, that he had been separated from his beloved.

The door shut, and he heard the key turning in the lock. From what the housekeeper said, he was in the top room of the oldest tower. And here, the marquess had told him, he would stay until he agreed to marry at his father's command. Not just until he was twenty-one, either. He would take the bride his father had chosen for him, or he would not leave this room until he agreed to the marriage. *Or,* Spen thought defiantly, *Until I am Deerhaven myself.*

Spen shuddered at the thought of how long that might be, setting off waves of pain in his wounds and bruises. Lying still was a good idea. He could use the time to plan an escape. But how?

Idly, he wondered what would happen with the other guests Lady Deerhaven had invited to the house party the marquess had ordered. The marquess would send them home, Spenhurst supposed.

Where was Cordelia now? Would she have ordered the carriage back to London? At least she had her aunt and her maid with her, and her outriders. She was not unprotected. Now that she was safely off Deerhaven land, her people would protect her. Spen hoped she knew he had not given up. That he *would* not give up.

If I have to, I will wait my father out.

AUNT ELIZA NEEDED to be nearly carried to the carriage after the Marquess of Deerhaven appeared in a gallery above the massive entry hall as they crossed it on their way out. He stood far above them, staring down at them and thundering for them to be off. Cordelia took rooms in the nearest village off Deerhaven's lands, and Aunt Eliza went gladly to bed. The stress had brought one of her migraines, and a carriage journey would be impossible until she recovered.

Just to be safe, Cordelia gave her name and Aunt Eliza's as Cruikshank, which had been the name of one of her governesses. She swore her servants to secrecy, and they agreed it was best not to draw the attention of Deerhaven.

Aunt Eliza remained in bed for the rest of the day and well into the afternoon of the next day, in a darkened room with a succession of damp clothes over her eyes to ease her headache.

Cordelia left her to the care of their maid and set off to make friends with anyone in the village who could be persuaded to talk to her. "I will have a footman with me at all times," she promised Aunt Eliza. She instructed Andrew, the footman, to sit outside the tavern, with a tankard of ale. He could see her wherever she went, except when she was inside a shop, so it was more or less true he was with her at all times. Within shouting distance, in any case.

Andrew went beyond his brief, chatting with the tavern's other patrons. Through him, Cordelia learned that Deerhaven was known as a hard man. High in the instep and convinced of his God-given right to trample on lesser people who got in his way.

Cordelia, on the other hand, persuaded some of the women to talk to her about Deerhaven's sons. Young Lord John had taken lessons with the vicar's sons before he went away to school, and was still a frequent visitor to the village when he was at home.

Lord Spenhurst was always polite, and very handsome, but they had seldom seen him since he finished school. Nor did they see much of Lord Deerhaven, even though he frequently deposited Lady Deerhaven at Deercroft and went off on his own. It was said he spent the Season in London, six weeks over the summer at Deercroft, and for the rest of the year traveled around the country, visiting his other properties, and attending house parties.

Lord Spenhurst usually went wherever the marquess went.

Apart from commenting that Lady Deerhaven stayed at Deercroft, none of them would talk about her, not the tavern patrons nor the village women.

That was as much as Cordelia knew when Aunt Eliza woke on the third morning with her headache much diminished and began worrying about them staying in the neighborhood.

"We need to go back to London, Cordelia," Aunt Eliza said. "What if the marquess finds out you are still here?"

"I am not on his land, Aunt Eliza," Cordelia reminded the poor dear.

"I do not like it," Aunt Eliza complained.

Cordelia was determined to stay until she could talk to Lord John, or at least until rumors trickled out from Deercroft to tell her how Spen fared. "You know how ill you get in a carriage when you've had one of your headaches, Aunt Eliza," she said, ignoring the twinges of guilt at using her aunt's frailties for her own purposes.

She set herself to soothe Aunt Eliza's worries. "You do not need to worry about Lord Deerhaven. His people shop in the village on his estate. He does not visit here, and nor does Lady

Deerhaven."

"But if he were to come..." Aunt Eliza fretted. "I was so frightened, my dear Cordelia. I thought he was going to hurt us!"

"He will not even know we are here," Cordelia insisted. "I want you to rest and get better. We will go back to London once I am sure you are well enough to travel."

Aunt Eliza hesitated, and Cordelia could tell she was thinking about how ill and weak she felt after a migraine passed. That had been Cordelia's intent all along, since she was hoping her aunt's desire to stay in one place would win over her fear of Deerhaven. If Lord John did not come within the next two days, however, Cordelia might have a real argument on her hands.

She decided to enlist the rest of her servants to collect information about Deercroft, its owner, and his family. Perhaps she could find a way to get a message to Lord John, or even to Spen.

Chapter Seven

THE SECOND DAY after a beating was always worse than the first. The insulating effect of shock was gone, the bruises were at their maximum, and the stinging cuts were still so raw the least and lightest of covers caused agony.

Spen lay on his stomach and endured. The housekeeper visited again, and Fielder popped his head in a couple of times, bringing food and drink and taking away the chamber pot. He remained sullen, but was, at least, no longer actively hostile.

Just after the second meal of the day, Spenhurst heard voices outside of the locked door.

"His lordship said no visitors," Fielder growled.

Spen strained to hear the response. It was John. Spen recognized his voice but couldn't hear the words.

"No visitors," Fielder repeated.

John's voice again, Fielder gave the same response, and then silence.

So. Spen was to be deprived of his brother's company. Probably as well. If the marquess caught John anywhere near Spen, it would go badly for the boy. John stayed safe by staying out of the way of the marquess, who was too proud to admit his wife's second son was not his get, but too volatile to be trusted not to kill the unwanted cuckoo in his nest when he lost his temper.

John, though, hadn't given up. Spen's dinner came with a note folded inside the table napkin. It was written on both sides and crossed to keep it small. Spen hid it until Fielder had taken away the tray, then puzzled it out by the fading light shining through the window from the sunset.

Spen, they won't let me in to see you. Can you come to the window tomorrow morning at half after six by the stable clock? I will be in the oak tree on the other side of the courtyard. Lady Deerhaven is still taking her meals in her room, but her maid says it is only a bruise on her face. The marquess is leaving again tomorrow. The schoolroom maid heard him order the coach for ten o'clock. I told Fielder that and asked to see you tomorrow, but he said his orders were to keep you there and not let anyone in. Your loving brother, John.

Spen hobbled to the window, but it was too dark to see the clock in the little tower on top of the stables. No matter. Dawn at this time of the year was before six. If he watched for the light, he would be up in time to see John.

That wasn't hard. He was in too much pain to sleep much at all, and restlessly pacing as soon as the sky lightened enough for him to move around the room without bumping into walls or furniture. The little tower room had once been a mirror image of the one at the other end of the building, but in recent times, it had been divided in two by an internal wall and had become a dumping ground for elderly chairs and sofas, all overstuffed and sagging. In addition, it held two chests of drawers, a desk, a couple of tables, a wardrobe with only three legs, and of course, the bed, which was also in disrepair, with one corner supported on bricks.

John should have waited until the marquess had left. He shouldn't be climbing the tree at all—though it was a good choice. It was as tall as the tower, and on the far side of the tower from the main house, so someone in the tree was likely to go unobserved.

Spen studied the tree as the sun rose. The growth was at its lushest, with young green leaves and catkins covering and concealing the branches, but Spen knew how strong those branches were. They had grown particularly robust on this side, thanks to regular pruning. The gardeners kept them trimmed to prevent them from spanning the path, so no one could enter the tower from the tree—or, for that matter, escape by the tree from the tower

Not that the bars on the windows made either of these actions possible. The marquess was nothing if not thorough.

Spen could open the window, however, and he did. His spirits rose. If John was careful, he might be able to get within perhaps ten yards of the tower, and he'd be impossible to see from the ground, should anyone be out and about this early in the morning. It was an easy climb, too. John shouldn't be attempting it with only one useable arm, but Spen didn't doubt his agility and balance.

The wait was interminable. Spen crossed the room twice to another window from which he could see the stable, and each time the longer hand had crept only a few minutes. No more. John would come, or he wouldn't. And if he didn't, Spen would worry about him for the rest of the day.

Despite his watching, he didn't see John arrive at the tree. The boy's head suddenly popped into sight, surrounded by leaves.

He was at the same level as Spen, but a few yards away. His intense determined look softened into a grin. "Spen! You're here! You're able to move around. The housekeeper said you would be up and about by now, but I was worried."

"I'm well," Spen lied. "Nothing for you to worry about, John."

"Good. What does he want you to do, Spen? The servants say he is keeping you locked up until you sign something, but they don't know what."

Spen never knew how much the servants told John, and how much John picked up from the conversations of others because he was good at moving around the huge old house as silently as a ghost. Certainly, though, John was usually way ahead of Spen at hearing any news. "What happened to Miss Milton, John? The housekeeper said she got away safely, but I was concerned the marquess might send someone after her."

John shook his head. "He didn't. Not that I have heard. I don't think she went far, though. Just to the inn at Crossings. The stable boy saw her horses at the inn when he took two of ours to be shod."

"She is off our land at least. But she must go back to London, John. To her uncle. He'll be able to protect her." Spen hoped. The marquess had a long reach though, as Spen and John both had cause to know. Their mother had died at the hands of highwaymen, or so the world believed. But the marquess had told her sons he had sent the villains after her and her lover when Lady Deerhaven had attempted to escape her miserable marriage.

"What does the marquess want you to sign?" John insisted.

"A marriage contract. Between me and Lady Daphne Ashburton, the daughter of the Earl of Yarverton. I'm not going to do it. I am marrying Cordelia Milton, even if I must wait until his lordship is dead. But the more I refuse, the more danger there is to her. Go and see if she is at the inn, John. If she is, tell her to go home to her uncle and stay safe. Tell her I love her, and I will come for her as soon as I can." Even as he spoke, his stomach clenched, and his heart seemed to flip in his chest. *Please, let her wait for me.*

"He will make your life miserable," John warned. He frowned. "We need a rope. If you had a rope, you could lower it and I could send up anything you need."

Spen looked over his shoulder at the room. No ropes lying around, and if he started ripping up the sheets or the bedcovers, his keeper would notice. "Maybe I could take the fabric off the backs of the chairs," he mused. "I don't know if I could get enough pieces to reach the ground, though. It must be close to fifty feet."

"How many chairs?" John wondered.

"Half a dozen, and three sofas."

John had a furious frown, a sign he was thinking. "Horsehair," he said.

Spen frowned. "Horsehair?" Then it dawned on him. A couple of years ago, a stable master at one of the estates had taught the pair of them to make ropes from horsehair from which they then formed halters, and even bridles and reins. "The chairs will be stuffed with horsehair," he realized. He could possibly make a rope long enough to reach the ground. It could work. Not only that, but it would at least give him something to do.

"I have to go," John said. "I need to be back in my room before the maid comes. I'll try to get to Crossings today, Spen. See you here tomorrow?"

Spen shouldn't let him do it. It was a dangerous climb. On the other hand, the marquess was leaving, and the house was always safer and more relaxed when he was gone. Besides, Spen needed to hear that Cordelia was safe.

"Tomorrow," he agreed.

He stripped the horsehair out of one of the chairs and tossed his clothes over the depleted remains. No one noticed its miserable state. Not the housekeeper who came to check his wounds. Not the estate steward, who stood in the door as the sun approached its zenith and read a letter from the marquess that informed Spen he had five days to recover his senses and his obedience.

"You will have nothing to do but sit here and reflect on your duty to me and to the Deerhaven name," his lordship had written. "One meal a day. Nothing to read. Nowhere to go. Sign the marriage contract, and you will be released to eat your normal meals, to follow your normal amusements, within reason. Within the confines of this house. Once you are married as I bid, I will allow you to resume your usual activities."

Any comment was pointless. His father was not going to change his mind, and Spen was not going to change his own. The steward did not wait for him to comment, in any case. He turned away, and Fielder shut the door between them.

The cord was under the bed, where Spen had kicked it each time he heard the bolts being drawn back on his door. He retrieved it and got back to work.

By the time Fielder came back with his meal, Spen was hungry enough to eat anything. Soup and bread and not much of it. A jug of ale and another of water. He was glad of it.

"That's it, my lord," the man said, with an uncharacteristic note of apology.

By the time it was too dark to continue, the cord stretched the length of the room four times. He'd paced the room out and estimated he had about eighty feet of double-twisted horse hair cord. It wasn't perfect. He'd hand-rolled the hairs together, using the double-twist method the stable master had taught them. The resulting cord was tighter in some places than others and thicker or thinner where he'd added hair as the strand grew longer.

It was long, though. He'd need more cords to make a rope strong enough to be of much use, but he had plenty of horsehair. Even twisted with two more cords to make a six-ply rope, the length he had should reach the ground.

He was back at the window at dawn the following morning. He'd pulled a wooden chair to sit on, leaving his hands free to work on the next cord. It was repetitive work but required little thought. The worst thing about his confinement was having nothing to occupy his mind, which seemed determined to dwell on all the things his father could do to compel his obedience.

He cannot kill me.

Still, Spen wouldn't put it past the old fiend to kill him and John both, except the title would then go to the branch of the family that had moved to the United States two generations ago, and the marquess might prefer to see John inherit than an American. No. Probably not. But as long as Spen was the only son with the man's blood, he, at least, was too valuable to kill.

Things might change if Lady Deerhaven delivered a healthy boy, but even then, removing a man past the age of the common childhood diseases in favor of a newborn baby would be a risk.

The marquess could do a lot short of killing Spen, though. He could hurt John, for a start. Once he realized he could use threats against John to blackmail Spen, it would be the end of Spen's defiance.

Spen's hands kept twisting, twisting, and the cord grew, slowly but surely.

He had lost track of time when he heard Cordelia's voice. "Spen!"

Astonished, he looked up from his work, and there she was, no more than a dozen feet away in the oak tree, where John had been yesterday. And there was John, a little higher up in the tree, grinning a welcome.

"You shouldn't be here, my love," Spen told Cordelia. "It is dangerous." He paused, trying and failing to think of any female acquaintance who could climb a tree. The thought of Miss Wharton attempting such a feat boggled the mind. "You can climb trees? Every time he met her, he found more to admire about her.

She smiled then. "As you see," she told him. "As to the danger, the marquess is gone, and I have my pistol."

What a resourceful, clever woman she was. How proud he was to love her. His heart warmed, especially when she said, "I had to see you, Spen."

He couldn't argue with that, considering how wonderful it was to see her. "Tell me you at least brought a groom or a footman with you."

"Of course. My footman is keeping watch to give us warning if anyone comes this way, and one of my outriders is below the tower with some things to send up to you if we can make it work."

"Cordelia has some ideas to help," John said. "She thought we could throw you a cord, and then tie a rope to one end of it for you to pull up. It will save you having to make one."

Spen held up his work. "I've made a cord. It is plenty long

enough to drop down to the ground." He fetched the cord he'd made the day before and fed it through the bars.

"My outrider will tug once to get you to stop, and twice to get you to start again," Cordelia said. *Good thinking.* Spen couldn't see the ground below the tower with the bars in the way, but he kept feeding out the cord until he felt a tug.

"I brought the rope," Cordelia said. "Also, some food, since John says you are not getting proper meals, some tools to try to loosen the bars, and a couple of books for you to read in case we can't get you free today. Is there anything else you need, Spen?"

He was responding to a double tug from below by pulling up the cord. From the weight of it, it was bringing something up with it. "I need you and John away from here," he told Cordelia. That sounded ungracious and the hurt that passed across Cordelia's face showed she thought so, too.

"I've been thinking about what my father might do to force my hand," he explained. "I can stand against him if the pair of you are safe. If he has you or John and threatens to hurt you, I will have to obey him. You don't know what a monster he is."

Cordelia nodded, thoughtfully. "I believe you. John has been telling me about him. I can see the rope coming up with your cord. Did you really make it yourself, Spen? Out of furniture stuffing?"

A moment later, the rope was in his hand. He hauled the end of it inside, untied the cord, wrapped the rope around the bed leg, and tied it to the bars to anchor it. Then he gave it a double tug.

"It's a bit of a knack," he admitted. "The first few yards are pretty rough, but I got better."

A moment later, a double tug told him to start hauling again. This time, the weight was heavier.

"We made two bags of it," Cordelia said. "The first one should be the tools and the books. The second one will be food and other comforts."

"I suggested the brandy," John advised.

The first bag came up—a cloth bag with several chisels, a

mallet, and three books. Spen had to take them from the bag one at a time to get them through the bars. He lowered the rope again.

"John told me you were staying at Crossings," he said to Cordelia. "You must see it is dangerous to be so close to the marquess. If you were to fall into his hands…" he shuddered. "He believes being a marquess means he does not have to obey the rules and laws that apply to lesser beings."

It appeared to be true, too. The law gave him the right to chastise his successive wives and his son, but his beatings when in a temper were excessive. So much so, that, since Spen grew old enough to fight back, he had left the beatings to servants he could trust not to kill Spen. And he had got away with murder, at least one Spen knew of, when he paid for the killing of his fleeing wife.

"He is away from home, and he does not know we are there," Cordelia assured Spen. "I used the name Cruikshank when I signed the register, and my servants won't betray me. John says the stable boy recognized my horses, but he won't say anything."

"Even so," Spen insisted. "I don't want you at risk. If you won't go for your own sake, go for mine. I don't want to be forced to marry Lady Daphne. Even if she was competent to marry—and I cannot believe she is—she is not you, Cordelia. I will marry you or no one."

"Lady Daphne is sweet," Cordelia commented.

The second bag reached Spen's level. "It doesn't matter what Lady Daphne is," Spen told Cordelia as he unpacked it. "I will marry you."

Boxes and parcels. Two bottles. A pack of cards. A sharp knife. A brief examination confirmed the boxes and parcels contained food. "I think you've thought of everything," he told his two accomplices.

"It was mostly Cordelia," said John.

"John thought of the brandy and the cards," Cordelia pointed out. "And the knife."

Spen raised his eyebrows. "What are you learning at school,

John?"

John just grinned, then turned his head to gaze at the corner of the tower. Spen couldn't see what had attracted his attention, but Cordelia said, "Draw the rope and the bag inside, Spen. John, keep quiet and still. Andrew and Charles know to hide until whoever it is has gone past."

After that, she said no more, and John, too, obeyed her command to be still. Spen, meanwhile, drew in the bag and pressed up against the bars to try to see the path below the tower.

The sill was in the way, but he could hear two men talking, their voices carrying clearly to his ears in the quiet morning. He didn't recognize them by the sound, but then the estate had several hundred servants, both indoor and outdoor, most of whom never entered the rarified sphere of the young heir.

"'E won't last. Pampered young lordling like that."

Was Spen the topic under discussion? It seemed so, for the other man said, "Maybe so, maybe not. 'E's been goin' be'ind 'is Da's back for years to look after the young 'un."

"Five shilling says 'e gets wed like 'e's told." They had passed the tower and turned onto the path that led across the park, ending up eventually at the home farm.

"Done!"

Spenhurst could see them now, coming into view between the branches as they passed under the trees. One was pushing and the other pulling a cart, but it could not have been hard labor, for they continued arguing as they moved away out of sight.

"We had better go," said Cordelia.

"I love you, Cordelia," Spen told her. "Get yourself and John to safety. Please."

She shook her head, stubbornly. "We have a couple of days. I will be here again tomorrow."

"So will I," John agreed.

They disappeared from view. Spen sat there for some time watching, but he did not see them depart.

Chapter Eight

SPEN HAD A point. If his father caught Cordelia still in the neighborhood of his estate or—even worse—on his estate, there was no knowing what he would do, but it would be bad. True, even the Marquess of Deerhaven would not get away with killing or even hurting Josiah Milton's niece. However, since he was far too arrogant to realize how much power Cordelia's uncle had, he would only find out his mistake after Cordelia was already in far more trouble than she wished to contemplate.

The wisest thing was to retreat and plan Spen's rescue from the safety of her uncle's protection. Uncle Josh might balk at extending that protection to John, but Cordelia was confident of her ability to persuade him.

Still, Cordelia thought it worth the risk to wait one more day, and when she got back to the inn, it became a moot point anyway. Aunt Eliza's migraine had returned, and there was no way they could travel today. Perhaps, if Spen was able to deal with the bars, they could all leave together tomorrow.

The following morning, she again walked to the tower in the early morning light, with Andrew the footman, and Charles the outrider. She took the path John had shown her the previous day, and he was waiting on the other side of what the boy had called "the home wood".

His face lit up when he saw her. "You came."

"Of course. Do you think Spen has managed to get through the bars?"

John shook his head. "I couldn't tell in the dark, but I think they are still there. They were there last night."

As he had the day before, he led them into the shadow of a tall hedge. They followed the hedge until they were close to the tower. They then had to cross an open space, but the tower already screened them from view of the house and the stable block on this side of the house was largely empty.

They would be visible from the windows of the tower, but John had already assured Cordelia that only Spen and his guard were within, and the guard occupied the house side of the top floor where Spen was incarcerated.

The only other danger was some early riser walking the grounds, but they saw no one, and no one sounded an alarm.

In the safety of the oak, Cordelia unlaced the skirt she wore over a pair of trousers her maid had managed to purchase when John first told her his plan to climb to Spen's level. Before yesterday, it had been more than six years since she climbed a tree, and she had never climbed so high.

She had been afraid, and perhaps John realized that, for he assured her he could do the climb and relay her messages. But there was no way she was missing her chance to see Spen again, so she gritted her teeth and made her way from branch to branch until she was high enough. Today was easier. She had already done it once. Once she removed her skirt, her footman made a stirrup of his hand and tossed her up to the first branch, and from there it was simple. Soon, she was edging her way out onto the branch she and John had chosen the day before.

Spen was waiting at the window. The barred window.

"I am scraping away stone a bit at a time," he reported after they'd exchanged greetings. "The sill is hard rock, and I don't know how deeply the bars are set, so I don't know how long it will take me. Not less than a week, but it might be much longer."

"We can wait in Crossings," Cordelia said, but she knew they could not even before Spen shook his head.

"He will use you and John against me," he said, "and then I will have to wed as he bids. Go, both of you. For my sake and for the sake of our future. Your uncle will be able to protect you? Won't he?" His tone made that a question.

Cordelia was certain of it. "Your father thinks his position allows him to bully anyone he pleases and trample on those who defy him. But my uncle has connections and influences of his own and is used to a far harsher world than your father could imagine. He will protect us."

Spen nodded. "Then you will go? You will take John with you?"

"Yes, but I will leave two of my men behind to see you have enough food and anything else you need," she insisted.

"Make sure they understand the danger," Spen insisted.

"I already have," she assured him. "The two men who helped us yesterday have volunteered. Their names are Charles and Andrew, and they will come every morning."

Cordelia had spoken to all the men in her entourage, footmen, grooms, and outriders. "I need two of you to leave my service and find positions in this village," she had told them. "Except, not really. In fact, you will still be employed by me, at double your usual wages." She went on to explain that the earl—her betrothed—was locked in a tower and that his father the marquess was unstable and dangerous. They had a friendly set of eyes and ears in Deercroft, however. The stable boy was on Lord Spenhurst's side and was willing to pass information on his visits to the village.

"Every second morning would be safer," Spen suggested. "Can you ask them to bring me writing materials?"

"Of course, and will you write to me, Spen?"

Spen's eyes widened. "What would your uncle say?"

Uncle Josh would ask Aunt Eliza, and Aunt Eliza would say young ladies did not receive letters from gentlemen. "We are betrothed," Cordelia replied. "Besides, I need to know you are safe. Write to me, Spen."

>>><<<

CORDELIA SENT THE shortest of the grooms out to meet John on the road to London with a spare suit of livery for John to wear. They had decided not to appear in the village together. As it turned out, he had quite a wait, since Aunt Eliza insisted on intervening with the servants who had decided to stay behind.

"But you have a good position with Mr. Milton," she insisted. "Why would you abandon it?"

Cordelia knew she had chosen well when neither of them indicated by word or look that they were not leaving their employment. Poor Aunt Eliza. Cordelia felt guilty for not taking her aunt into her confidence, but the lady had no gift for deceit and would let their secret out if she knew it.

The scene with her two spies had its uses, since the innkeeper, his wife, and several of his servants and customers witnessed Aunt Eliza's distress. No one would doubt Andrew and Charles had left her service. That and the false name she had used at the inn should help to keep them safe from the marquess's attention.

At last, her party left the inn yard—two coaches and a surrounding cluster of outriders. Cordelia and Aunt Eliza were in the lead vehicle with Gracie, Cordelia's maid, who also looked after Aunt Eliza on journeys since Aunt Eliza's maid was an even worse traveler than Aunt Eliza.

The second carriage, which carried their luggage, was under instructions to pause to pick up John and the groom at the spot just beyond—and out of sight of—the first tollgate. The carriage would pause for only a moment, and the road was dry. With luck, there would be nothing to show two people had joined the carriage.

The livery fitted well enough, Cordelia decided when she saw

John at the first stop for a change of horses. He had dispensed with the sling as part of his disguise, and she went over to tell him to put it on again.

"Your brother will be upset if traveling with me impairs your healing," she pointed out. "Please be careful, John. If the bone shifts before it is mended, it might not heal correctly." On an inspiration, she added, "How will you be a cavalry officer with a damaged arm?" That did the trick. He fished the sling out of his pocket and put it back on.

At the next change, they paused long enough to take lunch, then took to the road again. Aunt Eliza complained about the speed. "You insisted on staying in the village, Cordelia," she pointed out. "And now you cannot wait to get to London. Surely, we could stay somewhere overnight?"

Cordelia could not tell her she was anxious to have John under her uncle's protection. She was pleased when Aunt Eliza ceased her complaining and dropped off to sleep.

She signaled to the driver to stop and left the maid to watch her aunt while she joined John in the luggage coach.

"I hope you don't mind, John," she said. "I thought we might take the opportunity to get to know one another better. How are you?"

"I am well, thank you, Miss Milton," the boy said.

"Cordelia. I will be your sister," she insisted.

"I hope so, Cordelia," John said, though his face showed his doubts. "You love my brother and I think you will be good for him. But the marquess is going to be furious."

Cordelia shrugged. From what she had heard and seen of the marquess, he was a bully and a tyrant, but she did not intend to allow him to win. "I think your father overestimates his power," she said.

John shook his head. "He is not my father. I thought Spen would have told you. My mother played him false." His eyes blazed and his jaw was stiff, as if he expected her to repudiate him.

Cordelia wanted to reassure him and blurted out the first thing she thought of. "You must be glad. I know Spen is afraid of being like the horrid man, but you don't have that worry." Perhaps it wasn't the ladylike thing to say. In fact, it definitely wasn't. But it had banished the tight, grim look from John's face.

"That is true," he said. "I hadn't thought of that. But Spen does not have to be afraid. He will never be like the marquess."

Cordelia smiled. "That's what I told him, John. I reminded him how kind he is to those who serve him, and how much his friends like him. And you and I, too. We love him, and we have very good taste, do we not?"

John laughed and began telling her stories about Spen. It was clear Spen was a hero to his younger brother, and she also got the impression that—apart from Spen—John had no one who cared about him.

He now had her, too, Cordelia determined.

"What will the marquess do when he finds out you are missing?" she asked.

John shrugged. "With any luck, he will assume I have gone back to school, or taken off for Rosewood Towers. That's the estate in Cumberland where I spend my summers when the school closes for the holidays. The marquess never goes there." He smiled, a soft dreamy look. "Spen always spends several weeks with me in the summer."

"I thought Deercroft was your home," Cordelia observed.

"It is the marquess's seat, but none of us spend much time there. Except Lady Deerhaven, since her first confinement."

Cordelia was diverted by the comment. "I did not know Lady Deerhaven had an older child."

"The baby was born early and died," John told her, mournfully. "They say the marquess was furious. He has not let her return to London since then."

"The poor lady." Cordelia's distaste for the marquess could not grow any stronger, but this was a new low. To blame his poor, grieving wife for the loss of a baby. She hoped the lady would bear a live child this time. A daughter, preferably. According to the gossip Andrew had heard, Spen's chief protection from his father's anger was his position as his father's heir, and Cordelia was afraid of what might happen if the marquess had an alternative.

At least now John was out of the evil man's hands.

"I can't help but feel I should have stayed at Deercroft," John said. "Perhaps I could have helped Spen."

"You could have been used to hurt Spen," Cordelia pointed out. "Or do you not agree the marquess would hurt you to make Spen do as he is told?"

John sighed. "I do agree. It is just the kind of thing he would do. He has done it in the past. He once fired my governess because Spen had a bad report card. He beat me once because he wanted Spen to sing to entertain the guests at a house party. Spen said he would do it, but then…" John shrugged.

"He hates performing in front of an audience, he told me," Cordelia said.

John nodded. "He thought Spen was embarrassing him on purpose, so he sent me away to Rosewood Towers. The marquess thinks Spen's love for me is a weakness, but that has never stopped him from exploiting it."

"What a monster," Cordelia said.

John chuckled. "Spen uses it against him, too. He has only to suggest there's something I would hate, and then defy the marquess over something, and I get to do it. That is how he got me lessons with the vicar, instead of being left with no one to teach me what I need to know to be an officer. He let the marquess know I hated doing lessons."

He frowned and shifted uncomfortably. "Then the vicar wrote to tell him how well I was doing, so he sent me to that horrid school. Still, at least there were lessons. I am going into the army when I'm grown, Cordelia." He grimaced. "At least, I want to. The marquess probably won't buy me a commission."

Or he will jump at the chance to send you into danger, Cordelia thought but did not say. "We will keep you out of the marquess's hands as long as we possibly can, John—at least until Spen is of age and can wed against the old man's wishes. My uncle will provide you with refuge, and he will help us rescue your brother."

John looked doubtful, but Cordelia was certain. Her uncle had never refused her any reasonable request, and he hated tyranny.

Still, she worried. It was all very well to assure John her uncle would help in Spen's rescue, but what could they do? The marquess had the right to lock his son up if he wished, and even to have him beaten. Until Spen was of age, they could not demand his release, and her uncle was unlikely to agree to a less-than-legal approach.

She refused to let John see her doubts. Instead, she begged him for more stories about her beloved.

Chapter Nine

WHEN CORDELIA TOLD Uncle Josh what had happened at Deercroft, Uncle Josh shrugged. "Well, lass. Ye did reach high. But if the marquess won't have it, then that's that."

Cordelia shook her head. "Lord Spenhurst will marry me, Uncle Josh. His father will not prevent him, even if we have to wait until he has turned twenty-one."

Uncle Josh raised his eyebrows. "And if I won't have it?"

Cordelia's heart sank but she lifted her chin and said, proudly, "Then we will have to wait until I am twenty-one."

"No, lass," Uncle Josh assured her. "I'll not deny ye. If the lad proves true, I'll stand his friend."

"He has been beaten and remains true. He is locked up and is being starved and remains true. We have to help him, Uncle Josh." Cordelia went on to tell her uncle about leaving her servants in the village, with instructions to learn what they could and help Spen as much as possible.

"Uncle Josh, what do you know about the marquess? Is there anything we could use to make him let Spen go? And to stop him from hurting you, Uncle Josh? For he threatened to ruin you for imagining I might aspire to be Spen's wife."

Uncle Josh looked thoughtful. "Did he, now? As if he could! Well, if he tries it, he shall find out Josiah Milton is not helpless.

Perhaps I should dig around a bit, at that."

Uncle Josh was not sanguine about keeping John from his legal guardian. Cordelia pointed out the marquess did not care about John and had mistreated him, but Uncle Josh insisted it didn't change the legal position. John would have to go back either to Deercroft or to the school.

John declared he would take his chances on the streets of London rather than go back to the marquess.

Uncle Josh peered at him and must have decided he was serious. "The streets of London are dangerous, young lord. No soft beds or full bellies, and many bound and determined to take the shirt off yer back."

John met Uncle Josh's eyes. "A master at the school broke my arm, Mr. Milton. I've gone to bed cold and hungry many a time. Going back to the school is dangerous. The marquess even more so."

Uncle Josh narrowed his eyes. "Dee-Dee, take yerself off and let me talk to Lord John. See about a tea tray for us, will ye?"

Cordelia assumed Uncle Josh thought the story was not fit for her female ears, and perhaps he was correct, for by the time she returned with the tea tray, he was talking about hiring a tutor for John.

"I'm staying and I'm to be John Milton," the boy reported. "Your uncle is going to introduce me as distant cousin, Cordelia."

"If I understand ye, Dee-Dee, my sister hasna met John here." He shook his head. "What sort of chaperone be she, when she doesna see what's happening under her nose?"

Cordelia didn't answer that. She and Spen had enjoyed Aunt Eliza's incompetence as a chaperone, but she'd rather not tell Uncle Josh that.

Uncle Josh sighed. "It's for the best, mind. Lizzie never could keep a secret. That there marquess won't be asking me for the boy if he doesna know John is here."

"She will know John is not a cousin," Cordelia objected. One thing Aunt Eliza was sharp about was the names of every relative and all of their descendants.

Uncle Josh grinned. "She won't ask questions, Dee. She won't want the answers."

Cordelia didn't understand why Uncle Josh should think that, but Aunt Eliza herself gave the clue when she came downstairs for dinner, and Uncle Josh brought John over for an introduction.

"Lizzie, this be John Milton. John will be living with us. Yes, and dining with us when it is just family."

Aunt Eliza peered at John as she took his hand in both of hers and smiled up at him. "Then you are very welcome, John, but I do not precisely understand the relationship. Who is your father, dear?"

John cast a panicked look at Uncle Josh, who immediately said, "Now, then, Lizzie. Don't ye go fussing the boy." He clapped John on the back and added, "Not for female ears, Lizzie, and not the boy's fault, that's for certain."

Aunt Eliza's bright blush and flustered cascade of words about what might be for dinner and how inclement the weather was for this time of year showed she had jumped to the conclusion Uncle Josh had been reluctant to tell his maiden niece. Cordelia swallowed a gulp of laughter. So, John was to be her uncle's unacknowledged son, was he? Poor Aunt Eliza. It was unfair to embarrass her so.

<hr />

THE FOURTH DAY after Cordelia and John left started well and ended badly.

Charles and Andrew brought a letter from Cordelia in the morning, which confirmed she and John had reached London safely.

We all arrived this afternoon and will be staying in London for the moment. My traveling companions are well, though my aunt has taken to her bed with another headache, poor dear. My uncle is delighted to have us all under his wing.

She did not mention John—obviously fearing the letter might fall into the wrong hands. Wise girl. But it was clear Mr. Milton had accepted his brother, which was a weight off Spen's mind.

The letter was signed, "With all my love, Cordelia." Spen wanted to wear it next to his heart, but he allowed common sense to prevail and tucked it away into the pocket he had gouged from his mattress.

Just as well, for the marquess arrived later in the day, and was furious to find him still refusing the marriage. He ordered Spen beaten again and demanded Spen's one daily meal be halved. If Spen had been carrying the letter, Fielder would have found it when he stripped Spen's shirt off.

Fielder whispered an apology as he tied Spen for the whipping, and again when releasing him, but the beating wasn't so bad. Fielder hadn't laid on with enthusiasm as he had the first time but had not been able to avoid opening some of the healing scabs. All to the good, for the blood satisfied the marquess that Spen had been adequately punished, and he left, warning Spen there would be worse to come if Spen persisted in his defiance.

"I'll recall that brat from school and beat him in your place," he threatened.

Spen found it hard to contain his joy at the marquess's involuntary revelation. *He does not know John has been here, let alone that he is gone.*

It was Fielder who saw to Spen's wounds this time, carefully and gently spreading the salve. "His lordship has ordered I am the only one to see you, my lord," the man explained. "I'm sorry, my lord."

"I don't hold you accountable for the orders you have to follow, Fielder," Spen assured him. "I hope the housekeeper is not in trouble for nursing me last time."

Fielder shrugged. "The marquess does not know, my lord. Nobody told him." Which meant Fielder hadn't told his master. That was promising.

Spen decided to go fishing. "Has my brother returned to

school? Or has he gone back to Rosewood Towers?"

"I don't know, my lord." Fielder sounded hesitant, but after a moment, he added, "He is not still here at Deerhaven."

Spen pushed a little. "My father seems to think he is at school, but it is the summer holidays, is it not?"

Fielder thought about that. "I wouldn't know, my lord," he admitted after a while.

Spen waited to see if he had anything more to say and was rewarded when Fielder added. "He left suddenly. The kitchen sent up a dinner and a breakfast before the maid reported they had not been eaten, and the young master's bed had not been slept in."

Spen didn't have to pretend surprise. *It took nearly a whole day before anyone noticed John had gone?* "What did the marquess say about John's departure?" Disappearance, Spen had nearly said.

"Not my place to ask," Fielder grumbled. "Lord Deerhaven has commanded no one speak to him of Lord John."

Spen wanted to laugh. The marquess's distaste for any mention of John had given Spen's brother his freedom. He controlled himself enough to pretend concern. "I hope my brother is all right. Perhaps someone should write to Rosewood Towers to check whether he is there."

A safe enough suggestion. Spen doubted Fielder would do anything about it. Sure enough, the man said, "Not my place, my lord."

It had been the longest conversation Spen and Fielder had ever had, and it had broken the ice. After that, they always talked during Fielder's daily visit. At five in the afternoon by the stable clock, give or take a few minutes, Fielder would turn up with hot water for Spen to wash and Spen's one daily meal. Bread and water, by the marquess's command, and not much of that.

Fielder gave the room a cursory clean, gruffly expressing his thanks to Spen for keeping the place tidy. Spen felt a little guilty for accepting praise for hiding the evidence of his attempts to get through the bars and of the largesse delivered every second day by Cordelia's servants.

After he'd finished, Fielder removed any waste—the tray from the previous night's meal, last night's bucket, and the chamber pot. "Sleep well, my lord," he would say.

"You, too, Fielder," Spen replied. The poor man was nearly as much a prisoner as Spen, forced to live in the outer room of the tower prison, going nowhere and seeing no one except Spen and whomever the housekeeper sent to fetch and carry.

In fact, thanks to Cordelia's men, Spen was probably better off than Fielder. His days were long, but Andrew and Charles brought him plenty of food, books to read, drawing and writing materials, a pack of cards, and replacement chisels as he wore the others down chipping away at the stone sill. Bit by bit, he was making a hollow around one of the bars. Eventually, he'd have a hole large enough to slide it beyond the sill and let it drop.

He had not been able to chisel for more than a few minutes at the start. His hands, already red and sore from twisting his rope, blistered and then toughened. His wrists and arms ached. His shoulders, too. But day by day, they strengthened, and he was able to work for longer periods of time.

The biggest impediment to progress was the need to be quiet. He couldn't afford for Fielder to investigate any suspicious noises. Fortunately, the walls and the door were thick.

The relief baskets also carried letters from Cordelia and sometimes from John, and the men took away any food he hadn't been able to eat, and also the letters Spen wrote.

Spen would escape as soon as he could, but in the meantime, he was not uncomfortable.

He was not left entirely undisturbed. He had two visits from his father's steward in the next two weeks and gave the man the same answer he'd given the marquess. He refused his father's match. He would not change his mind.

The steward asked his questions and went away, leaving Spen to take out the chisel he had hastily hidden and return to his work.

Then came disaster.

Spen watched it unfold from his window. Charles was on basket duty and Andrew was in the tree when a group of footmen appeared from both sides of the tower and descended on Charles. He didn't resist, and it was over in less than a minute. Some of them hustled Charles towards the stables and out of view, and the others untied the basket and collected the other items Cordelia's men had brought for him.

Thankfully, none of them looked up into the tree. If Andrew stayed where he was, out of sight among the leaves, he should be safe. Spen could do nothing to help him, and there was work to do here.

The chisels and hammer went into a bag. He tucked Cordelia's letters in there, too. What else did he need to save? As much food as he could pack went into another bag. He couldn't keep the rope Cordelia had brought. It would need to stay hanging out of the window, for they knew it was there.

If he hid it, he was asking for them to tear the room apart, but they would not be looking for the one he had made himself, hand-twisting the cord and then knotting cords together in a tight strong weave. He had had plenty of time in the past few weeks to think of a hiding place they'd not find with the most careful of searches.

He took his bags and his coil of rope to the window that looked out over the roof. The bars here were even closer together, but there was room enough to maneuver the chisel bag between them and lower it down by the cord tied to the handle. He tied the cord around a bar. It was almost the same color and as close to invisible as it was going to get.

He did the same with the food bag and the rope. Only someone standing on the roof would be able to see them. As long as no one noticed the thin loops of dark cord against the dark metal of the bars, they would not be discovered.

That done, he concealed some of his books in the cavity in the mattress and more in the hollowed-out chairs. He put the rest, along with the remaining food and drink, the pack of cards and other entertainments, and his writing supplies, into drawers.

After a moment's thought, he spread the blankets Cordelia had sent onto the bed, hoping they'd be ignored by the searchers.

The sound of the key in the lock and of the bolts being drawn back told him he had run out of time. He sat on one of the lumpy chairs. They didn't keep him waiting for long.

The steward led the way into the room, with Fielder and several other footmen at his heels. "Search everything," he commanded. "Lord Spenhurst, it will go easier for you if you tell me who that man is to you, and what they have been providing."

Spen did his best to look relaxed. Better the marquess's hirelings than the marquess himself. "He is my man," he claimed. "I trust you will let him go."

"He was trespassing on Deerhaven land and feeding you when the marquess commanded you be fed bread and water only," the steward said. "He will be sent to the assizes."

"He has broken no laws," Spen insisted. "He was here at my command and following my orders."

The steward sneered. "Your father is in charge here," he pointed out. "He will decide, and your man will remain locked up until he returns."

Spen narrowed his eyes and spoke with all the hauteur he'd learned from his father. "You would do well to remember that one day, I shall be both marquess and magistrate."

The steward's eyes skittered away, but not before Spen saw the flash of fear and doubt. The man tromped over to the pile of books and other items that were accumulating on the bed. "How did you miss all of this, Will Fielder?" he demanded. "You useless git."

Fielder sent Spen a sullen glare.

"So did you," Spen pointed out. "No one expected me to have a servant of my own on the outside. Neither of you is to blame for not thinking to search the room."

Fielder gave Spen a nod, his expression a little less resentful.

One of the footmen had hauled the rope up and was untying it from the bed. Another wrapped what they'd discovered in one of the blankets to haul from the room. "No food tonight," the steward ordered Fielder. "Everyone out. We shall leave you, Lord Spenhurst. The grounds shall be patrolled after this. There will be no more servants on the outside for you."

With a final sniff, he led the way out of the room. William Fielder was the last to leave. He gave Spen a slow nod before he shut the door, and Spen took heart that Fielder, at least, still stood as much his friend as he safely could.

And the searchers had missed two of his caches and the bags and rope he'd hung from the window. It could have been much worse. He pulled in the bags and the coil of rope and re-hid them.

He hoped Charles would be all right. If Andrew managed to escape, surely, he would fetch help to rescue the other servant?

Spen settled by the window, chisel in hand, so he could scratch away at the sill while watching for Andrew to be caught or to get away.

CORDELIA WAS SPENDING the morning going through reports from her business managers. When she was fifteen, she had gone to her uncle with a proposition for a business using skilled embroiderers working from their own homes to embellish some of the high-end fabrics he imported, using designs she created herself. He had given her a loan to try the idea out, and advice when she asked for it, but had otherwise left her to figure things out for herself.

She began in a small way, grew the production side of the business while selling the resulting fabrics to dressmakers, and moved on to take orders for embroidering directly onto partially made garments. Eighteen months ago, she had paid off the loan.

She had competent people running the various branches of the business, but she still maintained a careful watch over it, and she was deep in making notes on the various reports when she heard a commotion, as feet trooped up and down the stairs, accompanied by excited chatter.

She came downstairs to find a bustle of preparation for a journey. Her uncle had not mentioned a journey yesterday evening, but it was not unusual for him to be called away to deal with a problem at one of his mills or warehouses. She had no reason to immediately assume the disturbance had to do with Spen, but her heart was already in her mouth when she followed the sound of her uncle's voice into the parlor and saw Andrew.

He sat slumped in a chair, but when Uncle Josh said her name, he straightened and stood. He looked dreadful. Part of that was because of his crumpled scruffy clothes in an anonymous muddy brown, but it was mostly because his face was drawn, and his expression defeated.

"Andrew! What has happened!"

"Now, Cordelia, I am dealing with it," said Uncle Josh.

"What has happened?" Cordelia repeated. "Andrew, sit down. You look exhausted."

"He rode all night from Deercroft," Uncle Josh explained. "They were found taking food to your earl, and Charles has been locked up. I've sent for Thompson, and we'll be getting him out."

Thompson was her uncle's solicitor. But how was Spen? She turned her gaze to Andrew, who had collapsed back into his chair.

"They didn't see me in the tree, miss," he told her. "It was hours before I could get down, and then I hid and listened to find out what they'd done with Charles and the young earl." He sighed and slumped still further. Cordelia held her breath. "They searched his lordship's room and took the stuff we'd brought for him. Charles is shut up in a storeroom in the cellars. He isn't hurt. Lord Spenhurst told them Charles was his servant and was just following orders. He reminded them he would be marquess himself one day. The man in charge said they'd better not do anything to Charles till the marquess gets home."

"So, there you are, Dee," Uncle Josh said. "Your young man is unharmed, but I need to get to Deercroft before the marquess. And before you ask, no, you are not coming with me."

Cordelia was going to argue that point, but first, "Has someone ordered food and drink for Andrew, Uncle Josh? And a hot bath, I think. Andrew, you must have ridden non-stop from Deercroft."

"Pretty much, Miss Milton," the footman admitted, "but I'm going back. I have friends in the village who might help us."

"You will go back fed and clean," Cordelia decided, and went to make the arrangements.

Uncle Josh would not change his mind, and even told the servants and Aunt Eliza that his niece and his ward John were to stay at home in London until he returned. They took their instructions seriously, so she spent the next five days confined to the townhouse, with a maid and a footman or two following her and John everywhere, even into the garden.

She had little to do but worry and plan. There must be some way to get Spen out of his father's hands. She and John discussed idea after idea, but all depended on help from inside the mansion and, though John assured Cordelia many of the servants were sympathetic, he also knew they were frightened of the marquess and would not defy him.

At last, Uncle Josh returned. The rescue had not succeeded but was not a complete failure. The local magistrate refused to demand the prisoner be handed over to him. However, he also took Andrew's evidence and agreed Charles had a defense of charges of trespass since he was working for Lord Spenhurst, who lived on the property.

"He has told the marquess's estate steward that Charles must be brought before him on charges within seven days or released. I've left my solicitor and several others to bring Charles home once he is free."

"What of Lord Spenhurst?" Cordelia asked.

Uncle Josh shrugged. "The magistrate can do nothing, Dee-

Dee. The marquess is the earl's father and the earl is not of age. He has no right to object to anything his father does, and the law cannot interfere. If it helps, as far as anyone knows, nothing has happened to him beyond being locked up."

"Uncle Josh will do nothing to help," she reported to John. "I am going to write to Andrew. I don't want him to take any risks, but if there is a way to get a note to Spen, and even better, a note from him, we would worry less."

"The stable boy might help," John thought.

Cordelia was certain she could do more if she was just able to stay in the village. But how to make that happen? For a start, she would make no further demands for Spen's rescue. She sought and received permission to show John some of the sights of London—escorted, of course. She accompanied Aunt Eliza on calls. She visited the modiste, though her appearance of compliance would have been destroyed had Aunt Eliza overheard her commissioning a special wardrobe.

Her chance came when Uncle Josh had to travel to Liverpool and Aunt Eliza succumbed to a cold.

Several days later, her plans were laid. "We will catch the mail coach that leaves at six in the morning," she said. "We can stay overnight and return the next day. If I say we are staying with my friend Margotta while Aunt Eliza is sick, Uncle Josh will never know we have even gone."

They did stay one night with Margotta, the daughter of another wealthy merchant. Cordelia had known Margotta all her life, though they had grown apart recently. Uncle Josh had insisted on Cordelia making her debut in the ton and Margotta had married a man of their own class. Her husband was heir to a mill owner, and Margotta had given him two sweet little children, a boy and a girl.

For the sake of their old friendship, she agreed to give Cordelia and John a room for the night. She even managed not to scold when she got up early to see her two visitors off to the mail coach and found Cordelia dressed in some of her new clothes from the modiste—a suit of clothing suitable for a young gentleman. With a cap on, Cordelia thought she made a fine boy. "Everything will be fine," she assured her friend. "We will be back before you know it."

Chapter Ten

SPEN HAD FINALLY managed to gouge a large enough groove in the sill. He slid the base of the bar into the room so that, with a bit of persuasion, it dropped down into his hands. He cleaned out the holes top and bottom so he could put the bar back up and take it out again, more easily this time. One bar wasn't enough—he could get his head through, but the space was too small for his shoulders and chest, especially since he would be wriggling outwards over a fifty-foot drop. But if he could remove one bar, he could remove a second.

Things were looking up. His stash of food had run out, but he'd woven more rope and would soon have a ladder. Furthermore, Fielder had clearly decided to side with Spen as much as he could without disobeying a direct order, and that included putting extra food into each day's single meal.

"You stand by those who work for you," he explained. "Your man Charles? Some of the marquess's men would have beaten and starved him because they could. The marquess wouldn't have cared. He might have rewarded them. But they didn't dare, because of what you said. And the servants who support you, my lord, made sure he was fed and cared for. Also, your friends from London are trying to get him released."

Spen didn't know for certain who had come from London to

advocate for Charles, though he assumed Mr. Milton organized it. They had not been immediately successful. The magistrate had not ordered the servants to turn Charles over.

However, he had made it clear Charles was to be treated well and turned over to the magistrate within seven days. If no orders arrived from the marquess in the meantime, the magistrate and the visitor's solicitor would be back for Charles tomorrow, when the deadline was up. *I hope their presence means Andrew got away,"* Spen thought. It must do, for someone sounded the alarm. Besides, Fielder didn't mention another captive.

Spen asked after the marchioness, who had been keeping to her rooms but whose maid reported she was as well as could be expected given the baby could arrive at any time. A doctor had been sent from London to take up residence. Poor lady. Shouldn't she have a woman with her, as well? She had no living mother or sisters, but surely, she had friends?

He could do nothing about it, however.

Nor could he trust Fielder enough to use him to send and collect letters, so Spen couldn't write to Cordelia. Fielder's main motivation in shelving his former hostility was that Spen would be his boss one day. Given a choice between the current marquess and the probable future marquess, Spen assumed Fielder would look after his own skin first.

Nothing was more certain than that the marquess would return. Perhaps even his steward did not know when. Certainly, the marquess's plans were not known to the servants or anyone else whose gossip Fielder related. It would be well for Spen if the old man stayed away a bit longer.

When his lordship found Spen was still defiant, Spen had no idea what would happen. He shivered at the thought. Perhaps the countess would give birth to a son and put his lordship in a good mood.

Fielder finished his evening tasks by picking up yesterday's dinner tray and returning Spen's good wishes for a pleasant night, before exiting the room and locking and bolting the door.

Spen took his usual seat by the window facing the oak tree. The sun would not set for hours. He would work on his ladder, which was nearly finished.

THE FOLLOWING MORNING, he was back at the window and making a start on a groove at the base of the second bar when a beloved voice spoke from the nearby oak tree. "Spen. Thank God you are well. You are well, are you not?"

How could joy and fear co-exist? Joy because Cordelia was within reach, and fear for the same reason. "You shouldn't be here, my love. What if you were caught?"

She took no offense, perhaps because of the grin he could not suppress and the longing that must show in his eyes. "I will be safe, Spen. There is a festival in the village today, and most of the servants have been given leave to attend. Also, I have servants on watch all about, and some of them are yours. You have more friends than you know, and they told me you are safe and being treated well. I had to see for myself, though. Did they take everything from you when they caught Charles? Have you had time to make another rope?"

"They only took the one you brought," Spen said, and added smugly, "I have made more and woven a rope ladder. I managed to keep the chisels and your letters, too. Look!"

He removed the loose bar. "I can't fit through, but one more bar and I'll be able to climb down out of here."

Cordelia narrowed her eyes as she considered the gap. "I could probably get through that gap. Drop your ladder, Spen, and I shall try."

"Do not think of it, my love." Spen was horrified at the idea of her attempting such a climb, even as he yearned to touch her, to hold her in his arms. "What if you slipped? What if somebody saw you?"

"There will never be a better time, with most of the household and grounds servants away. Drop the ladder, Spen. I'm coming up." She disappeared with a rustle of leaves.

I shouldn't let her take the risk. I should send her away and tell her not to come back. Even as he told himself he must not allow her to risk her safety, he was retrieving the rope ladder from its hiding place and tying it firmly to the bars.

He removed the loose bar and put his head through the gap to watch Cordelia come out from under the tree and wave up to him. She was dressed in men's clothes again—boy's clothes, really. A pair of workman's trousers and a rough baggy coat. She removed the coat and bundled it up. She used her neckerchief to tie it to the bag she wore on her back. A man in similar casual dress came with her, to take hold of the two outside ropes of the ladder and hold it firm.

Even with that stability and the freedom of movement trousers gave her, Spen's heart was in his mouth as she climbed, and he did not take a breath until he could reach out to help her, first to take her coat and bag from her and toss them behind him, and next to support her as she balanced herself on the sill and twisted and wriggled to squeeze through the narrow gap and into his arms.

She clutched him as if she wanted to merge their bodies. Spen's embrace, born of relief she had survived the climb combined with joy she was within reach, turned carnal in a split second. He had to deny the frantic urging of his own body to put her slightly away from him so he could see her beloved face, grinning with delight.

"It was not a hard climb," she boasted.

"The last bit was the worst," he admitted. "I did not think you were going to fit. If you had slipped…"

"You had me firmly held," she assured him. "I was not afraid. I am never afraid when I am with you." She leaned forward again, resting her face against his chest, and he tightened his arms to hug her close.

"We had better pull up the rope ladder," she murmured, "lest it attract attention. My servant will be back to hold the ends in two hours."

Spen let her go and bent to the task. It would be as well to keep his distance, but he didn't know if it would be possible. Not for two whole hours. He couldn't deny her, though. Quite apart from the fact her arms must be tired from the climbing, the servant to keep the ropes from swinging and twisting was already gone from view. Anyway, letting her leave him again was going to tear the heart from his chest.

***

Cordelia knew Spen was right. She shouldn't be here. But the last few weeks had made her desperate. Her uncle declared he had no power to get Spen released—the marquess was acting within his legal rights and was contemptuous of the circles within which her uncle had the most influence. And what little John said about the marquess made her fear the man would eventually win. He would find a way to force Spen to comply with his wishes, and she would have lost him forever.

Lost him before she had ever truly had him. They had kissed, of course. Even done a little cuddling that had set her on fire. Any more, he insisted, would come after they were married. It was nice he treated her with such respect. Indeed, it was. But she wished he had not been such a gentleman. If memories were all she was able to have of him, she wanted all the memories she could gather.

Unable to resist being close to him, she had arrived in the village late yesterday afternoon, certain she would be safe with the large contingent of servants Uncle Josh had left to guard and protect his solicitor. They were coming for Charles this morning and planned to leave with him after that, which gave her plenty of time for this adventure. Not that the solicitor and John knew where she was. They were still asleep when she left the inn. She had told only those of the servants she knew would not stop her.

When John's friend the stable boy had told her about the fair, she had leapt at the opportunity to see Spen one more time. Except now her plans had changed. Being able to enter the tower room was too much of a temptation to resist, and a two-hour delay would still bring her back to the inn before the solicitor left to fetch Charles. This was her chance to seduce Spen into taking her to bed, and she was determined to take advantage of it.

But now that she was here, she did not know what to do. The welcoming hug was promising, but the only kiss he gave her was nearly as decorous as their very first, which had been sweet and compelling but nothing to the knee-trembling assaults on her senses that had followed after she agreed to marry him.

He wanted her. He would not let go of her hand, and his eyes seemed to burn each time his gaze slipped from her face to study her curves before he ruthlessly dragged his eyes back up.

However, the two hours slipped away in conversation. She snuggled in his arms as they shared some of the spiced buns Cordelia had brought with her. She told him everything she and John had done while they were apart, he described Fielder's slow thawing, and they spent a delightful but wistful interlude speculating about their future marriage.

"It must be nearly time to go," he said, and when they checked the stable clock, it confirmed his assessment. "I am torn, my love. On the one hand, I want you back in the village or—better still—back in London, and safe. On the other, I wish you could stay as long as I must."

Cordelia squeezed his fingers. "I wish the second bar would conveniently dissolve, so we could escape together."

It remained as solidly in place as ever when they peered from the window to see half a dozen servants sitting on the grass within easy sight of the tower. They were passing around a jug of something and looked to be settled in for a long time.

"We will have to wait for them to leave," Cordelia said. "We might as well make the most of it, Spen. Kiss me again."

As the sun reached higher into the heavens, it became clear Cordelia had been mistaken to think the grounds would be deserted because of the fair. Instead, groups of people were coming and going between the house and the village all day long, making it impossible for Cordelia to climb back down to the ground without being seen. Her escort must have been frantic, but there was nothing she could do about it.

Not that the day felt long. In Spen's arms, whether they were kissing and cuddling or merely talking, Cordelia was unaware of the passage of time. Every moment felt eternal and yet the chime of the stable clock seemed to be sounding the minutes rather than the quarter hour, each ring following the other in far less time than she expected.

At noon, Cordelia finally overcame her fear of being thought wanton to place her hand on the part of Spen's anatomy that signaled his intense interest in what they had been doing. Spen shifted away, catching her hands in his. "If you touch me there, my love, I might not be able to resist you."

"I do not want you to resist," she told him. "Take me to bed, Spen."

"We should wait," he told her, while his eyes yearned and he gripped her hands tightly.

"For how long? For your father to die? I love you, Spen. I want a memory to keep my heart from breaking while we are apart." She blushed, suddenly embarrassed. "I have given you a disgust of me."

He folded her in his arms again. "Never that. You honor me. I am only afraid something might happen, and doing this will make it worse."

"I am afraid, too," Cordelia assured him. "Afraid I will never know what it is to be with you in that way. That would be worse, Spen. That would be far worse."

Spen groaned and was suddenly kissing her again. She had thought his kisses passionate, but he had been holding back. His hands were touching her in all the places that burned and somehow managed to soothe the intense longing while forcing it higher.

With caresses and kisses and soft moans, they stripped one another of their clothes and tumbled into the bed to explore one another's bodies.

What he did with his hands and his mouth set her soaring among the stars, but it wasn't what she had expected of a coupling. Of course, most of her knowledge had been gathered by listening to servants, but did his male part not need to enter the place where she was so wet? Gloriously wet, Spen had called it, when she had tried to apologize.

"But what of you, Spen?" she asked, as she lay in his arms, her body still vibrating with the music of her release. "Should you not have a turn?"

"I am happy," Spen told her, and he kissed her again. His mouth tasted a little salty, with a flavor of musk. Her taste, she realized. "Bringing you to pleasure has been wonderful."

Cordelia was not satisfied with his answers. "I want you to join with me. I want it all."

"I am told the first time can hurt," Spen warned. "I shall try to be careful, but I want you so much, Cordelia, I am afraid of losing control."

Cordelia rolled to her back and spread her legs. "I am ready," she proclaimed.

She wasn't. Not quite. Nothing could have prepared her for the intimate invasion. Yes, there was a sharp pinch, but the other sensations were—not pleasurable, precisely. Desirable, yes. This fullness had a rightness about it. She was his and he was hers.

He stilled, holding his weight on his elbows, kissing her deeply, and Cordelia stopped trying to understand the sensations and gave herself over to them. Soon, she was heading for the stars again, but Spen got there first, stiffening, and letting out a long, keening moan as she felt a flood of warmth deep inside.

He collapsed on top of her, his weight comforting, though

she could not draw a deep breath. She smiled in relief and triumph. She would remember the pleasure she brought him as much as the pleasure he brought her. A memory to give her comfort, however long they were apart.

After a few moments, he came to himself enough to murmur, "I am crushing you. Forgive me, my love." He shifted enough to lie on his side, bringing her with him so they were still joined. They dozed for a while until Spen began flexing his hips to slide in and out of her again. The second time was even more wonderful than the first.

Afterward, they washed in cold water from a jug and dressed again, a process impaired by their need to keep touching one another. "I can only offer you water, but there are still a few of your buns left," Spen commented. That reminded Cordelia she had also brought a bottle of cider. They shared it, drinking it from the bottle.

Fielder's arrival a short while later was almost a disaster, but Cordelia scooted under the bed and Spen stood in front of the window to hide the rope ladder, which was coiled on the deep sill. "What is happening outside, Fielder?" he asked. "People have been going back and forth all day."

"Fair in the village, my lord," reported Fielder. "Steward gave all the staff a half day. I went this afternoon, and I saw them folks what come for Charles this morning. Thought you'd like to know he is well, and pleased to be free, and he thanks you for asking. Said he'd be joining his friend in London, my lord."

Cordelia was touched Fielder had thought to check on the man Spen had claimed as his servant, and Spen sounded pleased, too. "Thank you, Fielder. That is good hearing. I hope you had a good half-day out. You deserve a break from this place. I like to think of you raising a glass with your friends."

"Well, sir, that is right kind of you to say," Fielder commented. "I hope someday soon I get to raise a glass to your freedom, my lord." His face colored, and he looked down at a toe that was tracing a pattern on the floor. "I bought you a jug of ale, sir. And a spiced bun. From the fair." He whipped off the cloth that covered the tray, and Spen thanked him, warmly.

From under the bed, Cordelia could see Fielder backing out of the room, chamber pot in hand. Cordelia wondered if he would notice it was a bit fuller than usual. Twice, Spen had sat on the floor on the other side of the bed while Cordelia made herself more comfortable. Despite the intimacy of what they had done together, she had blushed scarlet at attending to such a matter with him in the room.

The sound of the bolts sliding back into place brought Cordelia out from under the bed, trying to smooth the hair and clothes disheveled by the scramble into and out of her hiding place.

"Half a spiced bun, Cordelia?" Spen asked, but she suggested he save it for their supper.

"If the Deerhaven servants are still going back and forth to the village, Spen, I am going to have to stay the night. A pity Fielder didn't bring you a different sort of fairing, for you will be sick of spiced buns."

What she really wanted to ask was when they might go back to bed.

"I like spiced buns," Spen said.

Even as he spoke, the clank of the bolts and then the rattle of the key sent Cordelia diving for the other side of the bed, and Spen looking anxiously around the room and returning once more to stand in front of the window.

Fielder burst through the doorway. He was panting for breath. "My lord, get the lady out of here. The marquess is home and is on his way up the stairs." He grimaced at Cordelia, who was just lifting her nose above the bed. "I am sorry, Miss," he said. "I'll try to slow him down." He slammed the door shut with him on the other side of it.

Chapter Eleven

SPEN TOOK NO notice of the bolts sliding back into place. He was busy helping Cordelia through the gap where the bar had been removed. It was harder this time. Before, the risk was she would fall into the room. This time, she was trying to slither through a gap, hold onto the bars, and get her feet out of the room and safely onto the ladder, which he had pushed off the sill hoping gravity would drop it to the ground.

If she slipped or if she failed to hold onto the bars or the ladder, it was a long way down.

He could hear his father's voice shouting. "Then find the key, you idiot. Hurry up."

At last! Cordelia was secure on the ladder, only her head and shoulders, and her hands on the rungs of the rope, still in view. She mimed a kiss. "I love you, Spen. I regret nothing."

"I love you," Spen returned. "Hurry, darling!"

She disappeared from sight, and Spen put the bar back in place and raced to hide anything that might hint at her visit. He would regret nothing as long as she got freely away.

For the second time in minutes, the door burst open. This time, his father filled the doorway, lifting his head to sniff the air. "You have had a woman in here," he noted.

Cordelia must be about halfway down. A little more time,

and she would be able to escape. Provided the old tyrant hadn't thought to post people at the bottom.

Spen shrugged. "A tavern girl. A man has needs." Inside, he winced at comparing the glory of his afternoon to a meaningless transactional encounter.

The marquess stepped into the room and gestured to the footman who followed him. "Search the room. Find the girl."

"Do you intend to deprive me of all comforts?" Spen asked his father, to prolong the conversation and keep his attention from the window.

"I intend to do everything necessary to bend you to my will, you ungrateful scoundrel," the marquess replied. "Where is your brother?"

"How would I know?" Spen asked. "He was here when I was locked up. He was sent home with a broken arm. Has he gone back to school? Home to Rosewood Towers?" He couldn't help the scorn that colored his voice

He braced himself as his father swung a hand back for a blow, but one of the servants shouted. "There are ropes my lord. I think it's a ladder."

"Haul it up and look, man," the marquess scolded.

"I cannot, my lord. Someone is on it."

The marquess strode to the window, his eyes narrowed. "Coming up or going down? But why? Ah! I see." He grabbed the loose bar and pulled it out, then stuck his head through the gap to look down the tower wall.

Spen managed two paces towards the marquess before men grabbed him and dragged him backward again.

"It's a boy," the marquess was saying, sounding bewildered, then chortling, "No, a girl dressed as a boy." He pulled his head back and with glee in his eyes he said, "And I think I know her name." He held out his hand. "Someone. Pass me a knife."

"No!" Spen shouted as he struggled, but the two men holding him didn't let go. "No, my lord. Don't do it!"

The marquess managed to get one arm and his head out the

window. Spen could see him sawing back and forth as he continued to speak. "Did you think I would not hear Milton has interfered with justice for that trespasser who was spying for your little slut?"

He snorted. "The magistrate had the nerve to tell me I could not have had him hanged or transported for his villainy, and my imprisonment of the man was punishment enough. My illegal imprisonment! Can you believe it? Who does the magistrate think he is? Ah." A shriek from below, short and sharp, coincided with the marquess's sigh of satisfaction.

He moved to the second rope, and Spen imagined Cordelia clinging to the rungs as the ladder collapsed with one of its uprights gone, twisted, and turned. "Don't," he moaned.

"What do I find when I stopped at the village inn on my way here," the marquis went on, "but the magistrate with Milton's solicitor, and both of them demanding to know what I have done with Milton's niece. I told them I did not know what they were talking about. Now, of course, I do."

He pulled back again to grin at Spen. "Three-quarters cut through. Let us leave the bitch's destiny to fate, shall we? If the rope holds, she spins for a while until I feel like sending someone to retrieve her. If the rope breaks, she dies."

Another scream came as he finished speaking. The marquess looked out of the window again. "Oops," he said. His grin was wider as he turned back into the room. "Well, my son. It seems your impediment to the marriage I wish is no longer a problem."

<hr />

SPEN FACED HIS father with a facade of calm that ignored the storm of howling grief within him. "On the contrary, my lord. If you have killed the only wife I will ever have, the only woman on whom I will ever sire children, then you have also ensured John and his children will eventually be the future of this line. For I shall never marry as you desire."

"You shall, if I have to bind and gag you to get you to the altar," snarled his father.

Spen shook his head. "If you can find some venal priest to pronounce the marriage valid, I shall never beget children upon whatever unfortunate female you force to accept a cold and sterile marriage."

The marquis sneered. "My wife is in labor even as we speak, and if it is a son, you are of no further use to me," he stated. He turned to his lackeys. "Take him and lock him in the cellars. Fielder! Collect your things and get out and be grateful I don't have you beaten before you are thrown from the estate."

⇶⫷

IT WAS DARK when Cordelia woke with a terrible headache and a vague sense of loss. She must have been dreaming of Spen again. She sighed.

"Dee-Dee! Ye're awake." It was her uncle's voice, from beside the bed, and his must be the hand that grasped one of hers and pulled it towards him to drop a tender kiss on her fingers. "How do you feel?"

"Uncle Josh? Why are you in my room? Can you light a lamp? I cannot see."

"Dee," her uncle replied, with a sob.

"Uncle, what is the matter?"

"Can't ye see me, Dee-Dee?" her uncle begged. "My finger. Can ye see my finger?"

She felt his touch on her nose, but she could still see nothing.

"It is too dark, Uncle Josh," she insisted.

"Fetch that doctor back," Uncle Josh ordered. "Miss Cordelia can't see."

Cordelia squeezed her uncle's hand in shock, fear almost choking her. "I am blind? What happened, Uncle Josh? Have I been sick?"

"Ye fell, darling girl. Don't ye remember? Climbing down Spenhurst's tower and falling?"

Cordelia started to shake her head, but the thunderous headache took sharp exception. She had to swallow nausea before she could say, "But Uncle Josh, Lord Spenhurst is at Deercroft. We are in London."

But that, she found out, was not true. It wasn't until the next day she managed to piece together the whole story. She had no memory of catching a mail coach with John or of bribing some of her uncle's men to accompany her to the tower. Nor did she know what happened at the tower or how she came to fall.

John was able to give some details of the trip back to Crossings, and the servants who had accompanied her explained she had gone for a brief talk and taken the opportunity to climb the young earl's rope ladder. She had been trapped there, apparently, for the whole day, with too many people walking near the tower for her to descend. Cordelia wished she could remember the day.

To Cordelia's surprise, much of the rest came from Fielder. He had been present when the Marquess of Deerhaven had cut the ladder while Cordelia was on it—fortunately only a few feet above the ground. He was the one who had carried her home from the base of the tower.

John had told her the poor man had been dismissed without a reference, but Uncle Josh was going to employ him, so that was some recompense. John had also sent Fielder to talk to his former colleagues, to see if he could find out what had happened to Spen. Also, to the marchioness, who was having her baby, which was the reason the marquess had returned to Deercroft.

Cordelia was fortunate, her uncle told her. Fielder had found out that she dropped five feet from the ladder, but landed awkwardly, stumbled, and hit her head on the stone wall of the tower. She had some bruises and scrapes, but the worst harm was the blow to the head. She had been unconscious for more than a day—long enough for an urgent message to reach Uncle Josh and for him to race to her side.

The doctor told her uncle her loss of memory was normal with such an injury. "It might return, or it might not, but at least she knows who she is, so she is a fortunate young lady." As to her sight, the doctor had heard of a few rare cases of a sudden blow causing partial or complete blindness.

"You must have hope," the doctor said to her uncle. "Her sight, too, might resolve in time, as the brain heals."

He seemed to know what he was talking about, and Cordelia did her best to remain calm, but it was hard. Blind! She couldn't imagine never being able to see again. She wouldn't even think about what this might do to her future with Spen. Even if he could escape his father, she couldn't expect him to marry her now. Whoever heard of a blind marchioness?

She fiercely reminded herself that she might yet recover, but holding onto hope was hard in the sudden perpetual darkness.

Uncle Josh wanted her to be seen by the best doctors in London and demanded to know when she could safely be moved.

"Not for at least twenty-four hours," the doctor had decided. "Watch her closely. If the headache does not worsen and if there are no other symptoms, she might be able to stand the trip without harm. Provided you take your time. Travel slowly and for short periods with frequent rest stops."

The following day, he conceded Cordelia was no worse. Cordelia had thought Uncle Josh would insist on leaving straightaway, but he said she was to have another visitor before they could leave. He ordered tea served to the little sitting room that connected their two bedrooms.

"Are we waiting for someone who can tell us what has happened to Lord Spenhurst?" Cordelia asked, hopefully.

Her uncle's voice was grim. "Forget about Lord Spenhurst," he commanded. "After the way he has treated ye, I'll never let him near ye again."

"Whatever do you mean?" Cordelia demanded. "None of this is Spen's fault."

With a world of sorry in his voice, her uncle said, "It's my fault. I should never have tried to push ye into their world. The so-called nobility are not for the likes of us. Forget that rakehell, I say. I'll find ye a husband of our own kind, Dee-Dee. You will be happier, I promise."

"Spen is not a rakehell, Uncle Josh," Cordelia insisted. "You said yourself he was a steady young man. I don't understand what you think he has done wrong."

"I cannot speak of it," Uncle Josh insisted, the tightness of his voice confirming that he spoke no more than the truth. Ye must trust me, niece. He has not behaved as a gentleman should."

Cordelia was shaking her head when a knock on the door interrupted them. "Mr. Milton, sir? The midwife is here," said one of the servants.

The person who entered spoke. A woman's voice, warm and kind. "Miss Milton, how good to see you awake. Mr. Milton, I have brought the ingredients for the tea I mentioned."

"If ye would leave it with me," Uncle Josh said, holding out his hand. "How often a day should she take it, and for how long?"

The woman didn't answer. Uncle Josh broke the silence, saying, "My niece remembers nothing that happened."

Something was going on, and Uncle Josh intended to keep Cordelia in the dark. She was not going to have it. "Are you not going to introduce us?" she demanded.

Uncle Josh hesitated, but the woman said, "I am Mrs. Austin."

"And I am Cordelia Milton. What is the tea you mentioned, and what is it for?"

"Now, Cordelia," Uncle Josh said, "it is just a little something to help ye recover without any ill-effects." Three things gave him away. He was coaxing her, which never happened. He had called her Cordelia, which meant he was seriously rattled. And, she could hear him shifting in his seat.

"Someone had better tell me the purpose of this tea, or I will not be drinking it," Cordelia said. It was, she supposed, for her headache. Though if that was the case, why not say so?

"Ye will do as ye're told, young lady," Uncle Josh blustered. "If I had not given ye more freedom than was good for ye, we would not be in this situation."

Cordelia knew it was true she had been raised with more freedom than other young ladies, and she had taken advantage of Aunt Eliza's shy and retiring nature to take more. Not that she intended to cede the point to her uncle. "You have not explained what situation we are in, Uncle Josh. Is this about escaping the marquess?" she retorted. "For here I am, and unharmed apart from a bump on the head." And the blindness, which was such a loss that she could not bear to speak of it.

Mrs. Austin sounded disapproving when she said, "Do you not think she should be told?"

"There is no need," Uncle Josh insisted. "Not if there are no consequences."

"What should I be told?" Cordelia asked, turning her head in the direction from which she heard Mrs. Austin's voice.

Mrs. Austin replied to Uncle Josh. "Well, Mr. Milton? What do I tell your niece?"

Uncle Josh did not answer. The silence stretched until Cordelia was nearly ready to scream from the frustration of not being able to see their expressions to interpret what they were thinking.

At long last, Uncle Josh grumbled, "Very well, then. Tell her. I shall be in the next room." He strode off into his bed chamber, shutting the door behind him in what was not quite a slam.

"Please sit down, Mrs. Austin," Cordelia invited, "and tell me what has my uncle in such a lather."

"Your uncle is understandably upset," Mrs. Austin scolded. "Tell me, Miss Milton, is it true you can remember nothing of your day in the tower?"

Cordelia nodded, slowly. "Nothing even of coming to the village," she said. "The last thing I remember is arriving back in London three weeks ago."

"I see. Miss Milton, may I be frank?"

"I wish you would," Cordelia assured her.

Mrs. Austin sounded pleased. "The purpose of the tea, which contains pennyroyal and some other herbs, is to help your courses to arrive as they should."

Cordelia shook her head. She had no idea what Mrs. Austin meant. "My courses are always regular," she said, her cheeks warming at the intimate nature of the conversation.

"Miss Milton, when I examined you, it was obvious you had had relations of a marital nature."

Oh! The heat in her cheeks flamed higher. "You mean... You think Lord Spenhurst and I..."

"I assume it was Lord Spenhurst," Mrs. Austin said. "Your servant escorted you to the tower, and Fielder apparently brought you straight back after your fall."

Cordelia frowned. How unfair! She had succeeded in convincing Spen to bed her, and she remembered nothing about it, though now she came to think of it, that part of her body did feel a little tender, as if muscles had been worked that had never worked before.

"It will, of course, remain a secret between us," Mrs. Austin assured her.

"And my uncle," Cordelia clarified. "That is why he has turned against Lord Spenhurst. When it was my choice as much as his. More, indeed, for I was the one who climbed to his window. And, though I don't remember it, I daresay he needed to be talked into—well. My uncle is being unfair."

"Your uncle is concerned about the possible consequences," Mrs. Austin said. "Hence, the tea."

"What consequences," Cordelia wondered out loud. "If the three of us say nothing, who is to know and how can tea..." she trailed off as the answer occurred to her. "A baby?" She could not help but smile, and both hands drifted to her belly, where Spen's child might even now be growing. "It is unlikely, surely?" She must arm herself against disappointment.

Mrs. Austin's voice was sympathetic. "It is not easy having a child with no husband," she warned.

"Spen will marry me when he is able to," Cordelia said, more to the possible baby than to Mrs. Austin. "We just have to be patient until he is free and comes for us."

"He has gone," Mrs. Austin blurted.

That broke Cordelia out of her daze. "Gone? Where? How?"

Mrs. Austin shifted uneasily. "The marquess left and took his son with him. I attended Lady Deerhaven's confinement two days ago. The servants said the marquess was expected, and later that day he had arrived. I didn't see him, but when I went back yesterday to check on my lady and the little girl, they told me the marquess and his son were gone. I cannot tell you where, Miss Milton."

"A little girl," Cordelia noted. "The marchioness has a daughter." The poor lady. Cordelia remembered how kind and welcoming she had been. The marquess, obsessed as he was with having sons, would not be happy. "Are they well, she and her daughter?"

"The child is healthy," Mrs. Austin confided. "Her ladyship is... sad."

And Spen is safe. The marquess could not risk anything happening to the one legitimate son he had sired. No doubt he would try again, but Spen would be of age in just a few months. The marchioness could not deliver another child for at least ten months. Probably longer.

Mrs. Austin put a packet into her hand. "Here is the tea, Miss Milton. I daresay you do not intend to take it, but perhaps your uncle will be less angry if he believes you tried, and it failed. It is not always successful."

Cordelia shook her head. "I will tell my uncle the truth. He will not hurt me, Mrs. Austin. And he will not put me out on the street, either. He will shout, perhaps. Probably, in fact. But in the end, if I do have a child, I trust him to support us until Spen is able to come for me."

Mrs. Austin sounded doubtful. "I hope you are right, Miss Milton. I wish you well."

"Uncle Josh," Cordelia called out, "Mrs. Austin is leaving, and you and I need to talk."

Chapter Twelve

THEY TRAVELED FOR four days. Spen spent each day chained to a ring that had been bolted to the floor of the carriage. At night, he was released from the ring, but the shackles remained on his ankles. He was escorted to a room in whatever inn the marquess had chosen, then chained to the bed.

No one would tell him where they were going or even the names of the towns they were in. Not that Spen cared. All he could think of was Cordelia. The marquess said she had fallen to her death. The man would tell whatever lies suited him best. Spen didn't believe him. Couldn't believe him. Cordelia could not have paid with her life for their glorious afternoon.

Had she been hurt? Had she been taken captive? Was his father, for once in his life, telling the truth?

He kept recalculating how long it would have taken her to climb down the rope. The trouble was those moments in the tower room when the marquess had been sawing at the rope had stretched out into an eternity. She should have been able to make the descent in a couple of minutes, but had that much time elapsed?

Her scream had been short and cut off. A fall? A small one, perhaps. Or some other shock as she reached the ground.

His mind went round and round, covering the same thoughts

again and again. He had asked the guards, but they refused to speak to him. There were four, all unknown to him, two of them with him at all times, day and night. He assumed the two not on duty traveled elsewhere in his father's retinue or bedded down with the other servants. It didn't matter. By contrast to his desperate worry for Cordelia, what was happening to him seemed to be unimportant.

Towards the end of the fourth day, the coach pulled off the road and through a pair of tall wrought iron gates. They had arrived somewhere, but where was it? Through the rain that hit the carriage windows, all he could tell was that trees hemmed them in on both sides, but the change in the pitch and sway of the coach hinted they were now traveling a relatively well-kept carriageway.

Finally, the coach pulled up and someone opened the door. One of Spen's guards knelt to undo his chains while the other watched Spen for any wrong move. Spen had learned the futility of any resistance. He waited until the chains fell away from the ankle shackles, and even then, didn't move until the guard who had opened the door spoke. Spen thought of the man as Chatter, partly because he spoke so little and partly because he was the only one of the guards who spoke in Spen's presence. Chatter said, "Come along, Lord Spenhurst. We have arrived."

Arrived where, though? The house was large—what he could see was four stories high, at least, and perhaps one hundred feet across. It wasn't a place he had been before. The sun was setting behind the house, so the carriageway, at least, had brought them west. For a moment, curiosity roused Spen from his misery.

His father had already mounted the tall flight of steps to the front door and was entering the house. His guards conducted him in another direction. "This way, my lord," said Chatter, and they went through a secondary door at ground level, along a passage, and up several flights of stairs. Servant stairs—unadorned, narrow, and steep.

"Where are we?" Spen asked. As usual, the guards acted as if they had heard nothing. The guard in the lead opened a door on one of the landings and led the way into a more elegantly proportioned hallway. Still shabby and neglected, but clearly part of the main house. The third door on the left led into what might once have been a nursery, or so the barred windows suggested. The room they entered had two doors leading off on one side, and one on the other.

"A bath has been ordered for you, my lord," Chatter said. "We will leave you to settle in."

Spen pointed to the shackles that had been clamped on him at Deercroft. "Do I get these off?" He asked.

No answer. Chatter regarded him in silence for a moment, then walked to the door, two of the other guards following. The three of them left, and Spen heard the tumblers fall as they locked the door behind them. The fourth remained in the room, his arms crossed, his face blank.

Spen was not going to be left alone then.

Fine. It would not stop him from investigating his chambers—a suite of rooms with mismatched furniture. He found a living room, a bedchamber, a smaller room that had hooks on the walls for clothes, and another of the same size containing nothing but a pallet on the floor. Was one of his guards going to stay with him each night? Spen hoped not.

The door to the hallway opened and in came a procession of footmen with a bath, buckets of water, and a couple of trunks. A bath! A man could get clean with soap and a jug of water, which was all he'd been allowed since the day weeks ago when his father arrived home unexpectedly and confined him in the tower. But there was nothing quite like a good soak in a tub of water deep enough to get wet all over.

No one would tell him anything, but apparently his father was changing tactics, for the trunks proved to be full of his own clothes, and one of the footmen remained to put them away in the dressing room and to set out breeches, stockings, a shirt, and a banyan for Spen to wear after the bath.

The guards remained to watch, and no one would speak to Spen, even when he asked to have the metal cuffs removed so they would not get wet. When no one answered, he decided to ignore all of them in return. He stripped and got into the bath.

As soon as he relaxed back against the towel-draped edge of the bath, his pleasure in the warm water evaporated and he tensed up again. Cordelia was all he could think about. *She is my future. I have to believe she survived and is unharmed.*

His job was to remain unmarried and look for any opportunity to escape. If a guard stayed with him at all times, it would be harder, but eventually, their attention would slip, or his father would get tired of the battle, or would die, putting Spen in control. *I just have to hold on.*

He would be polite and cooperative with his gaolers. He would continue to refuse his father's choice of bride. He would listen and try to learn where he was. What else could he do?

Perhaps the guards had not expected him to get into the bath, but after he did his best to dry the shackles, the guard he had dubbed Big Nose went off to find Chatter, and they came back with a key. This meant Spen was clean and unchained when he sat down to the best meal he'd seen since his father ordered him to be starved.

He had little appetite, but he savored the tastes and enjoyed being served by a deferential footman. Amazing how he once took such luxuries for granted. And having the shackles off made him feel a full stone lighter.

When the marquess arrived to see him the following morning, he was leaning against the window ledge in the sitting room, looking out of the window. The park in front of him was unkempt and hedged around with trees. In the distance beyond the trees, he could see mountains, largely shrouded in clouds. He was no wiser as to where they were than he had been yesterday.

He had not turned at the sound of the door, but he came alert when his father spoke his name. "Spenhurst."

Spen inclined his head in response.

The marquess took a seat on one of the sofas, spreading his arms along the back to take possession of the whole thing. He did not invite Spen to sit. Spen considered doing so anyway but decided not to aggravate his father before he had to.

"Did you enjoy your privileges yesterday?" the marquess asked, ignoring their audience of three guards (two had arrived with the marquess) and the two footmen who were clearing breakfast from the table.

Spen inclined his head.

"I make the choices, boy," the marquess declared. "I decide whether you starve or whether you eat, whether you wash or go dirty, whether you are chained up or not. And I decide who you will marry."

So much for not aggravating his father. "I shall marry Cordelia Milton or no one, my lord," Spen replied.

"You can't marry a dead woman, boy," the marquess growled.

"Then I shall not marry. I shall never have legitimate offspring. The marquessate shall go to John and his descendants."

The marquess narrowed his eyes. "And if I told you the boy is dead, too?"

Spen refused to show any reaction. "Then I daresay some cousin shall eventually inherit." On his way to a night in the cellars, he had overheard the servants talking. His stepmother had given birth to a daughter.

The marquess leapt to his feet, his fist raised for a blow, then thought better of it. "The cow I married has proved able to bear children," he pointed out. "Sooner or later, I shall have a legitimate son of my own flesh to replace you. Meanwhile, you remain a prisoner until you obey my will or until you die."

Or until you die, Spen thought, but did not say. He would never change his mind, and they would see whose will prevailed in the end. Even if the marquess spoke the truth, and Cordelia and John were both dead, he would not give in. The marquess deserved far worse from Spen than simply refusing a marriage the old man planned, but he held the power. For the moment. The only revenge Spen could currently take was to refuse him and to keep refusing him.

Chapter Thirteen

UNCLE JOSH WAS not happy with Cordelia's decision, but his attempt to browbeat her into taking the tea ran aground on the shoals of his concern for her blindness. Once they returned to London, he called in doctor after doctor, but they either said to wait and see, or they proposed cupping or some noxious medicine, neither of which Cordelia would allow.

The darkness of both sight and memory oppressed her mind, but the greatest agony was not knowing what had become of Spen.

Two weeks after her fall, the darkness around her lifted a bit. At first, she could see only shadowy shapes, but slowly her sight returned, until six weeks after the fall she was able to move around again without fear of tripping over something unseen. One of the doctors had experienced another case like hers and assured her she could expect more improvement over time.

She hoped so. She still could not see well enough to read easily or to sew. She had tried to write to her friend Margotta, and to Regina, who had married and left London while she was away in the country. But even writing brought back her headache.

Her memory of her time with Spen had not returned. Nor had her courses. And she was finding it hard to keep food down.

What she had always heard called *morning sickness* was with her all day every day.

She had not yet told her uncle she believed herself to be with child. She could not begin to guess how he would react. They were barely talking. Cordelia knew his anger at Spen and his frustration with her reflected his love. He was shocked and distressed at her injury and wanted to rescue her from the consequences of her own choices. He would have been upset with anyone who got in his way. Even her.

She was frustrated in her turn. If he tried, she was sure he could find where Spen had been taken. Deprived of her usual good health and with limited eyesight, Cordelia had to depend on others to bring her news. Uncle Josh wouldn't. Aunt Eliza knew nothing and burst into tears if Cordelia questioned her. John wasn't available—he had been sent to stay with a tutor who was preparing him for school.

Uncle Josh was going to send him to a small school just outside of London—a public school set up to provide a gentleman's education for the sons of those in trade. John had apparently spent his school life to date alternately hiding from and then fighting with bullies and was delighted at the prospect of a different school experience.

There was Fielder, of course. Cordelia had not seen him since they left Crossings, but she knew Uncle Josh had given him work in the stables. So today, once her stomach was as settled as it got, she was going to evade Aunt Eliza and her maid and go to the stables.

It wasn't too hard. She had to hold on tightly to the banister as she felt her way downstairs, for her distance vision was still not functioning properly, and she couldn't judge the depth of each step by sight. Her ears were working well, however, and she stilled each time she heard footsteps or conversation.

She assumed no one came close enough to see her, for she reached the back door unmolested. Out in the sunlight, the world around her was clear. She was able to walk briskly down the garden path and out of the gate, then across the mews to the stable. The shadows of the stable seemed night-black by contrast. Slowly her eyes adjusted, and she found the head groom and two stable boys staring at her.

"Can I help ye, miss?" asked the head groom.

"I wish to speak with Will Fielder," Cordelia told him.

But it was all for nothing. Fielder had not heard from anyone in the village and had no idea what had happened to Spen. He dismissed her suggestion he might have friends in the marquess's townhouse. "Sorry, Miss. I ain't never been to London. No one I know has."

She must have shown her distress, though she tried not to, for Fielder said, "If you can tell me where it is, Miss, I'll walk over and see what I can find out. It's my half day tomorrow."

"I'll give you the address and some money for a hack," Cordelia promised. "No need to spend the whole of your half-day walking there and back."

"I'd do it for Lord Spenhurst, Miss," Fielder insisted. "He is a good man."

But Cordelia insisted he take the money. "Come to the back door when you are ready to leave, and I'll make sure it is ready for you, with a note giving the address."

The following morning, she sent Gracie, her maid, with the purse and note for Fielder. Gracie reported the man had asked her to read him the address three times before putting the note in his pocket along with the purse. It had not occurred to Cordelia that the man couldn't read, but at least he'd come up with a way to solve the problem.

She wandered her rooms restlessly all afternoon, waiting for him to return, and headed to the stables towards the end of the day, to hear his report. Before she could let herself out of the back door, a footman intercepted her to tell her that her uncle wished to see her in his study.

Cordelia ignored the arm Uncle Josh's messenger offered and marched back through the house. The footman followed. Was he told to make sure she obeyed? Did her uncle think she was going to run back up to her room and bar herself inside? She was not such a coward.

In the wide hallway that led to the study, the footman managed to pass, open the door, and announce her. "Miss Milton, sir."

Cordelia entered the room, which was well enough-lit that her sight was clear. She could see who it was unfolding himself awkwardly from one of the chairs that faced the desk from behind which Uncle Josh ruled this house and his business empire.

Fielder nodded, sheepishly. That put paid to any doubt her uncle knew exactly what she had been up to.

Uncle Josh waved to a chair, and she sat, as did the two men. "Ye will not let this go, Cordelia, will ye?" her uncle asked. He looked tired, Cordelia realized. She had not seen him close enough to really examine his face since her sight began to return.

"I love Lord Spenhurst, Uncle Josh," she replied. "I will search for him until I can find him."

Her uncle sighed. He had lost weight and the dark shadows under his eyes hinted he wasn't sleeping. "Even though the Marquess of Deerhaven has made it known his son is to marry Lady Daphne Ashburton, daughter of the Earl of Yarverton?"

Cordelia ignored the pang. "Lord Spenhurst has refused that marriage, Uncle Josh. He will marry me or no one, he says." She trusted Spen. She *had* to trust him.

"That's true, sir," Fielder offered. "I heard him meself."

"Aye, Fielder, so ye said." Uncle Josh sighed again. "Very well. Tell my niece what ye found out for her."

Cordelia eagerly turned her attention to Spen's former gaoler. "Did you discover where Spen is?"

Fielder shook his head, pity in his eyes. "No, Miss. I'm sorry, Miss. The coaches won't talk about it, but one of the footmen told the maids they had taken his lordship nearly to Wales and left him there. They had him chained in the carriage and in the inns at night, the footmen said. But he wasn't hurt or starved, like at Deercroft."

"That is something," Cordelia mused.

Fielder hung his head. "That's all I could find out, Miss. That, and where the coaches drink when they has time off. I figured I could maybe buy them a few drinks...?"

Cordelia still had plenty of pin money. She could afford a few drinks. She looked at her uncle, who was regarding her with sad brown eyes. "Uncle Josh, would you let Fielder...?"

"Who do ye work for, Fielder?" Uncle Josh asked the man. "Who brought ye to London and gave ye a job?"

Fielder frowned as if thinking. "You pay me, Mr. Milton. You made me your stable hand and I am grateful. I do my work. But I am Lord Spenhurst's man. He was kind to me even though I was his guard. Even though I beat him at the marquess's command. I will always owe him for what I did to him. I came to London because I couldn't go with my lord, and Miss Milton is his lady. I serve him by serving her." He met Uncle Josh's glare with a set chin. "Lord Spenhurst is a good man, Mr. Milton."

Uncle Josh nodded, but more as if confirming a thought of his own than agreeing.

"He is," Cordelia told Fielder. "I appreciate your service, Mr. Fielder. I do not know what would have become of me if you had left me at the foot of the tower." It wouldn't hurt to remind her uncle of Fielder's rescue.

Uncle Josh was scribbling a note. "Give this to the head groom," he told Fielder as he handed it over. "It gives ye my authority to spend the time ye need to find out where Deerhaven's coach took his son." He opened a drawer and pulled out a leather purse, which he weighed in one hand and then passed over. "This will cover yer drinks. Food, too, if need be. Report to me each morning. To my niece, if I am not available."

Fielder bowed to each of them as he left. Cordelia stood up. "If that is all, Uncle Josh..."

"It isn't," her uncle said. "Sit down, my girl. We need to talk."

She sank back into her chair. *Does he know? Has my maid been talking?* Cordelia had done her best to keep her condition a secret, but Gracie had cleaned away her used slop buckets and had not been required to deal with the rags Cordelia used during her courses. She had made no comment, but she must know.

Cordelia prepared herself to lock horns with her uncle once again. She was keeping her child. If Spen was not able to marry her before the birth, she would manage. She would have to.

Uncle Josh's first words proved her suspicions about the maid were correct. "Does yer condition change yer mind about my offer, Dee? I can find ye a husband to wed in the next couple of months and give yer baby a father. A marriage will protect both the baby and ye from talk."

That was fairly conciliatory, for Uncle Josh.

"The baby has a father," Cordelia pointed out. "Help me find Lord Spenhurst so he can marry me before the baby is born. He will reach his majority in less than two months and will marry me as soon as he does not need his father's consent."

"Ye're that certain of him," Uncle Josh noted.

Cordelia nodded firmly.

"Then we had better find out where he is and get him back. Fielder will do his part, Dee-Dee. Let me tell ye what I know so far." He pulled a stack of papers towards him and took a sheet from the top. "Here is a list of all the places Deerhaven owns. Or, at least, all the ones I know of so far. I'm sending a person to each one to find out if Lord Spenhurst is there, and if so, where he is being held."

He handed the list to Cordelia, whose eyebrows lifted as she saw how long it was.

"I've also, just today, confirmed the reason Deerhaven is so keen on the marriage with Lady Daphne."

The next sheet of paper, taken from the top of a thick folder, listed sums of money owed. Astronomical sums, and all owed to the Earl of Yarverton, father of Lady Daphne.

"Deerhaven has been neglecting his lands and tenants, dabbling in trade and canals and the like without understanding what works and what doesn't, and spending like there is no tomorrow to buy votes and support for the protégés he has in the House of Commons," Uncle Josh explained.

"Gambling, too, and keeping an expensive mistress. The earl, there, has been buying up his debts." Uncle Josh's smile put Cordelia in mind of the crocodile in the picture book she had had as a child—a broad grin with no humor but a good deal of anticipation.

He tapped a second folder. "Which has cost the earl a great deal of money and left him on shaky ground. He can recover, if he gets what he wants out of the marriage."

"Do you mean Lord Spenhurst?" Cordelia didn't understand how one man could be worth the vast sum the man had spent. Yes, he would be a marquess, but he was no cipher to dance to a tune of his father-in-law's making.

Though it was true Lady Daphne was unlikely to find a husband of such high rank in the normal way of things. She was, as Cordelia had told Spen, a sweet person, but her mind had not developed along with her body.

"That's a long-term investment—a marchioness's robes for his daughter and a marquisate for his grandson. I think there's a faster payoff. I just received the marriage agreements this morning. Here. Let's see if ye can spot it."

Cordelia didn't ask how Uncle Josh got his hands on all these private documents. Her uncle had his ways.

Cordelia accepted the folder he handed to her. The thick stack of papers within had clearly been copied quickly, for she had to make her way through ink blotches and imperfectly formed letters. She sat in the window where the light was best and read in silence, following the lines with one finger, turning the pages until something occurred to her, and hunting back until she could check what the current page said against what she remembered.

The usual headache from reading could be ignored. This was important.

"It's about this estate," she said. "It is a swap, one of several. Both peers benefit by exchanging estates of similar value, so their interests are consolidated into particular areas, and both contribute to the security of the bride and future children. But this one in Derbyshire is the only one that doesn't—at least on the surface—benefit the earl or his daughter. And, while several alternatives are given for the other estates mentioned, there's no alternative for this. What is in Derbyshire that the earl wants enough he will throw his daughter into the bargain to get it?"

Uncle Josh's grin was delighted. "Smart girl," he said, approvingly. "My guess is coal. The Shropshire estate he wants to swap for the Derbyshire one might also have coal, but if so, perhaps it is played out. Or perhaps they couldn't find any there. Either way, it isn't close to the manufactories in which he has an interest, whereas the Derbyshire one is."

"There will be more," Cordelia guessed. "If he can slide one bad bargain past the marquess, there will be others. He is cheating the marquess."

"I think so, too," her uncle assured her. "I have a man creating a portfolio on each asset mentioned in the agreement."

"So, we know why the marquess is so insistent Spen goes through with the marriage, but how does this help us, Uncle Josh?"

The crocodile look returned. "Shaky ground can be made shakier. And what has been purchased can be sold."

"The earl's debts?" Cordelia guessed. "But he won't want to lose his lever over the marquess."

Uncle Josh was untroubled. "All I have to do is find something he wants to lose even less. We will get yer young man back, Dee-Dee. And in time to put a ring on yer finger before..." he nodded in the general direction of Cordelia's womb.

"What can I do to help?" Cordelia asked.

"Stay out of trouble," Uncle Josh growled. "I do not want ye anywhere near these people. Deerhaven has already made a couple of attempts to hurt my business, and I expect him to make more. Especially when he realizes I am attacking back. These people think they have the right to trample all over our kind.

They won't hesitate to go after my family." He leaned across the desk and put his hand on Cordelia's. "I've told ye what is happening so ye'll not worry yerself to flinders and do something stupid. In fact, I don't want ye in London at all. Ye or yer aunt. Or young John, come to that, once they figure out what I'm doing."

Cordelia was going to argue, but her uncle spoke again before she could. "I don't need to be distracted by worrying about ye, Dee-Dee. Show some sense and let me send ye somewhere they won't find you. If ye won't take care on yer own behalf, Dee-Dee, think of yer child. If you get hurt, or worse, what will happen to the babe? If ye must do something, go through the papers I've given ye. Ye have a good mind for business. See if anything else strikes ye as odd. But above all, stay safe."

When he put it like that, what could she say? "Where am I going, Uncle Josh?"

"I've rented a house in Ramsgate. The three of ye will be going to the seaside for the rest of the summer. Don't worry. I will send ye reports so ye know what is happening. I know if I keep ye in ignorance ye'll just go looking for trouble."

Ramsgate, as far as Cordelia could remember, was somewhere on the coast of Kent. At least two days journey from London and far, far away from wherever Spen was, somewhere in the north. But Uncle Josh was right. She could not put the baby in danger.

"When do we leave?" she said.

Chapter Fourteen

THE MARQUESS HAD set Spen a course of study, or so Mr. Morris said when he arrived and explained he had been appointed tutor again. Carrying out his lessons at least saved Spen from death by boredom. A set of estate books were part of it, though the easiest, since he had been managing an estate since he was seventeen. Morris was also putting him through a course on British law and politics, and another on how to read financial reports.

Morris was lodging in the area and came three times a week to review what Spen had learnt and to set the work for the next week. He would answer no questions that did not relate to what Spen was studying.

Spen had also put himself on a course, this one of exercises. He had the vague thought that he might one day need to fight his way free, and he needed to be fit. He remembered everything he could from visits to Gentleman Jackson's where he'd watched the owner putting his aristocratic students through activities to build their strength, endurance, and flexibility.

He created a regimen on his own. Running on the spot. Lying prone and pushing his entire body off the floor so his hands were straight, and he was balanced on his toes. Lying on his back and using his abdominal muscles to pull himself to sitting without lifting his heels from the floor. Whatever guard was on duty watched without comment until the day one of them—Spen called him Eyebrow, because the defining feature of his face was one single bushy brow that crossed his face, curving over each eye—suggested a correction to his technique.

After that, they must have discussed the matter, for each of them, even Chatter, began to offer corrections and suggestions for further exercises. They still would not answer his questions or talk to him about anything except the exercise activities, but he was pleased to have their advice because they were clearly fitter than he was.

The fourth man—the only one for whom Spen had a name, for he had overheard Chatter call him Mickey—even sparred with Spen when it was his turn to be on guard. Shadow-boxed, at least. "Can't put a mark on that pretty face o' your'n," Mickey growled, but clammed up again when asked why.

Seven weeks after he was first brought here, Spen had no more idea where he was than he had when he arrived. According to the calendar he was keeping on the wall next to his bed, it was late August. It was also still summer in the world beyond his window, and not, he thought, far to the north. The workers who occasionally crossed his view were often in their shirtsleeves and sometimes shirtless. His guards and footmen wore coats and trousers of summer-weight fabric.

More clues to his whereabouts were in the estate books he had been ordered to study. They had records of winter wheat and barley crops being sown in October. In the north, September was more likely. If, in fact, the estate books belonged to this property, and he had no evidence for that one way or the other.

He was standing at the window looking out at a pair of men scything the lawn when his usual footman arrived. Was it time for a meal already? No, for he could see the position of the sun by the shadow it cast. It was not yet noon.

"I am to shave you, sir, and help you change for a visitor," the footman said.

"My father?" Spen asked and got the usual reply.

"I am not at liberty to say, sir."

Spen had not yet washed after a vigorous exercise session. He did so, permitted the shave, and changed into the clothes the footman put out. Apparently, he needed to be clothed in the kind of formal daytime wear he would have worn in London to visit court or an older person he wanted to impress with his maturity and respect for protocol. A fitted coat, cut away at the front to show his breeches, and the bottom of his elegant, embroidered waistcoat, clocked stockings, leather shoes with low heels, and a snowy-white cravat intricately folded and adorned with a jeweled tiepin.

Which meant the visitor was not his father, probably. His father did not care to be kept waiting, and washing and changing had taken, Spen estimated, something like three-quarters of an hour. Besides, the marquess only noticed what Spen wore if it reflected in some way on the marquess.

Mickey came forward once Spen was dressed and apologetically showed him a shackle. "Have to put this on, Lord Spenhurst. You're going downstairs."

A struggle would be undignified and ultimately futile. Spen sat and offered his leg. Was there ever such a contrast as the court attire and the felon's ankle bracelet? He shrugged. He could do nothing about it, and presumably the visitor, whoever he was, knew his circumstances.

Mickey opened the door into the hallway and stood waiting for Spen. His heart rate kicked up a step at the thought of leaving his chambers. He nearly rushed the door but managed to subdue the impulse, sauntering slowly out of the room as if nothing momentous was happening.

The other guards were waiting in the hallway and formed up around him. This time, they conducted him down another stair, to what must be the main reception level of the house, for in the hall at the bottom of the stairs was a set of large double doors that, if he was not mistaken, he had seen his father use to enter the house when they first arrived.

If this was one of the marquess's estates, it must have been purchased within the past two and a half years, for he had been taken on a tour of the lands belonging to his family when he turned eighteen, and he'd never been here before. If he'd been asked to describe the place, he'd have called it "tired elegance". It had once been a magnificent, and beautifully appointed, credit to the family that made it their home. Now, everything he saw needed cleaning, polishing, repairing, or painting.

They crossed the entry hall, and a footman opened a door. "Lord Spenhurst," he announced to those within.

Spen paused in the doorway to assess the opposition. And opposition it was. His father, the Earl of Yarverton, and the earl's daughter, Lady Daphne, all staring at him. The marquess glared. The earl smiled a greeting. Lady Daphne looked nervous as she curtseyed. Spen bowed to her in response and then took a few steps into the room. "My lords, my lady. Good day to you all."

Lady Daphne giggled.

"Well, boy?" the marquess said. "Is that all you have to say to your betrothed?"

So, they were to lock horns immediately, were they? Spen was willing. "My betrothed is not in the room, my lord."

"Your betrothed is Lady Daphne," the marquess said, sternly.

"No, sir," Spen insisted. "She is not. My apologies, Lady Daphne, but I have not and will not give my consent to this marriage." He bowed again.

Lady Daphne giggled.

The earl rose, his face suffused with color. "Deerhaven!" he growled. "You told me the pup had come to his senses."

The marquess also got to his feet. "You!" He was looking at Chatter. "Chain my son over there."

"Over there" was a sofa by the window. They had been prepared, Spen realized. A chain descended from a ring-headed bolt that had been embedded in the wall behind the sofa. Chatter indicated the sofa with an inclination of his head. Would it be more dignified to resist? They'd force him anyway. He couldn't fight all four guards, assorted footmen, and the two peers.

He walked over and sat on the sofa. Chatter knelt to lock the chain to his shackle. Spen fantasized about kicking Chatter on the chin and throwing himself backward out the window, but he figured the drop was about twelve feet to the paved courtyard. Not a good idea.

"Come," the marquess said to the earl when Chatter stepped back. "Let us have a private discussion on these matters." He looked around at the rest of the room. "Everyone out until I call for you."

"Not you, Daphne," the earl said to the lady. "Go and sit by Lord Spenhurst. Don't be silly, girl. He won't hurt you. You know what to do. Now do it."

Lady Daphne's giggle this time had an edge of hysteria, and tears started in her eyes, but she obeyed, sitting as far away from Spen as the sofa's modest proportions allowed.

Spen could guess what they intended. He forced back the heated words that wanted to boil out of him. Nothing he said would change his father's mind. But then nothing would change Spen's mind, either.

When the two peers left the room, he passed Lady Daphne his handkerchief. "Dry your tears, my lady. I am not going to hurt you."

The lady giggled. She was nervous, Spen realized. He'd known a boy in the village who giggled whenever he was frightened or embarrassed.

"I mean you no harm, my lady," he insisted. "I will not even touch you."

Lady Daphne's eyes filled again at that. "But you have to. Father said. I am to kiss you and let you do what you like, and not complain if it hurts. Then you will marry me, and I shall be a countess and shall have a new gown." She added, doubtfully, "I will like that very much, Father says."

"I am not going to hurt you, Lady Daphne, and I am not

going marry you," Spen insisted. "I am already betrothed to Miss Milton. I will marry her."

"Miss Cordelia Milton?" Lady Daphne asked, a spark of interest in her eyes. "I like Miss Milton. Father says she is a mushroom, but that's just silly. She doesn't look anything like a mushroom. I think she is pretty, and she was very kind to me."

"I like Miss Milton, too," Spen said, wondering how on earth either of their fathers could believe this pretty child was fit for marriage. That thought and every other went out of his head at Lady Daphne's next words.

"I do not suppose I shall see her again. She is blind, you know," she said. "She hit her head, and now she cannot see. She does not accept invitations anymore. I did not know one could become blind from a blow to the head. Did you know that, Lord Spenhurst?"

Cordelia is alive! The joy in that thought warred with his horror at her blindness. How she must be suffering! He had to go to her! If not for the chain on his leg, he would attempt the window, but he was trapped here in this house while his beloved needed him.

"Father says no one will want to marry her now," Lady Daphne added. "I am sorry, for I like Miss Milton."

"I want to marry her," Spen told her. "I will look after her and be her eyes."

"How can you be eyes?" Lady Daphne asked, staring at him with a wondering expression.

"I will take her arm and guide her where she wants to go." Spen imagined it as he spoke, and his heart yearned to be with his love. "I will describe what I see so she can see pictures of it in her mind."

Lady Daphne regarded him solemnly. "I think you are kind, too," she announced. "Oh dear. Father is going to be angry." She giggled again.

Spen felt the need to reassure the poor girl. It was not her fault her father was a villain. "Do not worry, Lady Daphne. I will take all the blame. I do not mind if your father is angry at me."

"He hits hard," the lady confided. "Try not to cry. He hits you again if you cry."

Spen was shocked. He took it for granted a man would beat his sons for any infractions or, in his father's case, just for being present when the marquess was in a bad temper. But surely no gentleman should raise his hands against his daughters. "I will take all the blame," he reassured Lady Daphne again. "Now tell me what else is being said about Miss Milton."

She amused him for perhaps thirty minutes with London gossip—it was not the gossip that amused him but her naive and blunt commentary. "Miss Wharton trapped the Earl of Ashton. It must have been a big trap, for he is a large man. She is married now and has gone away from London. So that is good because she is not kind. I am not allowed to speak with Mr. Wharton. He is not received any more. That is because he is a bad man. I don't know what he did that was bad. Do you think he is mean, like Miss Wharton? Miss Kingsley is Mrs. Paddimore now. I like her. She is kind."

The door opened without any warning, and the marquess and earl led the way into the room, their smug faces darkening when they saw Spen and Lady Daphne had not moved since they left the room.

The earl advanced on his daughter, who shrank back in her seat, giggling with fear. "I told you to kiss him," the earl thundered.

"I refused her," Spen said. "I will keep refusing her. I will not marry your daughter, Lord Yarverton." He paused. "Nor will I compromise her. It would be like taking advantage of a child."

"You will," the earl insisted. "The marriage contracts are signed, and she has been compromised."

Spen remained calm. "The marriage contracts have not been signed by me. I am not a party to any agreement, and I will not be a party to marriage with your daughter. If she has been compromised, it was not by me. I have not touched her, and I had no part in making her stay in this room." He lifted his ankle to emphasize his point.

The earl rounded on the marquess. "You told me you could make him obey."

Lady Daphne tried to fold in on herself as the two peers shouted at one another. Spen looked around the room. Chatter was the only person close enough to help. "Can you take the lady to her companion?" Spen asked the guard. "This is frightening for her."

Chatter's eyes softened. "If the lady will come with me," he agreed.

"Lady Daphne." Spen kept his voice low, so the warring lords were not distracted from their posturing and bellowing. "Lady Daphne, this is my friend. He is going to take you to Miss Faversham. Will you go with him? He will keep you safe."

"Is he kind?" Lady Daphne wanted to know.

Hardly, but Spen felt safe enough telling her, "He will be kind to you, my lady."

Chatter offered her a hand to help her to uncurl and stand. "Come with me, my lady," he encouraged, his voice gentle. And yes, kind.

The lady responded to the tone and allowed him to escort her from the room. *Well. Who would have thought Chatter had a heart?*

The earl and the marquess sent the servants and guards away and harangued Spen for hours. They even brought in a cleric and ordered him to perform the ceremony he was being paid for, but when Spen told the man he was being forced into the marriage against his will, the cleric refused.

"I'll find someone who will do it," the marquess told the earl after the cleric had gone away. The earl glared at Spen. "I will beat some sense into the boy," he growled.

The marquess waved a dismissive hand. "You can try. Just don't kill him. I need an heir." He walked out of the room, leaving Spen alone with the earl.

"I will use your coercion as grounds for annulment as soon as

I am of age," Spen warned the earl, who called in a couple of burly men Spen hadn't seen before. They each took one of his arms. Lady Daphne was correct. Her father hit hard.

Chapter Fifteen

AT RAMSGATE, THERE was little to do except walk the beach when it was fine and play endless games of cards or chess with John when it was not. Cordelia's sight continued to improve, but the doctor in Ramsgate agreed with the London specialist she must not do too much close work, including reading or sewing.

"Half an hour twice a day," he said. "We can increase it after you have spent a whole week headache-free." John, bless him, was happy to read to her in the evenings, and she could play tunes she had by heart on the pianoforte. It could have been worse, she supposed.

Uncle Josh had still not found where Spen was. John was full of plans to go looking, but Cordelia reminded him of Spen's fears John could be used to pressure him into agreeing to the marriage.

Then Cordelia received a letter from Lady Daphne, the lady Spen's father intended him to marry.

She tried to puzzle it out herself. Lady Daphne had a round hand, but the letters were slightly tipsy and Lady Daphne's spelling made reading even more difficult. After a few frustrating minutes, Cordelia went looking for John.

He read it through, using a finger to follow the uneven lines. "I think she must have seen Spen," he reported. "Here, I'll read it out loud."

"Dear Miss Milton, my father says I have to marry Lord Spenhurst. Lord Spenhurst says he will not marry me. He says he will only marry you. I think that is a good idea, but my father is very angry. People in London say you are blind. I hope you get better soon, but Lord Spenhurst says it does not matter. He will lead you and be your eyes. I thought you would like to know. Yours sincerely, Lady Daphne."

"You're right," Cordelia decided. "She has seen Spen. In London? She mentions people in London, but Uncle Josh would know if Spen was in London."

John was reading the letter again as if he could drag more meaning out of it with each rereading. "She has written the letter from Thorne Abbey," he said. "That does not sound like London. We need to see her."

Cordelia was more cautious. She had promised her uncle, after all, that she would leave the hunt to him. "We need to write to Uncle Josh and send him a copy of the letter. He will find a way to discover where Thorne Abbey is and to question Lady Daphne."

Her letter to her uncle crossed another from him saying he had to go to Liverpool, but she wasn't to worry. He hadn't given up on finding Spen.

"We have to go ourselves," John insisted. "But go where? How do we find Thorne Abbey?" John looked up the Earl of Yarverton in the library, but Thorne Abbey was not mentioned. "We have to find out. What if this lady can tell us where Spen is, but by the time we can question her, the marquess has moved him somewhere else?"

That might have already happened, Cordelia knew. She had already spent sleepless nights fretting that any delay might mean she lost her chance to rescue her beloved. But something about the name "Thorne Abbey" niggled at her. She had heard the name before, but she could not recall where.

Will Fielder arrived later that day with reports from her uncle's investigation. The covering note from Uncle Josh was brief. Cordelia knew part of his business in Liverpool concerned the two peers, or possibly just the earl. Uncle Josh didn't specify in writing what he was doing, but he did say all was going well.

The enclosed papers were in three bundles. One was about the earl and one about the marquess. What they owned, what they owed, and where their income came from, with analysis and commentary from her uncle's lawyers and bookkeepers. The third was the marriage agreement he had already shown her, as well as a report on it from those same experts. As soon as she saw the agreement, Cordelia knew where she had heard the name Thorne Abbey. It was the Shropshire estate mentioned in the agreement.

It seemed like a sign from heaven. Fielder would take them to Shropshire, and he would keep them safe.

Leaving Ramsgate was easy enough. Aunt Eliza was laid low with a summer ague and keeping to her bed. Cordelia told her aunt Uncle Josh had sent the carriage for her and John, and they would be in London for a sennight. Perhaps two weeks. Aunt Eliza did not question it. Indeed, she expressed herself, pleased Cordelia would have something to amuse herself with while she was ill.

Persuading Fielder was no more difficult. His commitment was to Spen and therefore, to Cordelia. He was eager to find out what Lady Daphne could tell them.

Cordelia enlisted Gracie as chaperone for the five-day journey. Gracie said she would come, "...for I know I can't stop you, Miss, but you must write to Mr. Milton and tell him what you are up to." Cordelia agreed, for it was a good precaution. If it all went wrong, she could trust Uncle Josh to come to her rescue.

"I am going to write letters to Uncle Josh every day," she told John and Gracie, "so he knows where to start if he has to look for us."

Cordelia had cause to be grateful to Gracie in the next few days. On the first night, the innkeeper was insolent and dismissive, asking what a young female like her was doing with only a maid, a boy, and a few menservants, and relegating her party to a set of tiny rooms on the third floor. The lukewarm meal that was sent up for them to eat after Fielder had been down three times to ask for it was the last straw.

The next night, Gracie appointed herself as their spokesperson, with Fielder at her shoulder. Claiming to be the widowed mother of Cordelia and John, she demanded and received better service for herself, her children, and her servants. Even so, it was a long and exhausting trip, the only mitigating circumstance that Cordelia's morning sickness appeared to have left her.

Once they reached Shrewsbury, Gracie enquired about rooms to let at the first inn they came to. She came back with the name and direction of a widow who let rooms by the week. "Very respectable, the innkeeper's wife said. She normally only takes females, but I am told she might make an exception for a boy of Master John's age."

Soon, they were settled in the rooming house—Cordelia and Gracie sharing one room, John in another. Fielder and the coachman bedded down in the carriage, which they were allowed to park in an outbuilding of the once grand house. The rest of the men, three grooms, and four outriders, had rooms at the inn that had given them the widow's direction.

The next day, Fielder and the other male servants spread out through Shrewsbury with orders to find Thorne Abbey. John went with them.

Fielder returned first, and Cordelia met him in the landlady's parlor, Gracie in attendance. He and the other men had, between them, learned of three places that might be the one they sought, one Thorne Hall, one Thorne Grange, and one Thorn Abbey. Unfortunately, each was perhaps two hours or more away from Shrewsbury in a different direction. Fielder suggested three groups set off tomorrow. By tomorrow night, they would have their destination. Cordelia braced herself for another long day of waiting.

Fielder had seen John and his groom at various times during the day, but John had not yet returned home, and the groom wasn't at the inn when Fielder parted from the other men. He was about to go out again to see what had become of the boy when John arrived home, white and shaken.

"Nothing happened," he assured Cordelia. "We are both unhurt." Disaster had nearly befallen him, though, and it was the close call that left him breathless and disturbed. He had seen the marquess and had, in fact, run around a corner and nearly bumped into the man. "He was just having a meal while they changed his horses," he said.

"I watched him leave in his coach and then questioned the ostler. His horses came from a place called Marton," he reported, "and he will change again at Telford, which is on the way to Birmingham. So, he is heading away from this county, Cordelia. If Spen is somewhere in Shropshire, as we believe, at least the marquess is not with him."

Marton! Cordelia turned back to their map, and sure enough, Thorn Abbey, spelled without the 'e', was within a couple of miles of Marton. "This is the one!" Cordelia said.

Fielder argued for a day of reconnaissance, but Cordelia was plagued by the worry that another day might be a day too long. They left the rooming house not long after dawn to make the two-hour drive before the residents of the house would be up and about. She did agree to John's suggestion to question the people in Rorrington, the nearest village to the estate. He and Fletcher went out to find out all the gossip that they could.

According to one of the footmen whose mother owned the local inn, Lady Daphne was there. Or, at least, there was a young lady who had arrived several weeks ago. It was the talk of the village that the local vicar had been called to perform a marriage for the young lady and a gentleman who was also, apparently, in residence. The footman had told gothic tales about the gentleman who was kept chained in a room. Even more intriguing to the village gossips, when the gentleman voiced his objection to the marriage, the vicar refused to perform the ceremony and was dismissed.

Neither the lady nor the gentleman had left the house. "That boy always did have an imagination, look you," said the woman at the general store, who served Cordelia a glass of elderberry juice and sold her three meters of ribbon and half a dozen fruit buns.

Another customer gave it as her opinion the young man should obey his father. "From what I heard, the lady is a simpleton and wealthy. He could do a lot worse."

Cordelia struggled not to argue.

Meanwhile, the inn servant who had brought Fielder and John a glass each of the local ale also served as much of the local gossip as they cared to hear. "Vicar is right upset, says his housekeeper." The reverend gentleman had been torn between his urge to see justice done and his fear of offending two powerful lords. "High-born types. Reckon their younglin's 'll have to do as they're told," the servant opined.

"Not him," a passing maid declared. "I hear tell he says he is married to another lady or as good as."

The other members of the party all had their snippet to contribute, including that the estate was closely guarded, and that the young gentleman had no fewer than four guards, all foreigners. By this, Cordelia took it to mean the guards were not from the area immediately surrounding the village.

The two peers had not remained in the house, but one of them had returned a couple of days ago, stayed a night, and left again. What his purpose was, and whether he had accomplished it, nobody knew, though that did not prevent the villagers from offering speculations.

While everyone in the village was sure they knew what was going on, no one except the vicar had spoken to, or even seen, the young lady or the gentleman. Meeting the vicar seemed a logical next step, but a knock on the vicarage door elicited the information he was away, and not expected back for several days.

Cordelia had no doubt in her mind they had found both Lady Daphne and Spen, but how to rescue them, or even speak to them? She could hardly march up to the front door and ask to be announced.

Long discussion produced no other plan for breaching the guards. Perhaps her first thought was worth trying. After all, if she marched up to the front door and asked to be announced, what would they do? Neither peer was in residence. The marquess had proclaimed her an enemy, but the earl barely knew she existed, and his servants had no reason to detain her, even if their orders were to deny all visitors.

Fielder and Gracie argued against it, but John agreed, and in the end, the pair of them prevailed, and they set out for Thorn Abbey

The outrider sat up beside the driver directing him along the lane to the house. They stopped around the corner from the main gates to split their forces. The outriders and two of the grooms would stay in hiding to sound the alarm and to stage a rescue, should anything go wrong.

Even with that precaution and all her rationalizations, Cordelia's heart was pounding as her carriage passed through the gate and along the carriageway, to pull up outside the house.

Fielder handed her and Gracie down and climbed the stairs to knock on the door.

Cordelia's palms were sweating inside her gloves, and Gracie was white with fright. "You can stay in the carriage if you wish," Cordelia told the maid.

"I am coming with you, Miss," the maid insisted.

Fielder was speaking through a narrow opening to the man who had pulled the door open just enough to speak through the gap. "...doesn't have visitors," the man was saying.

"No wonder. I daresay they cannot find Thorn Abbey." Cordelia was careful to shorten many of her vowels and crisp her consonants, imitating the accent of the most aristocratic ladies she knew. She climbed the stairs as she continued. "My poor driver has been traveling practically in circles along these lanes looking for the home of my dear Lady Daphne. Please let her know Miss Milton and her cousin have arrived and direct my driver to a place where he might see to the horses."

She didn't mention Spen. She could not think of an acceptable reason for an unmarried woman to ask to see an unmarried man.

The butler had let the door drift open during her speech, and John was quick to dart ahead and push it the rest of the way.

Cordelia stalked in through the doorway as if in no doubt the servant would step out from her path. He did, his mouth agape as first John, then Gracie, and finally Fielder followed her into a small entrance hall that badly needed cleaning.

A moment later, he had recovered himself enough to stammer, "If you would step this way, ma'am, I will see if Lady Daphne is receiving."

The reception room he led them to was in no better condition than the entrance hall. It was not much used, as the dust covers on the furniture made clear. The butler whipped one off a faded sofa and a cloud of dust rose. Cordelia took a seat, inclining her head in gracious thanks.

She gestured to the maid, who came to perch on the edge of the sofa. Fielder moved back against the wall, the picture of a footman waiting patiently for whatever command might come his way. John prowled the room, examining the few paintings that decorated the walls. In several places, a darker patch hinted at paintings that had been removed.

The butler looked at them helplessly, as if unsure of his next move.

"Lady Daphne?" Cordelia reminded him.

He jerked into motion and left the room.

Cordelia tried to stay calm as the minutes passed, but she could not help imagining all sorts of nasty scenarios. She should not have brought John and Gracie with her. Fielder could look after himself, and Cordelia was prepared to take the risk, but she should at least have left the other two with the carriage.

John continued to prowl, though he looked perfectly calm. The maid was rigid with fear, her jaw set and her eyes wide. Fielder's usually grim expression had darkened still further by the time the door opened again, and then Lady Daphne erupted into the room, followed by Miss Faversham.

Lady Daphne rushed to Cordelia and took her hands. "Miss Milton! You came to see me! No one ever comes to see me. How kind you are." She turned to her companion. "Miss Faversham, I told you Miss Milton was kind. Did I not tell you?"

"You did tell me, Lady Daphne, and I well remember how kind Miss Milton is," Miss Faversham assured her. "Do you remember what we do when we have visitors?"

The lady giggled, and her eyes widened. "Call for tea," she announced. She grinned at the butler. "We need refreshments for my guests. I have guests!" She bounced on her toes and giggled. The butler's smile held considerable affection. "Yes, my lady," he said.

"Lady Daphne," Cordelia said, "may I present my companion, Miss Simpson, and my cousin, John Milton."

"And who is that?" Lady Daphne asked, pointing to Fielder.

"Pointing is rude," Miss Faversham whispered, and Lady Daphne snatched her hand back and hid it in her gown.

Cordelia pretended she hadn't heard. "My footman's name is Fielder."

Fielder stared into thin air, and anyone who didn't know him would not realize he was amused. Cordelia, though, saw the small twitch in the corner of his lips and the slight crinkling on the outer edge of his eyes.

"Now you introduce me," Miss Faversham coached, and Lady Daphne obediently followed the instruction.

"Miss Milton, I would like to make known to you my companion, Miss Faversham. Miss Faversham, this is Miss Milton, Miss Simpson, and Miss Milton's cousin, Mr…" She trailed off to address Miss Faversham. "Should it be 'Mister Milton' or 'Master Milton'?"

"Call me John," John suggested, and Lady Daphne looked to her companion for permission.

Miss Faversham shook her head. "'Master Milton'," she dictated. "Now let us sit down, my lady, so Master Milton may also sit."

Once again, Lady Daphne obeyed her companion, taking a seat on a sofa set at right angles to Cordelia's. Miss Faversham sat beside her, and John selected a chair.

The butler entered with a tea service, followed by footmen carrying trays. While they set the tea makings and plates of food on a table by Miss Faversham, Cordelia wondered how to introduce her questions. Should she just ask straight out? Should she talk about Spen and hope that Lady Daphne would volunteer the information she wanted?

But once the door closed behind the butler and footmen, Miss Faversham took the initiative. "Is it true that you are betrothed to Lord Spenhurst, Miss Milton?"

"I am," Cordelia insisted. "Or, at least, I will be once he is of age. My uncle consents, but his father does not."

"Lord Spenhurst says he will marry you," Lady Daphne volunteered. "He does not want to marry me. My father says he will make him." Lady Daphne frowned. "You are not blind," she observed. "My father said you were blind."

"I was, but I got better," Cordelia explained. She turned her gaze to Miss Faversham. "What do the earl and Lord Deerhaven plan? Do you know?"

"Wicked things, Miss Milton. I believe you have come to find out where Lord Spenhurst is being held. He is here, Miss. If you are able to rescue him, will you please help, my lady?"

Chapter Sixteen

CHATTER PROVED TO be nearly as gentle a nurse as Spen's housekeeper. He set Spen's broken arm, bound up his cracked ribs, and provided poultices for the bruises. Spen had tried to defend himself from the earl, but the men the earl had brought with him held Spen's arms, and Spen had been handicapped by being chained in one place.

He seemed to recall that his own head guard intervened to stop the beating, but perhaps that was just a dream. Certainly, he had no memory of being carried from the room, and he had not seen either peer again since. Chatter told him they had left, but the little lady remained.

He spent more than a week of very uncomfortable days. On the third day, he insisted on the binding being removed from around his ribs. A good deep breath hurt but was not the stabbing pain Chatter warned him to watch for.

"You'll do, my lord," Chatter had assured him.

Spen certainly hoped so, because he still felt like one enormous bruise, quite apart from the sharp pain of his arm and ribs. But filling his lungs helped his general malaise. For the rest, it was just a matter of time.

The footman who served him was a little more forthcoming about what had happened after Spen was knocked unconscious.

He confirmed Chatter had rescued Spen, intervening when it became clear the earl was not going to stop just because Spen was unconscious.

"Lord Deerhaven was right peeved with Lord Yarverton," he confided. "Said he'd gone too far. Lord Yarverton stormed off. Lord Deerhaven went this afternoon when he knew you hadn't taken an infection, my lord."

"Did they beat Lady Daphne?" Spen asked and was relieved to hear the lady was unharmed, but locked in a suite of rooms just a little farther along the passage. "What is the name of this place?" he asked the footman. "Where are we?" But the guard on duty growled and the footman had paled and stopped talking.

The nights were the worst, when he lay awake thinking about Cordelia and wishing he was with her in between sessions of worrying about what his father had planned.

His father came to tell him. It was more than two weeks after the beating. By this time, he was able to move with some ease again, and to resume his exercise routine, but Mickey the guard entered his rooms in some haste and told him to put himself back to bed. The marquess was here, and they had told him Spen was still ailing.

Spen only had time to strip to his shirt and get back into bed.

"You are healing, I hope," the marquess said, in what sounded more like a command than a question.

"I daresay I will in time, my lord," Spen replied. "My arm is broken and several of my ribs, but nothing vital was damaged, I imagine, for I am not dead."

The marquess's face worked with anger, but whether at Spen or Yarverton, Spen couldn't tell. Both, probably. "You brought it on yourself with your own stubbornness," the marquess declared.

"Before you ask," Spen told him, "I will not agree to the marriage with Lady Daphne."

The marquess glared. "If you are well enough to argue, you are well enough to be wed," he replied. He turned on his heel and left the room.

That night, Spen fell to sleep easily, but when he woke in the early hours of the morning, it was as if the scales had fallen off his eyes. He had been waiting to be rescued. Even back in Deercroft, he had only begun to weave the rope and to attack the bars because Cordelia and John had suggested it. Since then, he had done not one active thing to help himself, apart from exercising to keep himself fit. And much good it had done him.

He had waited for his birthday as if the mere fact of reaching his majority would set him free. His father was not going to stop ordering his life merely because he turned twenty-one. His father probably didn't know Spen's birthday had been and gone, and certainly wouldn't allow Spen's age to make a difference. Saying "no" wasn't enough. He had to get free through his own devices.

By morning, he had come to terms with the fact he had, despite his age, been playing the part of a child, acting as if his only options were to obey or to defy. He'd been letting other people make decisions and then reacting to them.

Cordelia did not do that. Cordelia reached after what she wanted, even if it meant putting herself in danger. He lost himself briefly in memories of the day when what she wanted was his lovemaking, but if he was ever to enjoy it again, he would need to make it happen.

He wasn't worthy of her. He had not tried to argue his case with his father but had simply opposed him. He had not even made much of an effort to woo his guards to his cause. They were hired men, and unlikely to have any personal loyalty to the marquess, so it was worth a try.

He couldn't offer to double their wages. Spen had no money that had not come from his father, and that his father could not take. Would they turn their coats on a promise? One day, and it couldn't be more than a few years away, Spen would be one of the wealthiest men in England. He couldn't wait, however long that might be, to take control of his life.

He should make a list. Several lists, in fact. He had always found writing things down helped him to organize his thoughts.

What arguments could he use to convince his father? What had he noticed he could use in an escape? What might convince his guards to help with said escape? What jobs was he qualified to do to support himself and—if Mr. Milton would allow it—Cordelia from the time he escaped until the time he inherited the Deerhaven title and estates?

But before he could write a list, he realized, he had a problem. His broken right arm meant any lists he created would have to be held in his mind. *Although...* He narrowed his eyes and studied Mickey, the guard currently on duty. "Mickey?" he asked, "can you read and write?"

It turned out that Mickey was not literate. "Jim is," Mickey offered. "And Marsh, of course."

"When you go off duty, will you let them know I need someone to write for me?" Spen asked, wondering which of his guards were Jim and Marsh, and why Marsh was an 'of course'.

The question was answered when Big Nose arrived to relieve Mickey, and Mickey said, "Jim, his lordship here wants someone to write stuff for him."

So Big Nose was Jim. He regarded Spen thoughtfully. "We'll 'ave to ask Marsh," he said. Ah. Chatter must be Marsh. A surname, Spen guessed. "Please do," he said. "I have some lists to write."

Marsh arrived partway through the morning. "You want something written?" he asked.

"I do," Spen agreed. "I need to figure out a strategy to persuade my father to drop this marriage idea. I thought if I wrote down a few ideas—or at least got you to write them down for me—it might help. Also, even if he stops driving me towards Lady Daphne, he will not consent to the lady I have chosen, so I need a second list. In fact, you and the other guards—the footmen, too—could help with that list. Jobs I am qualified to do or could learn to do to support myself, and a wife and family, until I inherit."

Marsh's eyebrows twitched as if he was suppressing the urge

to raise them. "I will do it. When do you wish to start?"

It proved to be the longest conversation Spen had had with Marsh, who began by simply writing what he was told but was soon making comments and offering suggestions. Jim was drawn into the discussion, and when the usual footman arrived with tea for Spen, he was sent back for more cups and ended up sitting down with the three of them to offer his opinion.

It was Marsh who pointed out the obvious fact that there was no point in telling the marquess about how Spen's life would be affected by the wrong choice of bride.

"His lordship don't care about you being happy, my lord, if you'll excuse my saying so."

"You're right," Spen realized. "It's all about how it affects him."

"Some folks are like that," Marsh volunteered. "Other people don't matter to them. It's as if they don't see the rest of us as real. Just checker pieces to be moved around the board."

Spen had never imagined a day coming when he would be discussing the nature of man with Chatter. If nothing else came out of this exercise, at least he had changed the relationship with his guard.

"Does he plan to come and see me today?" he asked.

"Left after lunch," Marsh admitted. "Said he would be back in a couple of days."

The following morning, they continued with the lists, this time with all four guards plus the footman. They must have been talking for an hour when another footman knocked and was admitted. "Marsh, you are needed," he said. Marsh's face, which had been alive with amusement over Jim's suggestion Spen might be able to get work as a footman, changed as if someone had wiped a cloth over it to remove all expression. His eyes flat and his face blank, he stood and left without a word.

Spen figured they'd done enough for the morning. He thanked Jim and the footman, and asked if they would mind sharing any more thoughts they might have, then went back to reading a rather boring book about agricultural rotation he'd been given by his tutor Morris.

Not that he could settle to reading, or even to planning for the future. He was too concerned about whatever might have happened to draw Marsh away.

※※※

BEFORE HE LEFT the estate, the earl had spoken to Miss Faversham and informed her that she and her charge would remain. He had made it clear it was Miss Faversham's task to ensure Lady Daphne was introduced to Lord Spenhurst's bed where, the earl was certain, nature would take its course and Spenhurst, as a gentleman, would have no choice but to marry the girl.

"He seemed to think Lord Spenhurst would be eager to satisfy his male appetites because he has been unable to do so during his incarceration," Miss Faversham explained. "But even if the young lord was too bloodless to…" she blushed. "I cannot repeat the words, Miss Milton, but I trust you understand. The earl said he could arrange Lady Daphne was not, er, *intact* so Lord Spenhurst would have no grounds for the annulment."

She leaned forward, her eyes burning with outrage. "I cannot allow this. I have managed to put it off while the young lord was recovering, but the whole household knows he is now much improved."

Cordelia's heart stuttered in her chest. "He has been ill?"

"He was beaten, I have been told," Miss Faversham explained. "He defied the earl, and the earl lost his temper. The marquess's men had to intercede to rescue the poor man." She returned to her own concerns. "I must get Lady Daphne away, but what can I do? We are well-guarded. The marquess's men patrol the house and the earl's men patrol the grounds. And even if we could escape, I have nowhere to go."

"How did you arrange for the letter?" Cordelia asked. It was an assumption that Miss Faversham was behind the correspondence.

"I am sorry I could not be more specific," Miss Faversham apologized. "I thought of putting in a note of my own, but, though one of the footmen agreed to post the letter in the village, he insisted on reading it first, and I was afraid he would simply take my bribe and hand the letter over to the guards."

As the older woman spoke, Cordelia studied Lady Daphne, who was chatting cheerfully with John. An idea had occurred to her and as Miss Faversham finished speaking, she commented, "We are much of a height, and have similar figures," she commented. "My hair is darker, of course. In my bonnet... I think it would work."

"What are you thinking?" Miss Faversham asked, frowning in thought.

"How would Lady Daphne manage if I sent her away in my place, with my... my cousin and my servants? John and my maid Gracie would look after her, I assure you. They can take her to my uncle, who will keep her safe."

Miss Faversham's eyes widened. "You mean to swap places?" She pursed her lips as she looked from Lady Daphne to Cordelia and back again.

"The servants here might notice," she mused. "They probably would. But they are sympathetic to both my lady and the young lord. The earl never looks directly at his daughter but past her if you understand my meaning, as if she is of no consequence... If I bleach your hair... Are you a good actress, Miss Milton?"

Probably. Hopefully. Cordelia nodded. "I can try. And you can take me to Spen's room with an easy conscience, for we are betrothed."

"If we do this, I shall be your chaperone," Miss Faversham insisted. "After all, the lords are insisting on a wedding, and I take it you would not object, and nor would Lord Spenhurst."

Cordelia's mind had not gone there, but it was worth thinking about. "As long as my name was on the license," she commented. How to achieve that was beyond her at the moment, but perhaps something could be managed. She turned to address the others in the room.

"Gracie, Fielder, John, Miss Faversham and I have had an idea," she said.

After she had laid out the new plan and patiently countered everyone's objections, she sent Fielder and John out while she and Lady Daphne changed clothes. Lady Daphne thought it a fine joke, and Cordelia was concerned the girl's giggles might give them away. It occurred to her that perhaps they could manage to leave the house without being escorted by the butler.

When she opened the door to let the men back in, that minor worry was swamped by a larger one. Another man stood with them in the entry hall and followed them back into the room.

She looked anxiously at John. He and Fielder both looked cheerful. "Cordelia," John said, "This is Marsh. He is Spen's head guard, and he wants to help us."

Marsh was ignoring them. Lady Daphne had danced up to him in her cheerful way and taken his hands, and he was listening to her insistence she was going to be Miss Milton for a while and Miss Milton was going to be her. "I have to go away from my Miss Faversham, but Miss Simpson is going to look after me, and so is John," she explained. "I like John. He is kind. Like you, Marsh."

"That sounds like an excellent idea, my lady," Marsh told her, withdrawing one hand so he could pat hers. "You will be very good for Miss Simpson and Master Milton, I know."

Lady Daphne noticed Cordelia staring at them. "Marsh is kind," she announced.

Marsh told her to go to Miss Faversham before he addressed Cordelia. "My men and I would like to enter your service, Miss Milton. We've been talking to Lord Spenhurst, and he would employ us, but he is a bit short of the ready at the moment, and," he shrugged, "a man's got to eat."

Cordelia cast a glance at Fielder. Spen had charmed his support away from the marquess and now, it seemed, he had charmed this man and his colleagues.

The guard must have thought she was hesitating, because he explained, "I can't keep taking the marquess's money when I'm working against him, and my men feel the same. It wouldn't be honest. But it isn't right to help him with what he is doing. I didn't mind when I thought it was a case of a spoiled lordling who needed to settle down, but they never should have involved that sweet innocent there."

He shrugged. "We've been feeling stuck, Miss Milton. We didn't want to leave, because the men the earl hired are brutes who'll do anything for money. And we'd be walking away from what the marquess owes us, too. Then today, Lord Spenhurst suggested we could work for him, only he couldn't pay us yet. When I heard you were here, I thought maybe you wouldn't mind…"

He trailed off and Cordelia held out her hand, as her uncle did when he closed a deal. "I accept. You are now working for me, Mr. Marsh. How much pay does the marquess owe you, and how many of you are there?"

Marsh shook her proffered hand and answered her questions. *Oh, good.* She had enough money hidden in the carriage to give him the owed money as a token of good faith.

John was reluctant to leave, but they agreed it was dangerous for him to stay, especially when Marsh said the marquess had only gone as far as Birmingham where he knew of a minister who would accept a bribe to perform a forced wedding. Since John had seen him yesterday afternoon, he could be back as early as this evening.

Before long, Marsh and one of his men had escorted the visitors to their carriage. There, Cordelia, in her guise as Lady Daphne, climbed into the carriage, where she retrieved her money pouch from its hidden cupboard, then allowed herself to be persuaded back down again to wave joyously as the coach carried Lady Daphne, Gracie, John, and Fielder down the carriageway and out of the reach of both earl and marquess.

If her people managed to carry out their part of the plan, she and Spen would soon be free, too. Meanwhile—she gave an extra skip on her way up the stairs—she was on her way to be reunited with her beloved.

Chapter Seventeen

MARSH WALKED INTO the room with a broad grin. Spen had never before seen the man with even a real smile. He put down the book he was reading and stood. "What has happened?" he asked.

"I have accepted a new job," Marsh announced. "Would you like to meet my employer?" Spen had a moment to fear Marsh had once more joined the forces against him before the man stepped out of the doorway.

Miss Faversham entered the room, with Lady Daphne following. But even as the girl raised her head so her lace cap no longer hid her face, something in him knew it was not Lady Daphne but Cordelia.

It was impossible. She couldn't be here. But here she was, taking the few steps between him at a run. Here she was, as close to his body as she could get with their clothes between them, his uninjured arm around her.

"Cordelia! But how...?"

His thoughts stuttered to a halt as her lips reached his, and for a long moment nothing existed in the world except their seeking mouths, their bodies pressed to one another.

The sound of a clearing throat returned Spen somewhat to his senses. Miss Faversham said, austerely, "I promised Miss

Simpson that Miss Milton would be chaperoned, so if the pair of you would put a little space between yourselves, I would appreciate it."

Marsh snickered, which fetched a glare from Miss Faversham. Spen could feel himself blushing. Cordelia did not seem to be bothered. "Very well, Miss Faversham," she said. "Spen, we need to talk. We have a great deal to tell you."

⇉⇇

"And so, you see," Cordelia concluded, "It all hinges on whether or not the earl recognizes me. Miss Faversham is reasonably certain he won't, as he seldom sees his daughter and never really looks at her. And if he and your father believe I am Lady Daphne, we really cannot lose. If John and Fielder manage to reach my uncle, and he can organize a license, we have a reasonable chance of being married right under the noses of the marquess and the earl. If we have to go through a ceremony with me in the place of the bride named on the license, we will certainly have several grounds for annulment."

Spen could imagine a thousand things that could go wrong. "My heart, what if someone does recognize you? I thought we agreed you were going to stay out of the marquess's hands so he couldn't use threats to you to force me to obey him?"

"He cannot force your marriage when he cannot find the bride he intends for you, Spen," Cordelia pointed out. "By now, she and John are on their way to meet my uncle. They are surrounded by men loyal to the Miltons, and once they are in my uncle's hands, he will keep them safe. Especially if we carry on the masquerade. With luck, Yarverton won't even know Lady Daphne is missing."

"It is your safety I am concerned about," Spen said.

Cordelia shrugged one shoulder. "They might imprison me, but I doubt they are so lost to all sense they would do me physical harm. My uncle will move heaven and earth to retrieve me, and they must have heard the rumors about what happened to Richport."

"What happened to Richport?" Spen asked.

Cordelia smiled. "He had creditors who would not be refused. They called in certain debts, with menaces. He took advantage of the peace with France and fled across the channel. Rumor has it the creditors were in debt to my uncle, who disapproved of Richport's bet about me."

Spen raised his eyebrows. "Rumor speaks truth in this instance, I take it," he said. "As to this masquerade…" He heaved a sigh. "Are you going to do that when we are married? Throw yourself headlong into danger?"

"Hardly headlong," Cordelia objected. "Only after careful thought and doing what I can for our protection." She waved a hand to indicate Marsh.

"My men and I will do our absolute best to protect you and Miss Milton, my lord," Marsh assured Spen.

"If things go wrong," Spen told him, "Get Miss Milton out of here."

"If things go right," Cordelia corrected him, "we will win everything."

Spen had to smile. "I did not know I was marrying a gambler," he teased.

Cordelia was not amused. "I am not a gambler," she insisted. "But no one succeeds in any enterprise without taking risks. My uncle taught me to measure the risks against the benefits and to take all possible precautions. The risk of losing you is everything to me, Spen. Next to that, nothing else matters."

Spen's thoughts of the morning returned as he hugged her for that sentiment. Cordelia might be nearly three years younger than he was, but in many ways, she was so much older. So much more the adult. Though his was supposedly the advantaged class, it was the plucky determination and actions of the so-called lower class that had not only kept him alive but also full of hope. And of course, the best of it was easy to find in the woman he loved. "Just remember when you weigh those risks that you are everything to me, too, my love. Putting yourself in danger is not acceptable to me."

She rested her cheek on his chest and patted his back. "Danger is part of life, Spen. Did you expect me to leave you to your fate and bear your child without you?"

He was slow to parse that sentence. He had kissed the top of her head and started a reply when he realized what she had just said. "Wait. What did you say? Cordelia, my child?" He held her away from him so he could look down at her abdomen. Awe filled him as he moved one of his hands to lay it gently over her belly, moved beyond words at the thought of his baby, his and Cordelia's, cradled within.

His beloved blushed and slid her hands to cover his. "You are pleased?" she asked. She looked anxious.

"Thrilled beyond words," he told her, hugging her to him again. "And also, even more upset than ever you are here instead of safe under your uncle's care."

"We will win." Cordelia made it a fervent prayer rather than a promise, and Spen could only hope God was listening.

"We must win," he agreed, wishing their audience would go away so he could take his darling to bed and worship her body until she understood just how thrilled he was.

But they didn't disappear. Marsh was studiously staring at the plaster cornices. Miss Faversham was both blushing and frowning. Heaven alone knew what she thought of Cordelia's revelation. "It is time to return to our room, Miss Milton," she said. "Our meal will be served soon, and we do not want the staff gossiping about how long you have been in Lord Spenhurst's room."

She was correct, though Spen didn't like it. Cordelia clearly thought so, too, for she said, "I will return, my love."

"Not this afternoon," Miss Faversham fussed. "I need to bleach your hair, Miss Milton. We will not be able to carry off this masquerade if you are obliged to wear a spinster's cap in front of the earl. Now come along like a good girl."

Cordelia bristled, and Spen was about to rebuke Miss Faversham for her condescending attitude when Cordelia spoke. "Would you excuse me a moment, Spen? Miss Faversham, a private word, if you would."

She beckoned the woman to the far corner of the chamber and spoke for a minute or two. Miss Faversham blushed as she spoke in response, just a few words.

"I will return this afternoon," Cordelia repeated to Spen.

"I will read those papers you brought me. The reports on the marriage agreement, and the financial dealings of the marquess and the earl." He kissed the top of Cordelia's head. "Just a short time more," he told her, "and we shall be man and wife, and free of all this intrigue."

Miss Faversham stared at him. Spen returned her look. "You have the honor to be the temporary companion of my affianced bride and the mother of my child, Miss Faversham. The future Marchioness of Deerhaven is my partner in every way and has my respect and my confidence."

Miss Faversham's eyes dropped first.

Marsh opened the door for the two ladies and closed it after they had left the room. "I wonder what Miss Milton said to the besom," he commented.

Spen's keen ears had served him again. "She told the lady she is a grown woman and has had sole charge of her own business for the past three years. She said she understood Miss Faversham was accustomed to supporting a young lady who was childlike in her understanding, and Lady Daphne's affection for Miss Faversham was evidence she had performed her duties with affection and understanding. However, if Miss Faversham ever has the temerity to again admonish her as if she was a child, Miss Faversham and Miss Milton were going to have a serious falling out." He might not have remembered every word, but that was the sense of it. "She also told Miss Faversham that, if the woman could not be trusted, she would be locked in her room and guarded while we confront the earl and the marquess."

The head guard pressed his lips together and nodded. "Quite a woman, your Miss Milton," he noted.

That she was. And with her at Spen's side, he was almost prepared to believe they could pull this off.

Chapter Eighteen

CORDELIA HAD TO give Miss Faversham credit. She was not one to bear a grudge. Indeed, once they were safely in the suite of rooms assigned to them, she made a very handsome apology. She explained, "I have been with Lady Daphne since she was eight years old, and I suppose I am just not accustomed to independent young ladies. I promise I can be trusted, Miss Milton. Though I suppose I would say that even if I weren't."

"You are worried about her," Cordelia surmised. "Gracie, John, and Fielder will look after her, I promise."

"I console myself she has a happy nature," Miss Faversham said. "She no doubt will be pleased to see me when we are reunited, but I do not expect her to think of me while we are apart." She sighed. "Although I suppose the earl will dismiss me when this is over. And what will become of my poor lady, I do not know, though it cannot be worse than the earl intended for her."

"We must see if we can find a way to keep Lady Daphne with us," Cordelia mused. "And you, too, Miss Faversham."

"If you can manage that," said Miss Faversham, "you will be a miracle worker."

Cordelia was pleased to have cleared the air. She had enough to think about. When she went into Spen's arms, it was as if she had drawn a cork on her bottled-up memories and they had all gushed out. She'd managed to set them to one side in order to speak to Spen, but now they clamored for her attention, especially the ones of her in bed with Spen.

Fortunately, Miss Faversham was not inclined to talk, and Cordelia daydreamed her way through her meal. After they had eaten, Miss Faversham assembled the ingredients she needed to bleach Cordelia's hair. Ashes, lye soap, and urine. Cordelia wrinkled her nose. "It is disgusting, I know," Miss Faversham said, "but it works."

As she worked the paste into Cordelia's hair, she explained she had once worked as an apothecary's assistant. "He was a cousin of mine, and used to give me lodgings in exchange for my assistance whenever I was between positions. *Is* a cousin of mine, still, of course, but it has been a decade since I last required his protection. Still, I remember many of his recipes. This one was popular with actresses and such persons, but also with ladies who thought their marriageable daughters might be more successful if their hair was lighter."

The paste had to sit for a period to work. Miss Faversham wrapped a towel around Cordelia's head so she could enjoy a cup of tea while they waited and went out into the hall to order a bath and several spare buckets of water. Cordelia was looking forward to being rinsed. Her scalp felt itchy and raw. She hoped it would settle down once all the paste was washed off.

It took a number of rinses. Miss Faversham had her sit on a cushion on the floor with her head tipped back over the bath. She scooped jug after jug of water from the bath to run through Cordelia's hair, massaging it to remove as much paste as possible, then followed up with one bucket of clean water after another until at last, she declared the task done.

"It will look still lighter when it is dry," she said. "I believe it will be close enough, Miss Milton."

Cordelia was just pleased her scalp no longer felt as if it was burning. "Once my hair is dry, Miss Faversham, I wish to visit my betrothed again," she said. "We might not have a lot of time before the two fathers return."

※

Spen had spent the hours since Cordelia's last visit going through her uncle's reports. "The marquess has done me a favor in one way," he told Cordelia. "Three months ago, I would not have understood the mess both of these men are in. Failed investments here, dropping rural incomes there. I haven't told you, have I, that the marquess has sent me back to school?" He explained about the retired solicitor. "Perhaps the marquess should be put through Mr. Morris's exercises. Even without the commentaries, I can see we are on the road to ruin if we don't invest back into the land and the properties and stop chasing risky investments."

"Not ruined yet," Cordelia cautioned. "The marquess is still rich beyond the dreams of most people. He could sell some of the treasures of art and jewelry your family has collected across generations. Though I understand he will alarm the people who hold his mortgages and vowels if he starts doing that."

"He will not do it," Spen insisted. "He has an image as the perfect peer. Rich, powerful, never making a mistake, always in charge. He can't let people know about this." He grinned. "We might be able to use that, my love."

"We will need a long stick if we are going to poke the bear," Cordelia warned.

"If I'm reading this right," Spen said, "Lord Yarverton has taken out loans in order to buy up my father's debts. That seems a bit stupid to me."

"He has been very secretive about it," Cordelia conceded. "He has been careful to keep each of his loans manageable, and with different people. He will only be in trouble if his creditors call in all his loans at once. And he stands to make a great deal from the properties and concessions your father has promised in the marriage agreement."

Spen proved that he had been a good pupil. "So, his two risks are that someone will find out and buy up his debt, as he did to the marquess. And that the marriage doesn't go through."

With a satisfied grin, Cordelia told him, "Uncle is working on the first. The second is our job."

"Which brings us to the marriage agreement," Spen said.

Cordelia was inclined to think the marriage agreement was irrelevant. "You won't be marrying Lady Daphne," she pointed out.

"True. But they don't know that. Cordelia, I was thinking that maybe I could negotiate a couple of agreements of my own." His grin was decidedly wicked. "That's what business is about, isn't it? The marquess had something the earl wanted, and the earl had something the marquess wanted. But they both want something from me, and they both have something—or, rather, someone—I want."

Cordelia stared at him in wonder. "You want to renegotiate the agreement?" She realized even as he shook his head. "You want another binding agreement that will stand even after they realize you and Lady Daphne are not married. Spen, that is brilliant!"

Spen looked down, bashfully, a slight smile on his lips. "We need to figure out what I should ask for."

She could see his point. "John, of course, and Lady Daphne. But we need to bury those requests, so they don't know they are important. Will your solicitor tutor help us, do you think? Can he be trusted?"

"I think he is my friend," said Spen. Cordelia could believe it. He had shown a near miraculous ability to convert the marquess's hirelings into his friends.

"I think we have to risk it, my darling," Spen said. "He is due here tomorrow, so we have a bit of work to do, my love, to be ready for him."

Mr. Morris thought it reasonable for Spen to wish to get something for himself out of the marriage his father had arranged. He happily reviewed the two documents Cordelia and Spen had drawn up, with some help from Marsh and Miss Faversham.

They had decided not to take the man fully into their confidence. Marsh and Miss Faversham agreed there was no way to test his loyalty, and they should keep the conspiracy to substitute Cordelia for Lady Daphne to as few people as possible. Just the four of them, in fact, for Marsh had had little trouble convincing his men to work for Spen, instead of the marquess. Only Marsh knew they were actually working for Cordelia.

This meant Cordelia had to be in her Lady Daphne persona except when alone with her other conspirators. Spen thought she was good at it, though he had only a few meetings with the other lady to base his judgment on.

Certainly, Mr. Morris was convinced. Cordelia was present when Spen asked for the solicitor's help. He needed to do all the talking—or, at least, all of the relevant talking, for the fake Lady Daphne prattled and giggled, fiddled with her hair, and interrupted to pat Spen on the cheek and tell him he was kind.

Mr. Morris, in an undertone when "Lady Daphne" seemed to be distracted, asked, "Should you be going ahead, my lord? Her ladyship seems…"

Spen had an answer for that. "I am to be confined until I agree, Morris. And I feel sorry for the poor lady. At least I know I shall care for her as best as I am able." He shrugged. "Who knows whom the earl will choose for her if I continue to refuse."

Mr. Morris had tears in his eyes when he patted 'Lady Daphne's' hand, which she had just put on his arm so she could peer closely into his face. "You are a good man, your lordship. I am proud to be able to help you by making sure you and the little lady are independent of both your father and hers."

After Mr. Morris left with copious notes and a promise to send three fair copies of the two agreements, Spen tried to dismiss the praise as undeserved, but Cordelia did not agree. "You are trying to look after both John—who is at least your blood kin—and Lady Daphne, for whom you have taken responsibility simply because you are a good man. I am proud of you, too, Spen."

That deserved a kiss, but he did not want her to discount her own efforts. "And I of you, my heart," he told her. Spen might not have incurred the obligation to Lady Daphne, but his father certainly had, so how could Spen fail to help her when he had a chance to do so? Cordelia had taken John in for his sake but was helping Lady Daphne for no reason but *her* own goodness.

Though Spen had not been raised as a religious man, he was praying for enough time for Cordelia's people to reach her uncle and for Mr. Milton to organize a license. He had several ideas for managing a private word with the cleric to ask him not to mention the change of marriage license. A man who could be bribed could be turned with a larger bribe. Of course, that could go terribly wrong if the man decided to tell the marquess.

Apparently, God wasn't listening to his plea for a delay. Marsh came just as Spen was about to blow out his candle that night to say that both marquess and earl had returned, and they had brought with them a minister.

So, this was it. They had had the dress rehearsal. Tomorrow would be the main performance.

Chapter Nineteen

MARSH LEFT EARLY the following day to let the solicitor know that they needed the agreements he was preparing, and that Mr. Morris should take them to the manor as soon as they were ready. After that, Spen had only to wait to be summoned, as he had been last time. He spent the morning going over the notes they'd made yesterday, rehearsing what he would need to do and say, and wishing they had one more day. Cordelia was not going to visit. They'd agreed before she had left him yesterday that she would keep to her own suite once the two peers arrived.

Near noon, the message arrived, and the three other guards escorted Spen downstairs to the parlor where he had met Lady Daphne, and where the confrontation with the earl had occurred.

"Lord Spenhurst!" Cordelia, using her Lady Daphne voice, was the first to greet him. "Look, Miss Faversham. It is Lord Spenhurst. Hello, Lord Spenhurst."

"Keep the chit quiet," Lord Yarverton growled, but Spen ignored him, the marquess, and the others in the room to say,

"Good morning, my lady. I trust you are well this morning."

Her reply was a giggle, which was totally in keeping with what Spen knew of the lady she was pretending to be.

"Miss Faversham," Spen said next, taking a small measure of

pleasure in ignoring the two peers. "How are you today?"

She curtseyed. "Well, I thank you, my lord." Cordelia, with a sidelong look at her preceptress, also curtseyed and spoiled the dignity of the moment with another giggle. The earl sighed and cast his eyes up to the ceiling.

Spen then offered an abbreviated bow to the marquess and the earl. "My lords. Did you have a pleasant trip?"

Lord Yarverton made a harrumphing sound and the marquess barked, "Well, boy? Are you ready to do as you are told?"

"I am considering it, my lord," Spen said. "I wish to discuss the agreements." He relished the look of surprise on his father's face and of suspicion on the earl's.

"Your father and I have agreed on the terms of the marriage," growled that gentleman.

Spen bowed again. "I have read the terms to which you agreed, my lord. You and my father exchange benefits. I have no objection to that, though I do have a couple of questions about the details. However, as I have now turned twenty-one, your agreement should be with me, and not my father."

He held up a hand as both gentlemen protested, and they were surprised enough to fall silent and let him continue.

"It can hardly surprise you, my lords, that I want something to my own benefit from this match. With due respect to the bride you have chosen for me, you cannot deny I am making a sacrifice." Calm, firm, and reasonable, just as he had discussed with Cordelia. And it was working.

Before they could reject his proposal, at which point their pride would have them digging in their toes, he opened the package he had brought with him and gave each of them a thin sheaf of papers. "Mr. Morris, the tutor you assigned to me, Father, helped me to draw these up in legal form. One is between you and me, my lord," he bowed to the marquess, "and the other between you and me, Lord Yarverton," he bowed to the earl.

The earl was shaking his head, but the marquess was looking thoughtful.

"Are we going to get married, Lord Spenhurst?" Cordelia interrupted. "I am wearing my best dress."

What was she up to? "It is a very pretty dress, Lady Daphne," he said. Cordelia twirled, caught the earl's eye, and hid behind Spen, giggling. Without thinking about it, he put his hand behind him for her to cling to. The earl sighed and turned away. The marquess narrowed his eyes, watching the interaction.

"Well?" he said. "You are ready to marry the chit?"

"You are ready to sign my agreement?" Spen fired back.

The marquess lifted the papers and glanced at them. "It depends on what you are asking for, boy. After all," he waved a casual hand at one of the men who had come with him, "Mr. Parkins there is ready to perform the ceremony whether you agree or not."

"Yet my agreement will remove one of the grounds for annulment," Spen pointed out.

"True," said the marquess. "Very well, Spenhurst. I shall read your document."

He took it over to the desk by the window and sat down without further ado. The earl continued to frown, then sighed suddenly and sat down in the nearest chair to turn his frown towards the written pages.

"Miss Faversham," Spen said, "Perhaps you and Lady Daphne could arrange refreshments for…" he held out a hand towards the minister. "Parkins? Was it not?"

Parkins grasped his hand with one that trembled. Up close, Spen could see the bloodshot eyes and reddened nose of a man who overindulged in alcohol. "Yes, my lord. It is very kind of you, my lord."

The two peers did not look up from their reading. Cordelia and Miss Faversham had been right. Since they entered the room, neither of them had looked directly at the lady they thought to be Lady Daphne, which meant the conspirators had easily passed the first hazard.

Did the marquess ever look at John? Spen couldn't remember, but he was confident his father would have no problem with that part of the agreement in front of him.

He might quibble over the financial arrangements—an estate of Spen's own and enough money invested in the funds to give him five hundred pounds a year income, paid quarterly. Enough income for Spen to support his family and the other dependents he was determined to acquire if the marquess stopped his current allowance, which Spen fully expected. Yes, and the man would probably change his will to leave to other people everything not entailed to the estate.

Spen didn't care. He would not be dependent on the goodwill of the marquess or Mr. Milton. Better still, the agreement also gave him John as his ward. Spen didn't expect the marquess to care.

In the event, the marquess only asked, "Mr. Morris drafted this for you, you say?"

"I drafted it," Spen replied. With Cordelia's input and help. "Mr. Morris put it into legal language."

The marquess nodded. "It seems fair. I will expect you to continue learning about the estates, mind. Mr. Morris can continue to tutor you, and I shall instruct the stewards of each estate to do likewise. You can arrange to visit each of them in turn. I take it no prolonged wedding trip is necessary?"

"I would be pleased to continue to learn, my lord," Spen replied. If the marquess still wanted him to do so after he discovered the bride substitution. "I shall take my bride with me, of course."

The marquess cast a glance at the earl, and then stood and approached Spen, to whisper. "Not what you wanted, boy, I know. But good breeding, Spenhurst. It was mumps that damaged the poor girl. You need not fear for your sons. And the chit is pretty enough. You'll have no problems bedding her."

Spen swallowed his disgust, and merely said, "Lady Daphne is a sweet child."

"She is," proclaimed Lord Yarverton, who had turned in his

chair to stare at them. "Spenhurst, what are you up to? An estate for you from your father and an estate for my daughter from me? Do you mean to live separately?" His brows furrowed. "But you just said you would take your bride with you to visit your father's estates." He stood, his frown deepening as he shook the papers. "What do you mean by this?"

Spen hadn't expected the question. Perhaps he should find a diplomatic answer, but instead, he spoke from the heart. "My lord, I want security for your daughter. I know how you bought my father's debts to force this marriage. I don't want you or anyone else to have that power again. Not even me. A property and income held in her name, with trustees chosen from the most honorable men in Society. And acknowledgment from you I am her guardian."

The earl's nostrils were flared, and his eyes burned with resentment. "You will be her husband. You will own her."

Spen shrugged. "Then making her my ward will change nothing, but if anything were to happen to both you and me, the trust will already be in place to protect her."

The earl turned away for a moment, and when he turned back, his face was blank of all emotion. "I will choose the trustees," he said.

A negotiation. Good. "We will choose the trustees together," Spen proposed. "Each of us will have the right of veto, but we will stick with it until we can agree on three names."

The earl inclined his head gravely and let out a breath Spen hadn't noticed he was holding. "Acceptable." He sat again and picked up a pen. "I wish to add a clause to the agreement."

It was Spen's turn to frown. "Saying what, my lord?"

"You will promise not to set her aside or place her in confinement in your own home or in an asylum. She is simple, not mad."

That was a surprise. Spen could see no benefit to Yarverton of such an agreement. But it would help to protect Lady Daphne. Spen had no objection.

"I have no intention of setting her aside or confining her, Lord Yarverton," Spen told him. After all, he couldn't set her aside if he didn't take her in the first place. As to confinement, he was seeking guardianship to protect her from her father's threat. He wasn't himself a threat. "I agree to your clause."

The earl looked surprised. "Very well then."

Spen hoped he was right to do so. Was there a trap for him in the earl's change of mind? Or was the man truly concerned for his daughter? "Mr. Morris is here, my lord. I shall send for him to make the amendment."

He didn't wait for an answer, but opened the door and asked a footman to fetch Mr. Morris.

Mr. Morris, when he was told of the change, agreed it was fair, but pointed out Lord Spenhurst might, at some point in the future, wish to live apart from Lady Daphne. "I suggest, my lord, that Lady Daphne should be permitted, in that eventuality, to occupy the estate you settle on her, or another estate approved by her trustees, with suitable attendants and servants, also approved by the trustees."

Yarverton insisted that Spen agree not to live apart from Lady Daphne until after their first son was born. Mr. Morris wrote that into the agreement with Spen's goodwill, phrasing it that Lord Spenhurst agreed not to live apart from his wife. Spen, who had no intention of ever parting from Cordelia, was happy to agree.

The agreements had been the second hazard. A little more difficult, Spen reflected as each peer signed where indicated. There was food for thought in the unexpected challenges, but thinking was for later.

When they had signed the two agreements, Mr. Morris gave them the marriage agreement, saying he produced a new cover and signature page, as Spen had turned twenty-one since the two lords had attached their signatures.

"It will need Lord Spenhurst's signature, too, my lords, and it will look better—if the agreement is ever challenged—for the signatures to all have the same dates."

When it was Spen's turn, he signed the agreement with each of the fathers and initialed Lord Yarverton's proposed extra clause. He hesitated when Mr. Morris put the marriage agreement in front of him, with only the space for the three signatures showing. Mr. Morris gave him an encouraging nod. Did he trust the man, or did he open the document and check nothing had been added?

Did it matter? He had no intention of allowing the marriage to stand. He signed.

Now for the greatest hazard of all. Mr. Morris went to fetch the bride and the minister. Spen had no idea whether Cordelia and Miss Faversham had managed to bribe the minister—or, he supposed, to outdo whatever bribe the marquess had already offered.

In the next few minutes, he would be wed to either Cordelia or—at least by proxy and temporarily—to Lady Daphne. All he could do was his best.

Chapter Twenty

IF LORD YARVERTON was going to take a close look at her, Cordelia thought, it would be now. Surely any father would watch his daughter as she took her marriage vows? But Lord Yarverton did not even turn his head her way as she came into the room. It remained for Spen to cross from where he stood by the fireplace, offer her an arm, and conduct her back towards the hearth.

A table had been set there with a book on it. The marriage register, she assumed. Now, as everything she had hoped for was within her reach, it was hard to maintain the facade of Lady Daphne. She looked up into Spen's eyes, and he gazed warmly down into hers.

"Well, man?" barked the marquess, "Make a start."

The marquess and the earl were looking their way. That would never do. Cordelia giggled and was delighted when the two peers turned away.

"Witnesses, please," the minister said. Miss Faversham moved up beside Cordelia and Marsh beside Spen. The other three guards also moved forward, partially blocking the view of the marquess and the earl, who thankfully didn't comment.

The minister began the words of the marriage service. In the other parlor, he had stumbled over words and lost track of his thoughts as they presented their case for his support and tried to persuade him to their side. With a familiar script to deliver, he spoke smoothly and with feeling.

Cordelia could not help but be moved by the language, while part of her was alert to the actions of the two fathers. They had moved to the window and were holding a low-voiced discussion. Her heart lifted. The conspirators just might get away with this.

Then came the most crucial moment. The minister reached the question on which the whole masquerade depended, speaking their names—their true names—in a low voice.

Spen's whole face lit with joy when the man said "...take Cordelia Elizabeth Milton to be your lawful..." His 'I do' was so fervent Cordelia was afraid their adversaries would call a halt to the proceedings to find out why he was so happy about the wedding he had fought for months.

But they were still absorbed in their own conversation, and it was time for the minister to say her name again, "Do you, Cordelia Elizabeth Milton, take Paul James..." Like Spen, she could barely wait for him to finish the sentence. They had done it!

Well. Not quite. A few more exchanges. And now the two men left the window to watch, beaming with satisfaction, as Spen placed his ring on her finger. No names now. They were wed, with witnesses, and just had to keep her identity secret for a short time more. Just until they were out of reach. Marsh had pointed out that the best way for two such arrogant puppet masters to remove an inconvenient bride was to kill her. Cordelia would not put it past them.

"My lords, Miss Faversham, gentlemen, I present to you Lord and Lady Spenhurst," said the minister.

They turned to face the room. Miss Faversham embraced Cordelia, which was as well, for she was in danger of forgetting her part. She and Spen were married! But they were not yet through the woods.

"Who is Lady Spenhurst?" she asked, in Lady Daphne's child-like trill.

"You are Lady Spenhurst, sweet child," Miss Faversham assured her, and though it was part of the drama they were playing for the two peers, it was also the truth, and she could feel the thrill of it filling up her chest and shortening her breath.

To hide the emotion, she giggled, casting down her eyes, which would surely betray her, for they were glowing.

But perhaps she needn't have bothered. Lord Deerhaven and Lord Yarverton had barely looked at her. "The chit needs to make her mark in the book," Lord Deerhaven was reminding the minister.

Spen had been accepting the congratulations of his guard, but now returned to her side. "Come, Lady Spenhurst," he said. "We need to sign the register."

He escorted her to the table. Whoever had prepared the papers for Uncle Joshua had done a good job. If she hadn't known the page she was signing as Lady Daphne was a fake, inserted in the register so it could be removed and burnt without leaving any evidence, she would not have realized. There were even several records higher up the page for verisimilitude. She, Spen, and the witnesses would sign the true page as soon as they could do so without the peers watching.

Her new husband, of course, had no idea, but he followed her lead. His trust filled her heart to overflowing. March and Miss Faversham signed as witnesses. It was nearly done!

And Marsh proved to be right again. The marquess and the earl moved up beside them to check the record was correct. "Very good," said the earl. "I shall want a copy."

"One for me, as well," the marquess agreed.

Let them have one, Cordelia thought. *And much good may it do them.*

"Time for a drink, I think," said Lord Deerhaven after that. "Coming, Spenhurst?"

"Go ahead, my lord," Spen answered. "I will see to the comfort of my countess, first. This has been an exciting day for her. I have asked for tea and cake to be sent to her rooms."

"Oh," Cordelia said with a giggle. "I like cakes." The lords turned away to avoid looking at her. She might have discovered a formula for turning invisible.

The minister and Mr. Morris assured the two lords they would be along as soon as they had collected the paperwork, and in moments, it was safe to sign the real register, with Marsh taking charge of the false page to destroy it.

Once again, Spen followed her lead. "My uncle arrived at the village in time, with a license in our names," she told her new husband. "He sent Fielder with it, and also some money to bribe the minister. He is waiting over the border in Pool, and we are to go to him there as soon as it is safe. John is with him, and so is Lady Daphne." She smiled at Mr. Morris. "And Mr. Morris has been an absolute dear. When Miss Faversham and I told him what was going on, he jumped at the chance to help us."

Spen's heart leapt. "We did it!" he said and pulled her to him for a triumphant and celebratory kiss.

ONCE HE JOINED his father and Lord Yarverton, Spen was hard put to hide his jubilation. They had won! Of course, they were not out of the woods yet, as the cautious Marsh pointed out while escorting Spen to the parlor after they had taken Cordelia and Miss Faversham to Lady Daphne's suite.

Spen kept that advice in mind as he accepted a glass of brandy from the marquess.

"You'll bed the girl tonight, of course," Lord Yarverton said, as Spen took his first sip, and Spen nearly spattered it out again. The earl glared at him. "I want the marriage consummated before I leave here, and I want a grandchild on the way as soon as possible," he insisted. "I might not have been able to have a son, but by God, I will have a grandson!"

Spen managed to hold on to his temper sufficiently to say,

"Will blood on the sheets be sufficient, or do you require witnesses in the room?"

"I don't appreciate your tone, boy," the earl growled. "I have paid out a great deal of money to buy a marquess's heir for my daughter, and I expect value in return."

"You trust the bitch you have playing herd on your daughter, don't you?" the marquess asked.

"Faversham? She has been with Daphne since the girl was a child," the earl replied. "Yes, I can trust her. Treats the girl like her only chick. Which I suppose is true." He smiled at his own joke.

"Very well," said Spen. "Miss Faversham can speak to Lady Spenhurst in the morning and confirm I have carried out my side of the bargain."

"We've been talking, Spenhurst," his father said. "Once we have the reassurance we both need, we'll be off to make the arrangements for your estates and your income. I have it in mind to give you the Herefordshire estate. Easy access to London from that one. And Yarverton here is thinking of this estate for his daughter. What do you say?"

Spen bowed. Having looked at Milton's records, he knew that his father had mortgaged the Herefordshire estate without Spen's knowledge, and the one Yarverton proposed had shown falling incomes for the last decade. "I would like to see the financial records, my lords. And the estates would need to be free of encumbrances, of course." He took another sip of his brandy while the pair of them did their best to look innocent.

"The agreement you signed had no such conditions," Lord Yarverton argued, and the marquess nodded.

"Mr. Morris, will the courts consider that a property with a mortgage meets the terms of the agreement?" he asked.

"The terms say 'free and clear possession', Lord Spenhurst," said the excellent solicitor. He shrugged. "The income of the estate in question was not a condition of the agreement, however."

The marquess glared, but the earl puffed out his chest. "There, Spenhurst. You see? I will make this property over to my daughter."

"I was hoping for the Oxfordshire property," Spen commented. It was half the size of the one offered, and the income was lower, but Lady Daphne had lived there all her life except for the few months of her unsuccessful Season, and the last few weeks here in Shropshire. "My lady has an affection for the place."

"A piddling property," Lord Yarverton scoffed, and then a look of cunning crossed his face. "But if you would prefer it, boy, it can be arranged."

"I believe my wife would prefer it," Spen assured him.

The earl looked surprised and almost approving. "It is good of you to consider her feelings, Spenhurst," he said, some of that surprise leaking into his voice. Spen forbore to say *somebody needed to*, since it seemed to him nobody apart from Miss Faversham ever had bothered to care a whit for Lady Daphne or her feelings.

"I thought she and I could stay here for a few days while I make the arrangements for the tour of my father's estates," Spen said, next. He looked at his father. "Sir, may I keep Marsh and the others to be our outriders on the journey? My wife is accustomed to them, and Marsh is very good with her."

The marquess half closed his eyes over his brandy as he considered. "I will take their pay out of your first quarter income under the new arrangement," he proposed. "They will be your servants and your responsibility."

"If the allowance is paid in advance of the quarter," Spen responded.

"Half in advance and half in arrears," said his father.

"Accepted," Spen replied.

"I'll let my own men go in the morning," the earl decided. "You can keep on as many of the extra servants as you wish to see to your comfort, Spenhurst. My wedding present to you."

The marquess, not to be outdone, offered Spen the carriage

and its driver and grooms that had brought him to Thorn Abbey. "You can take me back to London, Yarverton, can you not?"

It was time for Spen to return to his new wife. He thanked the reverend gentleman, who had been sitting quietly in the corner with the brandy decanter. He was into his third glass. Spen wondered if he could be trusted not to spill the entire plot, but when Spen spoke to him, he stood and swayed. "Best be on my way," he said. "Delighted to be of service, Lord Splendid, er Spender, er..."

Mr. Morris took his arm to steady him. "I shall see him safely to the inn in Marton, my lords. Also, I shall prepare that list of estates to visit, Lord Spenhurst, and bring it to you when it is done so we might consult over a map."

"My thanks, Mr. Morris." Spen could not have hoped for a better advocate.

He bowed to the peers. His father nodded vaguely in return, but Yarverton grabbed his arm. "Spenhurst, you will be kind to her, will you not? My wife thought the world of her. Made me promise I'd not give her to anyone who would not treat her kindly. If only..." He shuddered. "Mumps. Terrible thing. Went right through the whole house. Lady Yarverton and my son died. Daphne and I survived, but poor Daphne... I need a grandson, Spenhurst. I know she was not fit to go on the market. Vultures and wolves. It was like staking the poor child out. You were the only gentleman who was ever civil to her. You understand?"

"Not really, my lord," Spen told him. "You must know it was cruel to subject her to Society."

Yarverton shrugged. "I *need* a grandson. If my son had lived... But he died, and my wife died, and my clever, beautiful daughter might as well have died, for her mind was damaged. She looks just like her mother, you know. But that dreadful giggle. I've tried to beat it out of her, but she can't seem to help it, poor girl." He shuddered. "I can't bear to look at her—but you will be kind, will you not?"

Spenhurst had not expected to feel any sympathy for the

man. Yarverton was still a brutal villain, whose obsession could have destroyed the daughter he thought he loved. But at least he'd made a considerable effort to purchase her a husband who would not hurt her.

"I will, my lord," he said, bowing with more feeling this time. Then, at last, he was able to return to Cordelia.

They wanted him to consummate his marriage? In that one thing, he was eager to oblige them.

Chapter Twenty-One

BOTH PEERS WERE gone by mid-morning, grumbling about the distance to London, and how much they had neglected because of Spen's recalcitrance. Miss Faversham reported she had managed to use the truth to satisfy their demand for information. "I can confirm, my lords, the bride is no longer a virgin."

The earl took with him the guards from around the house. In their absence, Fielder arrived from the village with letters for Spen from his brother, for Cordelia from her uncle, and for Miss Faversham from Lady Daphne.

Spen sent to the stables to have the carriage brought around, but then dismissed the driver and grooms. "My wife and I are going out for the afternoon," he told them. "One of Marsh's men will drive, and all four of them will come with as grooms and guards, so you may have the afternoon off."

He did not want any risk their reunion with those waiting in Pool would be reported back to Lord Deerhaven and Lord Yarverton.

※※※

UNCLE JOSH HAD taken an entire floor for his party in the Welsh town of Pool. John was delighted to see Cordelia and Spen, and Lady Daphne ran into Miss Faversham's arms.

Uncle Josh greeted Cordelia with a scowl. "Well, Miss? What do ye have to say for yersel'? Running off like that and deceiving your poor aunt."

"I had to do it, Uncle Josh," Cordelia replied. "Spen needed me, and our baby deserves a father."

Her uncle turned the glower on her husband. "Lord Spenhurst. So ye've married my niece, have ye?"

"I have, sir, and I am grateful," Spen said. "For your niece, for your help, and for your trust. I know I have not deserved it, but I promise you, on my honor, she and our children will never know want, and will always be my first priority."

"Good," Uncle Josh proclaimed. "Then ye won't object to signing the marriage agreement I had drawn up."

Cordelia slipped her hand into Spen's. "We will read it first, Uncle Josh," she insisted, and one corner of her uncle's mouth twitched in a smile. "That's my girl," he told Spen.

"She has an excellent head on her shoulders," Spen confided, and Uncle Josh's smile grew.

"Trained her meself," he boasted.

"Let's get that done first," Cordelia suggested, "and then we can talk about our plans."

She didn't expect it to take long. She and her uncle had gone through his proposed marriage agreement before she went to her first Society engagement with Aunt Eliza. She knew the size of the dowry to be paid to her husband, the money to be set in trust for each child, and even a sum in trust for the potential eventuality the marriage became untenable.

She also knew she was her uncle's main heir and would one day—she hoped far into the future—be a very wealthy woman.

Added to that, the agreement also included the unusual provision of leaving her own personal business interests in her hands rather than allowing it to become her husband's property. She did not know whether the clause was enforceable, given the agreement was being signed after marriage and therefore after they became legally Spen's possessions, which by law occurred the moment he put his ring on her finger unless the parties had agreed in writing beforehand.

When Uncle Josh took her and Spen into a smaller parlor, she read the document anyway, and partway through, looked up in shock. "Uncle! No dowry until I am twenty-five? Nearly seven years?"

Spen, who was reading another copy of the same document, commented, "I have no objection." He took Cordelia's hand. "Sweetheart, your uncle wants to know I have married you for yourself, and not for your money. He wants to see what I'm made of I suppose. I cannot blame him, and I do not care. I can look after my own family."

Cordelia didn't agree. "It is not fair. None of what has happened has been your fault. You didn't ask your father to incarcerate you and attack me. You didn't ask me to climb the tower and seduce you. In fact, you told me not to. And you certainly didn't ask me to abscond from Ramsgate and cross England to marry you."

Spen kissed her hand. "I'm glad you did. I cannot imagine life without you at my side."

"Ye will not be destitute," Uncle Josh grumbled. "I will give ye a job with one of my enterprises, lad. Ye'll be paid enough to keep a comfortable home for my niece and her children."

Cordelia opened her mouth to tell him they did not need his help, but Spen spoke first.

"Thank you, sir," he said. "It will be good to have a job to fall back on if my own plans fail. However, I have arranged an agreement with my father that gives me an estate, with its income, plus a further five hundred pounds per year. I am familiar with the estate and know it is self-supporting and produces a small income. In future, it will provide even more. As to a job, I will be apprenticing to the stewards of my father's estates, each one in turn, and learning my own trade, so I can take over when my father dies and do a better job of being a marquess."

Uncle Josh nodded thoughtfully. "Good lad. Good lad. Yes, with an estate, even one that only supports itself, plus a small income, ye'll do well enough. And the dowry will come to ye in time. Ye can use it to patch up some of the mess yer father has made. Mark this, though, Lord Spenhurst. Ye too, Cordelia. If I have reason to believe ye cannot be trusted with money, I'll leave the rest of what I have in trust for thy children. I'm not seeing what your grandmother, your father, and I slaved for frittered away. Ye hear me?"

Spen must have anticipated Cordelia's reaction, for he squeezed her hand again before she could return a sharp answer. "We will make you proud, sir," he said. "I hope I can soon prove I can be trusted, if just to set your mind and your heart at rest. I know Cordelia is the most precious person in the world to you."

It was true. Cordelia deflated with a sigh. Uncle Josh loved her, and if he was being pompous and overprotective at the moment, it was because of that love.

"If my husband does not object, Uncle Josh," she said, "then I do not." Still, she needed to mention a fact her uncle had left out—deliberately, she was certain. "Spen, I haven't shown you the financial statements from Milton Embroidery."

"No need, my love," he told her. "That business is yours." He tapped the agreement he was in the process of signing. "And 'all assets and incomes appertaining thereto'." He shrugged. "It is only what we agreed between ourselves, after all."

That day in the tower. The day their child was conceived. Cordelia realized her hand had crept to her belly and removed it, blushing slightly. "I have been putting the income back into my expansion plans, but this year, for the first time, I have been building savings. I have not yet taken an income from the business, but I can afford to do so."

He looked as if he was about to object, but she was determined to make her contribution to their comfort. "I know you will permit me to spend my own funds on my own comfort, should I want more servants, or furniture or gowns, or the like."

Spen gave a bark of laughter. "Well played, my love. Game, set, and match. Am I to act the pompous husband and deny you your pleasures for the sake of my pride?" He lifted the hand he still held and kissed it. "You shall do as you please with your own money, and if it adds to my comfort, too, I shall be very proud of my clever wife."

Cordelia hoped she had not bruised that pride, but Uncle Josh seemed pleased and Spen had changed the subject, so she put the matter to one side to discuss with her husband in private.

Once they returned to the rest of the company, she and Spen took it in turns to tell the story of their great deception, and Spen explained to John he was now John's legal guardian. "Cordelia and I would be pleased if you make your home with us," he said, "but I need to wait for the papers that give me ownership of the estate in Herefordshire."

Over tea and cake, they talked about the provisions of Spen's agreements with the marquess and with Lady Daphne's father, and about the proposed trip around the marquess's estates to, as Spen had already indicated to Uncle Josh, 'learn the trade of marquessing'.

Sooner or later, the two peers would realize they had been tricked. "I'd prefer to defer that revelation," Spen said. "They have had a lifetime of bending the world to their shape and I can't predict their reaction. At the very least, I want to wait until they've carried out their side of the agreements they made with me."

"Best to put it off as long as ye can," her uncle agreed. "I've a few plans of my own to hobble them, but a month or two more will help to weave the net tighter."

"You'll be careful?" Cordelia was anxious about Uncle taking on men who could rouse the entire peerage against them.

"Don't ye worry, love, yer uncle was not born yesterday," he assured her. "I learnt in the cradle that cornered rats bite."

She had to be satisfied with that since he refused to discuss his plans. "Least said, soonest mended."

John would return to the school Uncle Josh had chosen for him and would continue using the name, John Milton. As for their other ward, "I'll escort Lady Daphne and Miss Faversham to Ramsgate, if it suits ye, Miss Faversham," Uncle Josh decided. "I'll need to talk to my sister in any case. Reassure her about Cordelia."

"We will write to you there and in London," Spen told Uncle Josh, "and Mr. Morris's London servants will always have our direction."

Chapter Twenty-Two

Before autumn ended, the young married couple managed to travel to an estate in Lancashire, to Rosewood Towers in Cumberland, and to another estate in Peebleshire in Scotland. After that, they headed back across the border to the North Riding of Yorkshire, to a small estate in Durham, and to Cottlesworth Lodge in Leicestershire, where they intended to spend Christmas.

Cordelia was delighted that their long journey was nearly over. Her rapidly expanding waistline had made long periods in the carriage more and more uncomfortable. Their route had taken them farther away from Spen's father and Lord Yarverton, whose principal estates were in the south and who would probably spend autumn and winter, as they usually did, at those estates or at house parties in the home counties. They seldom traveled out of easy reach of the House of Lords and the Court.

According to Uncle Josh's reports, the two peers continued their usual activities, whatever that meant. Uncle Josh was not forthcoming about his own progress towards checkmating the two men.

So far, no one had questioned Cordelia's identity. In truth, they had made little effort to maintain the deception that she was Lady Daphne. Cordelia's maid had managed to purchase a white-blonde wig in Liverpool for Cordelia to wear while her bleached hair grew. Spen always addressed her as "Lady Spenhurst", or "my lady", or "my love", when in company.

But Cordelia did not continue using Lady Daphne's mannerisms, nor did she act as if her understanding was limited. After all, one day she would be the marchioness in charge of all these estates. The people who served in the Deerhaven houses would be under her direction. The welfare of the wives and families of the tenants who worked the land on the estates would be hers to cherish.

It was unlikely, they agreed, that the stewards would describe Lady Spenhurst in their reports to the marquess. "I get the impression his lordship does not read his stewards' reports, in any case," Spen said. The stewards were all touchingly delighted to have the heir taking an interest in their work. Spen had worked his usual magic with the coachman and grooms assigned to their carriage, charming them and then promising them continued employment.

The gentry they met were likewise not a danger to them. Neither Spen's father nor his supposed father-in-law would be in correspondence with mere gentlefolk. The few members of titled families they came across were more of a risk. Spen did not know who might be an intimate of the marquess. Or of the earl, for that matter.

The closer they came to the home counties, the greater the possibility of some chance introduction blowing their masquerade out of the water. Go south they would, though. Cordelia was due to give birth in mid-April, and she wanted her Aunt Eliza to be with her at the time. As far as Deerhaven was concerned, it didn't matter. Aylesbury Court, the estate in Herefordshire, had been transferred and the allowance established.

The Earl of Yarverton had been dragging his feet on the decision about trustees, and refused to transfer the ownership papers for Lady Daphne's estate until that was done. However, he and Spen had finally come up with a list of three names they both agreed on, and two of them had already consented.

Once the third had been settled, they would make their marriage known to the Duchess of Haverford, Lady Corven, and a few of the other great ladies of society, and the subterfuge would be over.

They wanted to announce the news themselves, rather than have it leak out before they had done so. The servants, and particularly the neighbors of the Herefordshire estate, might well pass information to the marquess.

Even a letter of congratulation on his new grandchild would be enough to send the man storming up from London. After all, Spen had not been housed with Lady Daphne until September, and the wedding had been in October.

In Leicestershire, on their way to Cottlesworth Lodge, they had an encounter with a particularly nasty group of Society gentlemen. They had been strolling in an inn garden, while their horses were changed, holding a laughing conversation about baby names.

"No," Cordelia was saying over her shoulder as they stepped through the archway that led from the garden to the stable yard. "Rumpelstiltskin Wolfsbane Forsythe does not have a ring to it."

"You are right," Spen responded, mournfully. "The little mite should have at least four baptismal names. What about..." He stopped, looking over her head, his eyes widening and cooling even as all humor drained from his features. "Don't look around," he whispered. "Quick. Back into the garden."

It was too late. The voice spoke from right behind her. "Spenhurst, it *is* you! And your lovely bride, I assume. The Earl of Yarverton's daughter, isn't it? We were all surprised, because we thought the little Milton bitch had her hooks into you." The man burst out laughing as if the observation was hilariously funny.

Cordelia ducked her head, hoping the obnoxious oaf would not look directly at her. Spen put a protective arm around her shoulders. "We are nearly at the end of a long trip, Stocke, and my wife is tired. So, if you will please step aside, we shall be on our way."

From under her bonnet brim, Cordelia saw several sets of boots. Of course, the rest of them would be there, too. Viscount Stocke, heir to the Earl of Selby, was seldom seen without his equally unpleasant friends. Entitled arrogant do-nothings with wandering hands, low minds, and a contempt for those who lacked their aristocratic bloodlines.

In her Season, Cordelia had quickly learned to stay away from them. They had tormented her anyway, calling her names and mocking her plebian origins, her connection with trade, her looks, and anything else that came into their fertile and nasty imaginations.

Spen shepherded her past them, using his free arm to move Stocke and then one of the others out of his way. All might have been well if the horrid men had not been in the mood to poke some more, demanding an invitation to Cottlesworth, and continuing to make rude remarks about poor Lady Daphne.

Spen must have sensed that Cordelia was about to burst with rage, for he asked Marsh to see her to the carriage, and the rest of the encounter happened out of her sight but within her hearing. Marsh's verdict had been, "The lad has bottom, my lady. And he's turning out to be none too bad in a fight."

Spen was bruised, his clothing scuffed and torn, but he glowed with satisfaction. Men were peculiar.

Cordelia was concerned that Viscount Stocke had recognized her, since she had looked back when the fight began. However, no gossip had leaked out, so her pretense of being Lady Daphne must have fooled the men. The next encounter, later that day, was even more worrying.

When they arrived at Colchester Grange, it was very clear the marquess was already in residence. The main rooms of the house glowed with light as they pulled up to the house, and a crested carriage was being wheeled into the carriage house.

Chapter Twenty-Three

December 1802

"THE MARQUESS IS here," Spen told Cordelia.

She lifted tired eyes to him. "What should we do?" She never complained, but Spen could tell she found travel uncomfortable, and if they left here, they would have to travel at least to the next inn, which they would more than likely find full of people they knew from London.

"We will have to brazen it out," Spen decided. "We both need to rest. Besides, if we left now, he would suspect something and might come after us. Or send someone after us, more likely."

"I daresay the servants have told him we are expected," Cordelia commented.

And so, it proved to be. When they entered the house, it was to be told the marquess had arrived, ordered a bath, and would be down for dinner.

Spen grimaced. "A bath for my countess and one for myself," he commanded the butler. To Mr. Morris, he said, "Please let the marquess know we will be having dinner in our rooms, but I will join him for an after-dinner drink."

Cordelia kept her head down, saying nothing. Would she agree? If not, he was sure she would let him know once they were in the privacy of their own rooms. She approved, however. "The less time I spend with your father, the better, Spen. And if I am not present, he will not expect to see Miss Faversham."

An hour and a half later, he went down to the dining room on his own, to find Mr. Morris cradling a brandy while his father, already well into his cups, was describing the day's hunt in excruciating detail.

He offered Spen a jovial greeting and poured him a glass of brandy. "Married life suiting you, boy? Morris, here, says you are doing well. Learning the estates. Meeting the tenants. Reading the books. All that bull dust. Hope you've been plowing that wife of yours, too. Yarverton and I expect an heir as soon as possible."

"Sir," said Spen, "I am happy to discuss any matter you wish, except Lady Spenhurst. Someone insulted my wife this afternoon, and I punched them. I cannot punch my own father, but I will leave the room, my lord."

For a moment, the marquess looked stunned, as if Spen had spoken gibberish. Then he burst out laughing. He clapped Spen on the back, and then Mr. Morris for good measure. "Very pretty speech, Spenhurst. But she's just a female, when all is said and done. Not worth two men falling out over."

"Speaking of females, my lord," Spen said, keen to change the subject, "How is Lady Deerhaven? And how is my sister?"

The marquess made a dismissive gesture. "Lady Deerhaven is well enough. At least she has proved she can carry a brat to term. I'll get a son on her next. Might have done so already, and if not, not for lack of trying." His laughter invited Spen and Mr. Morris to admire his prowess. Spen took a sip of his brandy, and Mr. Morris looked as if he was trying to shrink out of sight.

"And the little girl? Does she thrive?" Spen asked. "What have you named her?"

The marquess shrugged. "Well enough, they tell me. Lady Deerhaven named her. 'Hi' something. The blue flower." He shrugged again. "I didn't see the point. What use is a daughter?"

Spen was trying to think of a blue flower that began 'Hi'.

"Hyacinth?" Mr. Morris asked.

The marquess was pouring himself another brandy. He gave another wave of his hand. "Lady Hyacinth. Silly name." He gulped a mouthful of the drink, and then another, staring into space as if thinking deeply. Perhaps he was considering his infant daughter. Or perhaps he wasn't thinking at all.

Spen was wondering if he could go to bed as soon as he had finished this glass of brandy. His father was no pleasanter to be with, but at least he wasn't being abusive or critical.

Perhaps Morris felt the pressure of the silence for he broke it with the comment, "In some cultures, children are not formally named until they are ready to take on adult responsibilities. Their mothers give them cradle names."

The snorting noise from the marquess may have been a comment on that alien practice, but Spen rather thought his father had forgotten his audience and was lost in his own thoughts. Indeed, from the looks of the man, it might have been a snore rather than a snort. He appeared to have gone to sleep.

"I imagine little girls are given flower names in many cultures," Spen said to the solicitor. "Yes, my lord," Morris agreed. "I understand that to be the case." Another glance at the marquess confirmed that he had been lulled by a conversation that bored him and was indeed asleep.

Spen and Morris chatted for a few minutes about what they hoped to achieve on this visit. Colchester Lodge had been a productive estate at one time but had been neglected, all but for the breeding kennels started by Spen's great uncle, which had continued ever since. "The current kennel master is the great-grandson of the first kennel master," Morris told Spen. "The family are passionate about what they do—hunting dogs, mainly. Pointers, lurchers, terriers—the estate breeds the lot. A Colchester dog is certain to fetch a good price, and your sires are very much in demand to cover the dams of other breeders."

"And the cattle?" Spen asked.

"Less so. I believe the tenants have been asking for some

changes, but they have not been forthcoming. I understand from the steward the farmer who is in charge of Colchester's herd of longhorn cattle is one of those who has requested an audience tomorrow, my lord."

"We have a few wanting to speak to me," Spen acknowledged.

"Yes, my lord. Will you wish to cancel them, sir?"

"Not at all," Spen retorted. *Why should he wish to canc*—Ah! Of course. "I daresay my father will be hunting as many days as the hunt is out, and when he is not hunting, he will almost certainly be visiting friends or sleeping. I suggest we carry on with our plans, Morris. I suggest we see the steward first, the kennel master next, and the cattleman in the afternoon. If the day is fine enough, I could take my lady with me in whatever suitable light conveyance they have. She would enjoy an outing in a gig or the like, rather than being shut up in a carriage."

"A good idea, Lord Spenhurst. Our lady likes to be active, now she is no longer out of sorts in the morning."

"Out of sorts in the morning?" The marquess cracked open one eye. "Is the girl increasing, Spenhurst?"

"My wife is with child, my lord," Spen confirmed.

The other eye flew open. "Splendid! Well done, Spenhurst. I knew if I sent you off on a tour of the properties with a warm body and no other such easy option, you'd not disappoint me. Well done. Oh, to be a young man again. Ready to bed anything, am I right?" He slapped his hand down on the table and stood to shout for a footman. "Champagne! We need a bottle of champagne!"

"Not for me, sir," Spen insisted. "I was planning to make an early night of it."

"Nonsense, my boy," the marquess replied. "This is wonderful news. The future of the marquisate." His mood darkened. "Not another damned daughter, if you please, Spenhurst. I need sons."

"Sir, if people were able to choose, you would have had a

dozen sons," Spen pointed out, hoping his and Cordelia's child might be a daughter, just to spite his father. He would like to have a son sooner or later, of course, if he was so blessed. But his father didn't deserve to know he'd been successful in bypassing John as an heir.

The butler arrived, cradling a bottle of champagne, and made a performance out of opening it. "A Ruinart, my lords, sir," he said, bowing to the table. "A fine wine for a celebration."

"Well, pour it, man," the marquess said, impatiently. "Here. Hand it to me."

He grabbed the bottle and tipped a stream of faintly pink wine into the nearest glass, and then the other two. It foamed up over the top and bubbles streamed down the sides of the glasses, as the butler stood impassive except for eyes closed against the sacrilege of his master's rough and impatient pouring.

The marquess handed a glass to Spen and another to Morris and lifted his own high. "To my grandson," he pronounced, and tipped the glass up, swallowing the contents in a gulp.

Spen sipped more judiciously. He was not a great fan of champagne, but this was pleasant. The foam had receded, leaving the glass about a third full. His father was already pouring himself another and pushed the bottle over the table. "Help yourself, Spenhurst. You, too, Morris. This is a happy day."

He tipped his glass again and frowned. "It had better be a boy," he grumbled.

CORDELIA, TIRED AS she was, could not sleep until Spen came up to bed. She was sitting by the fire with a lap desk open on a little table in front of her when Spen came into the room. "I hate this," he said to her. "I'm proud to have you as my wife, Cordelia. I want to shout it from the rooftops. I want to go downstairs and tell my father this minute, except he is probably too drunk to remember in the morning."

Cordelia put the lap desk to one side and walked into his arms. "We agreed to wait until Lady Daphne's estate is hers without question, Spen," she reminded him.

He sighed. "Yes, and until we are safely on our own land. I don't want to risk you or the little one. It just annoys me we have to avoid people we know and pretend something that isn't true, just to protect ourselves from two selfish old men. When the one downstairs insults you and poor Lady Daphne, I just hate having to stand there and not rub his face in the fact we have beaten them."

"We haven't quite beaten them yet," his wife reminded him. "We could go from here to visit Regina Paddimore at Chelmsford and then straight to Aylesbury Court. I know Mr. Morris's plan calls for us to visit two more estates before we meet Aunt Emily there, but we can change it, can we not? And perhaps have some time just the two of us before Uncle Josh and Aunt Emily arrive?"

Spen kissed her. "We can, wife of mine. Of course, we can. I suspect Morris is as tired of traveling as we are and will be happy to stay in one place for a while. I will talk to him in the morning. And I will do my best to be pleasant to my father, or at least not to tell him to…" He caught back what he was going to say, and finished, "At least I'll try not to tell him where he can put his opinions."

As it turned out, Spen did not need to exercise heroic patience. It was raining the next morning, and the marquess decided to give up his planned day of hunting and instead travel on to the house party where he planned to spend Christmas. He sent a message to Spen suggesting Spen could come with him, but not the countess, since the other ladies who had been invited were not respectable. Spen sent down a polite refusal and asked Marsh to let him know when the marquess was ready to leave.

Instead, he came to find them. Cordelia and Spen were in the drawing room with papers spread out over a table by the window. Working side by side had become their morning habit.

They responded to their correspondence—reports from stewards and managers as well as letters from friends and families, sharing snippets of information and discussing problems and strategies.

Marsh announced the marquess with just enough warning for Cordelia to push back from the table and stare vacantly at the ceiling.

"Spenhurst," the earl said. "I came to say goodbye to you and your wife."

Spen bowed. "My lord. We wish you a pleasant journey."

"Young lady, I am going away now," the marquess shouted, speaking slowly as if his volume and speed might help her supposedly limited understanding.

Cordelia leapt to her feet and curtseyed. "Goodbye," she said.

The marquess directed his gaze some two feet over her head. "You have been a very good girl. Very good. Going to have a baby, eh?" He clasped each wrist with the other hand and made rocking motions, and shouted, "A baby?"

Cordelia giggled and patted her abdomen, wondering if he would even see, since he was now staring at the door. "A baby is growing," she agreed. "Spen will look after me. Spen is kind."

"Good," Lord Deerhaven agreed, vaguely. "Well, Spenhurst, that's it, then. Send me a message when the baby is born. I will increase your allowance if it is a boy. What do you say to that?"

"I will be happy if the baby is born safe and well, and even happier if my wife has an easy time of it," Spen said. "If our first one is a daughter, she will be very welcome. We are young and have plenty of time for more."

Cordelia giggled.

The marquess cast her a disgusted glance, shuddered, and set off for the front door. His carriages and servants were waiting outside. "Don't know how you can stand it, Spenhurst," he said over his shoulder. "Doesn't that inane giggle drive you crazy?"

Spen refused to take the bait. "I wish you a pleasant journey, my lord. And the compliments of the Season."

Marsh opened the door for the man and closed it with unnecessary firmness. "Nasty old man," he commented, to the horror of the manservant who lived with his wife in the house. They were butler and housekeeper when Spen or his father were in residence, and caretakers the rest of the time, which was most of the year.

He looked even more aghast when Spen agreed with Marsh. "Horrible," Spen said.

"I think he is pitiful," Cordelia offered. "A sad old man who has alienated his family and is in competition with most of his friends."

Spen put his arm around her and pulled her close to drop a kiss on her forehead. "Lady Spenhurst is kind," he observed.

Chapter Twenty-Four

Ayleswood Court, Herefordshire, early February 1803

AYLESWOOD COURT IN Herefordshire was a pretty Jacobean house extended in the previous century with two wings forming a U shape. The wings stretched back from the original house, so the building was wrapped around a formal garden laid out in terraces, a central fountain, paths, , and beds that slept in the cold, huddled under a blanket of straw.

Cordelia spent days exploring the house, usually in Spen's company. The garden, too, when the weather allowed. It was wonderful to stay in one place and to know it was now her home. At least until the time, hopefully far in the future, when she had to take on the intimidating pile that was Deercroft.

She enjoyed the nights, too. She and Spen had shared a bedroom every night since they were wed, but they had been either traveling or buried in a whirlwind as they tried to meet all the tenants at each stop and every neighbor of note, as well as comparing the estate's records with what they could see before them.

Not that they had been celibate—far from it. But they had gone tired to bed and risen early to a day full of engagements or travel. Either way, the days were full and passed in the company of other people.

Now, at last, they could go up to the same bed night after night. Early, if they wished. At different times during the day, too, which was both a surprise and a joy to Cordelia. Sometimes, Spen even locked the door to the study or the drawing room, and if the servants guessed why, nobody commented.

Spen was very inventive in making sure her broadening girth was not a hindrance to her enjoyment. He also described other ideas for their mutual pleasure that would have to wait until after the baby arrived, and she looked forward to trying them all.

Two weeks after they arrived at Aylesbury Court, they received a letter from Mr. Morris confirming the last person asked to be Lady Daphne's trustee had accepted the role, the trust documents had been signed, and their ward's home and income were now indisputably hers.

"At last," Spen said.

"Daphne will be delighted," Cordelia agreed. "She has enjoyed Ramsgate, Miss Faversham writes, but she often asks when she can go home."

"*I* am delighted," Spen growled. "I can finally announce to the world you are my wife."

He began that very afternoon drafting a letter to his aunt, while Cordelia worked on some embroidery designs that had occurred to her as she studied the wintry landscape.

The following morning, they were at breakfast when Marsh came in. "My lord, my lady, a messenger has come from Mr. Milton. He says it is urgent."

"Something is wrong!" Cordelia exclaimed.

"Bring him in, Marsh," Spen said.

Marsh nodded and left the room. They had arrived to find the butler had inherited an inn, and he and the housekeeper had married and decamped to run their new business. Marsh asked to be appointed acting butler. He was a little unorthodox, but keen to learn, and nobody could be more loyal. Furthermore, the other servants all seemed happy to answer to him. Cordelia thought they would probably confirm him in the appointment when his month's trial was over.

He returned with the messenger. A groom by the size of him, and one who had spent many years running errands in all weathers, by his leathery complexion. "Mr. Milton's messenger, my lord and my lady," Marsh said.

"You have a message for me?" Cordelia asked.

The messenger stepped forward, holding out a package. "For you and the earl, my lady. I was told to put it into your hands, my lord."

Spen's competent hands crumbled the seal and untied the binding even as he said, "Thank you. Marsh, take this man down to the kitchen for a hearty breakfast and to warm by the fire, and then find him a bed." To the messenger, he said, "I don't know if this needs an answer, but if it does, I'll send a groom. Sleep, man."

Before Marsh and the messenger had reached the door, Spen was spreading the contents of the package out on the table before them. Newspapers and gossip sheets. On some of them, Cordelia could see items circled in red crayon.

Spen pushed them to one side. "Letter first?" There was a letter in Uncle Josh's writing, covering several pages, tied by a string through a hole in one corner to a report in a far neater hand.

Cordelia nodded. He undid the string to separate the letter from the report and laid it out on the table. Her uncle's epistolary style didn't sound much like him, the "proper" way to write a letter having, to hear him tell the tale, been beaten into him by the tutor his ambitious mother had employed as soon as she could afford such a luxury.

It was more likely he chose to sound as educated as he truly was in formal correspondence but as a contrast to the way he spoke. Keeping rivals and allies off balance was part of his business strategy.

Whether or not her uncle's story was true, the influence of that schoolroom tyrant had not extended as far as the way her uncle formed his letters, which reflected his expansive personality, being large, round, and sprawling.

"My affectionate greetings to my dear Cordelia and Spenhurst," she read.

This correspondent regrets the need to pass on unpleasant news. The story has spread that the pair of you have been traveling the country together. Some pup of a lord recognized Cordelia at an inn somewhere in Leicestershire.

Since Yarverton and Deerhaven have both talked about Spenhurst's marriage to Lady Daphne, people are assuming you are in an illicit relationship. Opinions are divided about whether Lady Daphne is part of your baggage train or has been parked somewhere in the country.

The speculations are too varied to repeat without making this letter unnecessarily long, but the enclosed newspapers and caricatures will give you some idea of their content.

If the matter of Lady Daphne's inheritance has been settled, as one might hope, this might be an opportune moment for your own announcement. Meanwhile, to avoid the newspaper reporters and other scandalmongers, your doting uncle is joining your dependents in the town about which you know, where, it is to be hoped, they can safely stay until the dust of your revelation has settled.

There is no need for concern about the two lords. They may react impulsively in the heat of the moment, but they will be best served by an assumption of pleasure. Measures are underway to point that out to them. A report is included.

To other news, my dear children…"

Uncle Josh dropped the formal tone and gave them a chatty update about both John and Daphne. Aunt Eliza and Miss Faversham were keeping house for the two young people in a town near London, where John was attending school as a day pupil. The remainder of Uncle's letter was full of things the four residents of the house had said and done on his last visit.

Spenhurst, your brother has a mind for things mechanical, he had written. *I will have a position for him in a few years if he can be dissuaded from this damn fool idea of going for a soldier.*

As for Daphne, Uncle Josh said she had made many friends at

a local charity school for the daughters of fallen officers—men who had died leaving their families in poverty. The school gave board and keep to the girls and taught them skills a gentlewoman might utilize to earn a living.

Both Aunt Eliza and Miss Faversham had volunteered their services as teachers. Aunt Eliza took a weekly class in fine needlework, and Miss Faversham taught a decorum class. Meanwhile, Uncle Josh said, Daphne played with the youngest girls—those who were not yet considered old enough for formal lessons.

It was clear Uncle Josh had taken all three to his heart. As so often happened, Spen echoed her thoughts, a chuckle warming his voice as he said, "I'm not sure we're going to get Daphne or John back, wife of mine. Your uncle has adopted them."

"He will keep them safe," Cordelia said.

Spen sighed. "We had better take a look and see what is being said. I should have hit Stocke harder."

He picked up the first of the caricatures and snarled, "I should have hit him much harder." His glance at Cordelia was somewhat abashed. "My first instinct is to keep these from you, my love. I suppose you will not allow me to protect you from seeing such filth?"

"You suppose correctly," Cordelia said. After all, how bad could it be? The answer was pretty bad, but after all, Cordelia had been attacked before for her low birth and supposed high ambitions, even if not in such crude terms and with such salacious illustrations.

Still, her main emotion was irritation, which ripened to anger as she read some of the articles. Not so much on her own account, but on Spen's. "Truly, dear heart, can they not make up their minds? In one sentence they accuse you of being too weak and stupid to resist my evil wiles, and in the next, you seduced not one, but *two* poor innocents, and have us both in your thrall, becoming the worst rakehell of your generation. Really? Have they never heard of the Duke of Richport?"

Spen gave her a leering grin. "I am only a rakehell with you, light of my life," he assured her. "Remember…" and he whispered in her ear something he'd suggested two nights ago, the memory of which set her flushing.

She did her best to sound dignified when she told him, "I am your wife. Some would say it is your duty to… keep company with me."

His bark of laughter was accompanied by a squeezing hug. "Keeping company? Is that what we are calling it?"

"You are trying to distract me from the dreadful things they are saying about you," she accused him, with narrowed eyes.

"I am trying to distract you from the dreadful things they are saying about *you*," he admitted. "We will circulate the truth, my love—or, at least, the version of the truth we have agreed. Most of this will die down, after that. And if some people continue to believe it, they can do so. We won't care."

Cordelia nodded. She was not as confident their scandal would be forgiven, but she and Spen had gone into this knowing the possible cost of their subterfuge. If the price was the high-sticklers would shun them, she could do without their company and hope a score of years and a lofty title—along with Cordelia's and Spen's wealth, which as of now promised to be considerable thanks to the business senses of them both—would be enough for the mud not to stick to their children.

"Let us finish our letters and send them," she proposed. "It is our turn to give our side of the story."

※

ONCE HE AND Cordelia had finished that chore, Spen sent a groom to Uncle Josh telling him what they had done, and enclosing copies of the letters, which were mostly the truth but contained what Cordelia bluntly called a lie and Spen insisted was honest at its core, for both she and he counted their marriage as starting when they said it did.

They were wed, according to their version, one day in July, while Spen was confined by his father and Cordelia was visiting him. They kept their marriage a secret to protect Cordelia while Spen was still a minor. Then Spen was taken away and put under cruel pressure to marry Lady Daphne.

So, they came up with a strategy that would safeguard both them and the two minors being threatened to force Spen's compliance.

The rest of the story was exactly as it happened, and if they implied a second marriage in Scotland while they were there on the marquess's business, it was close enough to the truth even Cordelia's tender conscience did not suffer more than a slight twinge.

Spen was sure they would receive a compassionate hearing from the Duchess of Haverford. Also, Lady Georgiana Winderfield, the daughter of the Duke of Winshire. He was less certain about Lady Sefton, whose role as a patroness of Almack's gave her opinions considerable weight, but with whom he was not well-acquainted. Lady Corven he thought, would be furious about their deception, but would rally behind them for the sake of the Deerhaven reputation, as would his own father once he had calmed down.

What Yarverton would do when he heard was a mystery. As it turned out, one that was destined to be solved, for Yarverton arrived two days later, still believing the false reports put about by Viscount Stocke.

Chapter Twenty-Five

CORDELIA WAS RELAXING in the morning room. Spen had received a note from a neighbor about a breach in a fence through which his sheep had invaded a field of mangelwurzels. He had ridden out in the light rain to mend metaphorical fences with the neighbor while his shepherds mended the physical barrier.

He had said hesitantly Cordelia could go with him, and they would take the carriage, because of the rain. But it seemed silly to prepare the carriage for a journey of less than a mile. "You will manage faster on your own, my love, going across the fields on a horse rather than along the lanes," she had told him. "Besides, I am feeling much too lazy. I shall recline like a lady of leisure and read the book you brought me for Twelfth Night."

Her nights were increasingly unsettled, as her child seemed to think night the perfect time for vigorous activity. Also, her back and hips ached, and she needed to rise several times in the night to use the chamber pot. She felt swollen and ungainly, and she still had two more months to go! At least Spen gave her no reason to doubt he still found her desirable.

Although Cordelia had the book open on her knee, she was drowsing rather than reading. She thought of going back to bed, but that would mean getting up, and she really did not want to bother.

The couch on which she reclined was turned to face the window, which looked west across the park to the cattle stud. She had seen Spen and his steward riding away a little over half an hour ago. She didn't expect his return for at least another hour, so when the door behind her opened, she assumed it was Gracie or Marsh bringing her a warm blanket, or yet another cup of tea—if she drank any more this morning, she would be afloat—or some other comfort they felt impelled to press on her.

"I am warm and comfortable," she assured them, without moving enough to see who it was.

She didn't recognize the gravelly voice that said, "Whore," but the hand that buried itself in her hair and yanked her head back, and the sharp cold blade laid to her throat, were enough to stop the scream that rose in her throat.

"Make a noise, and you die, harlot," the man growled. "What have you done with my daughter?"

He let go of her hair and moved into her view, the knife shifting only slightly. It was Yarverton! He looked terrible—as if he had aged ten years, and not slept for a week nor changed his clothes for even longer. She stared at him, trying to form the words that would save her. That would save her baby.

Without thinking about it, she covered her belly with her hands. His eyes followed the movement and flared with rage. "You slut!" He shrieked and slapped her.

She was already pressed against the back of the couch, so the blow knocked her sideways, and there she stayed for a moment, mind reeling. Yarverton had leapt to his feet, pacing to and fro, and screeching at her that she had stolen his grandson.

He moved the knife. That was her first thought. It was dangling from one hand as if he had forgotten it. *And someone will have heard his shout,* she realized. She had to keep herself and the baby alive until help arrived.

Should she beg? Should she explain? Should she sit as she was, curled around her precious burden, trying to be invisible? Her pride revolted at the last option but her first movement drew Yarverton's attention, and he took a hasty step towards her, gesturing with the knife to emphasize each word he said. "Do. Not. Move."

Cordelia stilled, her eyes fixed on the knife, her muscles tensing even as she forced her face into an expression of fear. As soon as he came close enough, she must throw herself on that hand, and cling on with all her might, screaming at the top of her voice. He was taller and stronger than her, but he was also much older. And tired. So tired. *Please, God, give me strength. Not for my sake, but for the baby.*

He continued to wave the knife, but he didn't approach close enough for her to risk the attack. Instead, he demanded, "Where is my daughter? Not here. I have been watching the house, and there are only you and your servants. Where has your lover gone? I saw him riding away."

He was facing away from the window, at a slight angle, and out of the corner of her eye she saw a movement there. She made her eyes focus on Yarverton so he would not wonder what was behind him.

Now, Cordelia. Talk to him now. Keep him focused on you. "Lady Daphne is with Miss Faversham in a safe place where she is cared for and happy. I took her place before the wedding, and we sent her away. Spenhurst could not marry her because he was already married to me."

What was happening outside? She could not quite see. Nor could she risk looking. Yarverton was raving and pacing again, but his gaze was still fixed on her. Fortunately, for he had only to turn his head slightly and he would see whatever it was that was happening outside. If there was anything. Perhaps it was all her imagination.

"Lady Daphne is safe," she said again, both to keep Yarverton's attention and in the forlorn hope of calming him down.

He waved a dismissive hand. "But what of my grandson? Deerhaven promised me a grandson, and Spenhurst cheated me out of the child. And an estate. And my daughter." His eyes narrowed, and he stopped, facing her fully. "You lie. Or if you do not, then…" His frown deepened. "You must die so Spenhurst can marry my useless chit," he mused.

The knife came up. Cordelia tensed again, ready to fight for her life. A slight sound behind her had Yarverton looking at the door. Cordelia threw her book at him to distract him, and even as it hit him, the window exploded inwards in a crash of glass and wood, and the door behind Cordelia crashed open.

Suddenly, the room was full. Marsh was grappling with Yarverton, and Spen was shaking off shards of glass before taking Cordelia in his arms.

SPEN HAD NEVER been so frightened in his life as the ten horrendously long minutes after Marsh met him at the stables with the news Yarverton was alone with Cordelia, threatening her with a knife.

The sheep breakout had been all but resolved by the time he got to the breach in the boundary, with the beasts retrieved and moved to another field, and promises made about wall repair. The neighboring landowner had been grumbling about compensation when Spen arrived. Spen agreed and offered to discuss what was fair after dinner if the neighbor and his wife would favor him and his countess by coming to dinner later that night.

By this time, the rain had been strengthening. The neighbor agreed, hastily, and they parted ways for the warmth and comfort of their own homes.

Thank goodness. Two of Marsh's men were away with Spen, but Marsh, Jim, and another two men who claimed to have been sent by Mr. Milton would have subdued Yarverton without Spen, but Cordelia needed the man who loved her, and Spen needed to know he'd had a part in the rescue.

Cordelia had contributed, too. They could have done nothing if Yarverton had remained bent over Cordelia with a knife to her throat, but she must have said something to make him let go, and then she kept him talking until Marsh and Jim had the door open enough to see Spen's signal from the window. In the end, Cordelia gave the signal herself, throwing a book at the man just as he noticed the opening door.

Spen cradled his precious wife in his arms, ignoring the struggle behind him. "You are safe? He didn't hurt you?"

"We are both well," Cordelia reassured him. "Yarverton is crazed, Spen. He kept raving about how you had stolen his grandson."

Yarverton stopped screeching, and Spen turned his head enough to see the man slumped in Marsh's grasp. "He banged his head on the butt of my gun, my lord," Marsh explained.

A familiar voice spoke from the door. "Dee-Dee? Spenhurst? What has happened here? Cordelia, are you hurt?"

Spen helped Cordelia rise so she could see the newcomer but kept his arm around her. "She is unharmed, Mr. Milton, thank goodness."

"Uncle Josh, what are you doing here?" Cordelia asked.

"We are always pleased to see you, sir, of course," Spen added. "And thank you for the men you sent."

"Yer own seem to have managed well enough," Mr. Milton conceded. "Though I'd like to know how they allowed that villain into the same room as my niece."

"A fire in the kitchen," Marsh growled. "By the time we realized it had been set, the earl was inside."

"He has been watching the house," Cordelia offered. "He saw you riding away, Spen. I wonder if he made the hole in the fence as well?"

"It seems he may have. And then when I took two of Marsh's men with me," Spen acknowledged. "He saw his opportunity."

"He must have signaled his accomplice," Marsh mused. "The kitchen boy. He admitted it all when he realized the danger our countess was in. Yarverton had told him it was a joke. That he was a family friend come to give the lady a surprise."

Cordelia shuddered. "I was certainly surprised."

Mr. Milton opened his arms to his niece and Spen reluctantly released her to hug her uncle. He was inordinately comforted that she kept holding his hand.

"You knew he was here, sir?" Spen asked.

The man sighed. "He should not have been. I was having him watched. When those lies about the pair of ye came out, he eluded my watchers, and we have been on the hunt for him ever since. Then, yesterday, we found out he had left London."

"You guessed he would come here," Cordelia said.

"It seemed logical. He had no way of knowing where Lady Daphne was, and he was seen talking to Deerhaven just before he disappeared. I take it, Spenhurst, yer father knew ye were here?"

Spen nodded. He assumed so. After all, he had made no secret of it. "I suppose we can expect a visit from the marquess next, but meanwhile, we should get a doctor and the local magistrate to look at the earl."

"What are they going to do against an earl?" Mr. Milton grumbled. "Yer sort gets away with violence of our sort every day."

"That is shamefully a fact, but he didn't threaten one of your sort with a knife," Spen pointed out. "He threatened *my* countess."

Chapter Twenty-Six

THE LOCAL MAGISTRATE seemed somewhat intimidated by the rank and prominence of the earl but was horrified by the man's actions. "He will need to be held in custody," he agreed. "Perhaps as a guest in my house, on his word of a gentleman, he will not try to escape?"

"Would a gentleman have threatened to kill a woman with child?" Spen asked. "One who is, furthermore, my countess *and* the daughter-in-law of the Marquess of Deerhaven?" Invoking his father's title was a risk, and when the magistrate made it clear he had read the London newspapers, Spen thought it had been a risk too far.

"I understand he might have had some reason to believe the lady was not your wife, my lord." He bowed to Cordelia, flushing a little. "Begging your pardon, ma'am."

"When I convinced the man I was Lord Spenhurst's legal wife," Cordelia told him, "he lifted his knife and said that I must die, so your mitigating argument does not stand, sir."

"I would not accept his given word," Spen said. "And I am the one whose wife is in danger."

The magistrate reluctantly agreed to keep the earl locked up. "In a room in my house, however, as is appropriate for his status."

The doctor approved the earl's removal to the magistrate's house. Apparently, the man had some kind of a heart condition, though he wouldn't discuss it with the doctor. "I do not think the head injury is serious, but the man's pulse is running far too fast, and his ankles are very swollen. Any extra worry or overactivity could kill him."

So, the earl left, under guard, and Spen was pleased. He did not want him in the same house as Cordelia. They still had to decide what to do about him, though. Mr. Milton was in favor of negotiating a banishment. "I think we can convince him to leave England permanently," Mr. Milton argued. "If the case goes to Lords, the scandal might destroy him, but it will also dirty the twain of ye. Besides, it will become political, and justice flies out the window when politics comes in the door."

Spen thought the earl should be treated like anyone else, which Mr. Milton said was morally true, but that Spenhurst should not expect life to behave as he would like. The earl would be treated like an earl, and that was that. "If he has any sense, he will negotiate," Spen's uncle-in-law insisted.

"If he had any sense, he would not have broken in here with a knife," Cordelia pointed out.

In the end, it didn't matter. The earl was sent back to London, to be imprisoned in his own house pending trial. He died a couple of nights later. Mr. Milton, who had returned to London as well, found out his London physician had been expecting it to happen for some time.

Which left the marquess. Mr. Milton told them not to worry. Apparently, the marquess had negotiated. He had had little choice. Mr. Milton now owned ninety-five percent of his debts, including mortgages on his unentailed estates, bank and other loans, and gambling debts. "I will call them in if he harasses ye and my niece," Mr. Milton told Spen. "If he leaves ye alone, I will leave him alone."

Spen frowned. "I will pay you back, sir, once I inherit," he promised. "Every penny. But I hope you will give me time."

"Do not worry yer head, lad," said Mr. Milton. "I've brass enough and then some to spare, and just the one ewe lamb. Ye'll get it all when my time is done."

"My wife will inherit," Spen pointed out.

Mr. Milton chuckled. "We will work something out."

Was the marquess check-mated? Spen was not so certain. Then, on the same day, they heard about the earl's death, they received a letter from Deerhaven's secretary, which said, once the polite phrases were pruned out of it, that the marquess had canceled Spenhurst's allowance and would not acknowledge Spen or his countess in public. In effect, he was going to ignore Spen's existence, though a paragraph right at the end of the letter demanded information when Cordelia gave birth to a boy.

Spen and Cordelia enjoyed more than a month of peace. They met their neighbors, though Cordelia's condition allowed them to avoid formal dinners and other such entertainments. Spen threw himself enthusiastically into planning for the spring planting, and Cordelia brought her managers out from London for a weekend.

Letters from London assured them of the support of the sponsors of Almack, the Duchess of Haverford, and enough of the others to whom they had written to give them confidence their next appearance in Society would not see them shunned.

Even Lady Corven wrote to say she would reluctantly accept the marriage, for the sake of the family.

At the beginning of April, Mr. Milton arrived with Aunt Eliza, John, John's tutor, Lady Daphne, and Miss Faversham. "No stolen moments in the library for the rest of the month," Spen said to Cordelia as he rubbed her aching back in the bath that night.

"It is good of them to come," Cordelia replied, "and I shall be glad of Aunt Eliza and Miss Faversham before the month is out. Besides, my love, I am too ungainly for stolen moments in the library, but everyone will understand my need for a daytime nap!"

"I like your thinking," Spen agreed. "As a loyal and loving

husband, I shall make myself available to assist in any daytime nap you may require."

A few days later, the new Lord Yarverton arrived without prior notice. He had been a country solicitor somewhere in Yorkshire until the earl died. He had known he was heir to the earl but said he had assumed the man would marry again and displace him.

Once he had met Spen, Cordelia, Lady Daphne, and the rest of the family, he was quite frank about his motivation in calling. "My lawyers insisted Lady Daphne is happy in her current situation and is well-protected by the trust my predecessor set up for her. But I wanted to check for myself. I am her cousin, after all. And you, Lord Spenhurst, are not a relative."

He didn't mention the scandalous rumors, but he had clearly heard them.

Spen wondered if he was after Lady Daphne's inheritance, but the man seemed to be sincere about feeling responsible for her. Cordelia invited him to stay, and after a couple of days and a couple of serious conversations with Spen and Mr. Milton, they parted with mutual respect and the intention of furthering the acquaintance.

In the third week of April, Cordelia brought her baby into the world, supported by the local midwife, Aunt Eliza, Gracie Simpson, and Miss Faversham.

Spen had been relegated to the drawing room with Lady Daphne, Mr. Milton, and John. The normally placid and compliant Lady Eliza had turned into a birth-chamber tyrant. "Now, Spen dear, Cordelia has work to do, and she cannot be worrying about you."

Even the youngest of the maids acted as if she had more to do with the affair than he had himself. He sent her upstairs to enquire after Cordelia, and she came down to tell him all was proceeding as it should. When he commented that it seemed to be taking a long time, she gave him a decidedly superior smirk. "First births tend to take longer, my lord," she deigned to explain, as if at twelve years old, she was an expert on the subject.

She is the eldest daughter in a family of seven, Spen thought, so *perhaps she is*. Certainly, she could not be less knowledgeable than he was.

In the end, it took eleven hours from the moment Cordelia woke in the early morning with the first hard cramps until the moment, late in the afternoon, when Gracie came to fetch him. She refused to answer any questions about the baby. "My lady is well," she said. "She wants you to see for yourself, my lord, and for you to show her uncle and Lord John."

When he arrived in the room, Cordelia glowed with joy. She looked up from the bundle in her arms as he entered, and her smile broadened, before her gaze flicked straight back down to the tiny face turned up to hers. He went straight to them, ignoring everyone else in the room. "We have a daughter, Spen," she told him, not taking her eyes from the tiny creature.

Spen stiffened his suddenly weak knees so he could bend over these two most precious people in the world to drop a kiss on the astonishing lock of dark hair and another on his wife's lips. He felt as if his heart had swollen to twice its size, taking away his breath, but he managed to choke out the words, "I love you, Cordelia."

He stroked a finger down the petal soft cheek of his new daughter. "I love you, Mary Elizabeth." That was the name on which they had agreed. Mary for Cordelia's mother, and Elizabeth for her aunt. The baby turned her face towards his finger, her mouth open and working. He drew his hand away, wondering what she wanted. Her lashes lifted and dark blue eyes stared vaguely in his direction before being veiled again.

"Did I upset her by touching her?" he wondered out loud.

"She was born knowing to turn her head when her cheek is touched," the midwife told him, surprising him, as he had forgotten that he, Cordelia, and the baby did not exist in a world of their own. "At feeding time, my lady will bump her little ladyship on the cheek with her, um…"

"Breast?" Cordelia supplied, her voice warm with amusement.

"Exactly," the midwife agreed, "and the baby will open her mouth for my lady to feed her."

Cordelia did not want a wet nurse but was determined to feed little Mary herself.

"If you will let Lord Spenhurst take Lady Mary down to meet her uncles, my lady," said the midwife, "we shall finish getting you cleaned up."

There followed several minutes of fussing as four women coached Spen in the proper way to hold a newborn baby, which did nothing to make him feel more confident. He was already nervous enough. His last experience with a child so small had been sitting in the nursery when he was seven with John clutched in his arms while a nursemaid hovered on each side.

When he edged his way cautiously down the stairs, she was cradled in both arms, her head supported by one rigid elbow and her bottom cupped by a hand. She was so tiny. Had John been that little? Was there something wrong with her? None of the ladies in the birthing chamber seemed to be concerned.

A footman stepped forward to open the door to the drawing room. Before doing so, he took advantage of the moment to peer at the baby. Spen stopped to lift the shawl away from her face and the man grinned like a loon. "Lady Mary," Spen said.

"Lady Mary," repeated the footman, with reverence. "I won a shilling, my lord."

"Betting on whether the baby was a boy or a girl?" Spen asked.

The footman seemed to realize he'd put his foot in his mouth. "Begging your pardon, my lord. No offense intended. Just a bit of a laugh, like."

"No offense taken," Spen assured him.

"Better get back to work, Albert, or I'll dock that shilling off your wages," growled Marsh, and the footman scurried off. Marsh took his place, smiling down at the baby, all the grimness gone from his face.

"Lady Mary, eh?" he asked. "Congratulations, my lord, on behalf of all the servants. And my lady? Is she well?"

"Splendid," Spen said. "Tired, but splendid. Tell the servants the news, Marsh. And perhaps a glass of wine with their dinner?"

"Very good, my lord. Better take her little ladyship in to meet her uncles. They are climbing the walls, my lord." Marsh opened the door.

<hr />

THE MESSIEST PART of the cleanup was over by the time Spen brought Mary back upstairs. The midwife encouraged Spen to sit beside Cordelia on the bed with his arm around her shoulders and showed her how to hold the baby for feeding. "Some babies have to be taught how to suckle well," she observed, as Mary opened her mouth wide, closed it over Cordelia's nipple, and began to suck vigorously. "Not Lady Mary. I will be in the next room if you need me, Lady Spenhurst. Just let her suck until she goes to sleep and stops."

Lady Eliza nodded. "We will give the three of you some privacy, Cordelia, dear. Come, Miss Faversham, let us go and see what my brother and young John make of our precious girl."

Gracie said nothing, but followed the midwife into what had been intended as the room of the mistress of the house and was now a nursery. Spen and Cordelia preferred to share a room and a bed.

"Are you happy?" Cordelia asked her husband.

"Blissfully so," he said. He watched little Mary with soft eyes and a gentle smile. "And you?"

She repeated his words back to him. "Blissfully so."

Spen bent to gently kiss the baby's downy head.

She shook it slightly, as if to remove an annoyance, but didn't stop sucking. "I cannot believe how tiny she is, but I can tell you she is going to be empress of this house. Marsh and Albert both met her when I went to the drawing room. Almost every other servant in the place was waiting when I came out. They are all besotted. And so are her two uncles."

"It was worth it, wasn't it," Cordelia said. "The agony of the separation, the masquerade, the anxiety."

"Even the beatings," Spen agreed. "Which is not to say they should have happened. If the marquess had been a reasonable man, we would still have married, my love. Sooner or later."

"Later, probably. He was never going to agree to a quick marriage. We would not be here, today, feeding Lady Mary." The baby had fulfilled the midwife's prediction and fallen asleep, her mouth still open, a little milk dribbling from the corner of her lips.

"Do you know, Mary Elizabeth?" Cordelia told her daughter, "You have a very clever father. He is a first-class estate manager and smart about all sorts of animals and crops, and other things, too. You would not be here today, except your Papa knew how to weave me a rope."

Epilogue

London, April, 1807

"WHEN WILL UNCLE John come?" whined Lady Mary.

"Soon, darling," Cordelia told her.

Mary had been banished to the couch next to her mother, after administering a physical reproof to her sister, Lady Gina, for sitting too close. In her defense, the almost-four-year-old had claimed, "Her smell was getting mixed up with my smell."

Her punishment was being banned from the carpet until John arrived, which Cordelia devoutly hoped would be soon, for it had already been more than twenty minutes—an eternity to an active little girl, even one with a new picture book to look at.

Gina was on the floor with the block set she had received as a present on her recent birthday. Spen was on the floor, too, with Lady Vivienne splayed prone along his forearm, tucked against his body, her legs spread on either side of his elbow and her head cradled in one hand. With the other hand, he was stacking blocks for Gina to knock down again.

At two years old, Gina was in heaven, and had completely forgotten the altercation with her bossy older sister. Until the next one. The two were chalk and cheese. Cordelia could only hope they developed a greater appreciation of one another as they grew older.

A stir outside the room heralded the much-longed for arrival, and the book was cast to one side as Mary flung herself from the couch and across the room, to throw herself into her uncle's arms as soon as he came through the door.

John swept her up and sat her on one resplendent shoulder as Gina arrived and demanded, "Up, Unca. Up."

With one girl on his shoulder and the other held under his opposite arm, he galloped them around the drawing room as they giggled, then plopped them both down on the floor. "Now what might I have for my favorite rascals?" he wondered, and in a moment, Mary had a package wrapped in fabric and tied with a ribbon, and Gina had a smaller one.

"You gave Gina a present," Mary pointed out, inclined to be indignant, "but it is not her birthday, it is *my* birthday."

"And what did you get from Uncle John on Gina's birthday, hmm?" Cordelia asked.

Mary's pugnacious chin retreated. "I forgot," she mumbled.

"You two sit with your presents, while I greet Vivi and your parents," John ordered.

He gave Cordelia a kiss on the cheek and another for Vivi, who was still asleep on Spen's arm, though Spen had now joined Cordelia on the couch.

"You look very splendid in your uniform," Cordelia told her brother-in-law.

"I didn't expect the old devil to go through with actually paying for it," John commented. "I thought I was going to have to take you up on the offer of a loan, Spen."

"He does it to annoy me. He knows I have tried to talk you out of going," Spen grumbled.

Cordelia knew there was no point, though she, like her husband, would worry about the dear boy. Young man, she supposed. John had recently turned eighteen, but he had been set on becoming a cavalry officer for as long as she'd known him.

John's smile was full of mischief. "I rather counted on that when I wrote and asked him." He looked up to heaven in an ill-suited assumption of innocence. "I may have mentioned to Aunt Corven that you adamantly refused to help me."

Spen laughed. "You rogue. So, he purchased your commission, paid for your uniform, and what? The rest of your kit? Your horses?"

"Everything except my sword and the horses," John told him. "Spen…"

"Yes, John, I will buy you a couple of horses." Vivi stirred, and Spen began rocking his arm.

"As to the sword," Cordelia said, "would you object to a family sword? I found a selection when we were going through the attics at Ayleswood Court. If one of them would suit you, John, take it."

John looked uncertain for a moment. "A family sword? Should I? I mean…"

"You are my family," Spen told him, firmly. "Still my heir, too."

"Count it as a borrow," Cordelia suggested. "Keep it until you can afford one of your own, then send the family one back."

John refused to be distracted. "I don't want to be your heir, Spen. You know that."

Spen shrugged. "Nothing I can do about it, John. The marquess acknowledged you as his son when you were born, and not he, nor I, nor you, nor anyone else can change the way the succession works."

"Have a son," John begged. "Have a couple of sons. Let me off the hook." His wry grin showed he knew he was being unreasonable. "Sorry. I know that isn't a matter of choice, either."

"We are quite happy with our daughters," Cordelia told him. "In fact, Spen says he would have liked to have been a fly on the wall when his lordship got the news we'd had a third daughter. And Lady Deerhaven has given him two. Our family seems to run to daughters."

"Especially since Daphne has had a boy," John observed, with wicked glee. They had all been surprised when young Lord Yarverton had approached Lady Daphne's trustees asking to be permitted to marry her. Cordelia and Spen knew from Miss Faversham that he was a frequent visitor, but not that the gentle girl had won his heart.

Spen could still not understand it, but the pair were clearly happy—as was Miss Faversham, who was now devoting herself to the next generation of Yarvertons.

"I hope to have a son one day," Spen acknowledged. "Preferably after his lordship has gone, which is petty of me, but true. But you're right, John. Cordelia and I cannot do anything about it, and if all we have is daughters, we will still have been richly blessed."

Spen meant it, every word. Cordelia knew that, and she did agree. But for the sake of both the husband she adored and the brother-in-law she loved, she hoped they would one day be blessed with a son. Perhaps next time.

***

June, 1817

"I REMEMBER WHEN we first did this fourteen years ago," Marsh said to the Marquess of Deerhaven, whom he had served faithfully since the day Lady Deerhaven had hired him and his men away from the previous marquess.

His lordship was pacing. "I've been through it seven times before, and each time is as bad as the first. I don't know how Cordelia does it. I truly don't."

Marsh had been a soldier for twenty years before he came into Deerhaven's service, and was by no means convinced men were the strong ones. Not emotionally and mentally, anyway. He had seen army wives and mistresses who were tougher by far than their rugged husbands, whose resistance to danger, fear, pain, and risk was greater than any of the London fashionable crowd could even imagine.

It was late in the afternoon, and if ever a man needed a drink, it was Marsh's master and friend. He crossed to the decanters. "Brandy?"

"Just a small one." Lord Spenhurst didn't stop pacing. No. Lord Deerhaven. He had been the marquess for ten years, so Marsh should be used to it by now. "It is twins, you know," Deerhaven said, for perhaps the tenth time that day. "The doctor and the midwife both agree."

"Yes, my lord," Marsh commented.

"My brother is hoping at least one of them is a son."

That, Marsh knew. Lord John—*Captain Forsythe*, as he preferred to be called—didn't want to be Spen's heir. Especially at the moment. He was honor-bound not to draw back from a misguided betrothal, but the shark of a female who'd captured him would throw him overboard in a flash if he was supplanted in the line of succession.

"Don't mention sons to Cordelia," Deerhaven commanded. "I keep telling her I don't care, but she worries. And Clare doesn't help." Clare had been Lady Deerhaven before Marsh's own lady. Stepmother to Deerhaven and Forsythe, she had given the previous marquess two daughters. Two delightful sisters, much beloved by both Deerhaven and Forsythe. With her second husband, she had had three sons and had been known to crow about that fact.

The door opened. "My lord?" It was Gracie. "They are asking for you upstairs."

Deerhaven crossed the room in half a dozen fast steps and disappeared out the door.

"Is all well, my love?" Marsh asked.

"It is," Gracie reassured him. Gracie was now Mrs. Marsh but retained her position as Cordelia's maid and Marsh was still the marquess's butler. Their three children shared the schoolroom with the daughters of the house.

Gracie disappeared back upstairs. Marsh thought about pouring himself another drink. Deerhaven wouldn't mind, but Marsh was careful not to presume their friendship. He waited. How long was Deerhaven going to be?

And then the man was there, grinning from ear to ear. "Marsh," he said. "Meet my son. My heir, Mark, Lord Spenhurst," he lifted his right elbow to indicate the wrapped bundle who slept along that arm.

Marsh didn't think Deerhaven's grin could be any wider, but the man managed it as he lifted his left elbow. "And this, my friend, is his brother, Lord Martin."

"Boys!" Marsh said. "Captain Forsythe will be pleased."

THE END

This novel is set fourteen years before the first of the four novels in this series published in 2023. Deerhaven and Cordelia appear in those novels, with their brother John and some of their children. Indeed, the twins are born during the first novel just in time to save John from a horrible marriage. I've loved discovering their story in *Weave Me a Rope*.

John finally finds his happy ending in *Perchance to Dream*, the fourth novel in the series.

AUTHOR'S NOTE

This book was inspired by the story of Rapunzel. Like the other stories in the series *A Twist Upon a Regency Tale*, it is firmly planted in early nineteenth-century England, reverses the roles of hero and heroine, and reinterprets the magical elements of the fairy tale into natural happenings.

The obvious first element to reinterpret was the long hair. Rapunzel's, according to the folk tale, was long enough for the witch, and later the prince, to use as a rope to get into the tower. I gave my hero a room full of old chairs and sofas, stuffed with horsehair, which makes a strong rope in crafty hands.

What else have I kept, but reinterpreted?

Cordelia's temporary blindness and her hunt for her beloved—in some versions of the folk tale, the witch throws the prince into a thornbush, thus putting out his eyes, and he wanders blindly around the world until he stumbles across Rapunzel, whose tears bathe his eyes and cure him.

Cordelia's pregnancy—in the first edition by Grimm, the witch discovers the prince's visits after Rapunzel wonders openly why her clothes no longer fit her.

For the rest, I blame the plot elves.

A couple of legal notes. Yes, it is true that the marquess could not simply cut John out of the succession. The law assumed that any child born within a marriage was the child of the husband unless the father could prove otherwise. That was not simply a matter of denying responsibility, he had to produce evidence that the child could not be his, for example, that he was in another country for the entire period in which conception was possible.

And yes, fathers could and did beat their children bloody. Their wives, too. English law is based on Roman law, which gave the *pater familias*, the father of the family, power of life and death over his household. By the modern era in Great Britain, that power no longer included the right to deliberately kill a wife, offspring, or servant, but:

> "[T]he Lord Chief Justice of England, Sir Matthew Hale (1609–1676) wrote that the common law permitted the physical discipline of wives and that husbands had immunity from prosecution if they raped their wives (*Historia Placitorum Coronae*, Hale, 1736 @ pp 472–474). He also said wives, servants, apprentices, and children could be subject to 'moderate correction' even if such discipline caused death."
> (https://womenshistorynetwork.org/history-law-violence-for-women-children-17th-century-notions-are-inexcusable/0)

The same views were still in vogue one hundred and fifty years later.

The term "moderate correction" was open to interpretation, of course, and various people tried to codify it. The phrase *rule of thumb* comes from one such attempt, which held that a man could beat his wife with a stick no thicker than his thumb.

There seems to have been a general agreement that causing permanent injury went beyond moderate correction. Indeed, in extreme cases, wives could go to the courts and seek legal protection. If they won their case, the court might make an order restraining the husband from immoderate correction.

The mind boggles. What wife would be brave enough or desperate enough to take a case against a husband, knowing that, if it failed, she would be obliged to go home with him and live under his power again? This is the man who has been embarrassed in front of his neighbors but told, in effect, that he still has the right to administer as many beatings as he likes, as long as he uses a thinner stick. One can only imagine how bad things must have been for those who applied to the courts for help. As for wives, even more so for children, in a culture in which beatings were supposed to maintain the harmony of a home—for the head of the household.

To be fair to the time, corporal punishment was the norm. Schoolboys were beaten. Soldiers and sailors were beaten. Whipping and scourging were punishments for criminal behavior. However, from the middle of the nineteenth century, this would change, and the change had already begun in the home.

Already, by the Regency period, it was widely considered unbecoming for a gentleman to hurt someone weaker than himself, particularly someone completely dependent on him for food and board. Which, of course, made life better for those in the households of men who wanted to live up to this standard.

However, since no one wanted to interfere in what was seen as a private matter, abusers could safely see the new idea of marital and child abuse as a social wrong. They had nothing to fear from public censure or the law.

Even in the supposedly enlightened West, it would be a very long time before laws were changed to give protection to those abused by family members. And even now, this type of abuse still exists. Perhaps abusers don't face prosecution and the abused cannot find safety because of lack of police presence. Perhaps because witnesses such as neighbors, teachers, wider family, and even some police officers believe that domestic abuse is a private matter and that they should not interfere. Perhaps because abused women and children are shamed and frightened into hiding the abuse.

Abuse happens to people at all socioeconomic levels, of all education levels, of all professions, of any religion or faith, and to any gender or identification.

But help is available. Those suffering in the hands of abusers can find it. If you or someone you know is suffering from domestic violence, you can reach out for help to one of the following organizations:

https://www.domesticshelters.org/resources/national-global-organizations/international-organizations.

While it's a step in the right direction that our modern world provides more in the way of help for abused people and families, organizations like this will continue to exist until there is no corner of our society in which people are prepared to accept or ignore physical or emotional violence in what should be a haven of love and acceptance, the family.

ABOUT THE AUTHOR

Have you ever wanted something so much you were afraid to even try? That was Jude ten years ago.

For as long as she can remember, she's wanted to be a novelist. She even started dozens of stories, over the years.

But life kept getting in the way. A seriously ill child who required years of therapy; a rising mortgage that led to a full-time job; six children, her own chronic illness... the writing took a back seat.

As the years passed, the fear grew. If she didn't put her stories out there in the market, she wouldn't risk making a fool of herself. She could keep the dream alive if she never put it to the test.

Then her mother died. That great lady had waited her whole life to read a novel of Jude's, and now it would never happen.

So Jude faced her fear and changed it—told everyone she knew she was writing a novel. Now she'd make a fool of herself for certain if she didn't finish.

Her first book came out to excellent reviews in December 2014, and the rest is history. Many books, lots of positive reviews, and a few awards later, she feels foolish for not starting earlier.

Jude write historical fiction with a large helping of romance, a splash of Regency, and a twist of suspense. She then tries to figure out how to slot the story into a genre category. She's mad keen on history, enjoys what happens to people in the crucible of a passionate relationship, and loves to use a good mystery and some real danger as mechanisms to torture her characters.

Dip your toe into her world with one of her lunch-time reads collections or a novella, or dive into a novel. And let her know what you think.

Website and blog:
judeknightauthor.com

Subscribe to newsletter:
judeknightauthor.com/newsletter

Bookshop:
judeknight.selz.com

Facebook:
facebook.com/JudeKnightAuthor

Twitter:
twitter.com/JudeKnightBooks

Pinterest:
nz.pinterest.com/jknight1033

Bookbub:
bookbub.com/profile/jude-knight

Books + Main Bites:
bookandmainbites.com/JudeKnightAuthor

Amazon author page:
amazon.com/Jude-Knight/e/B00RG3SG7I

Goodreads:
goodreads.com/author/show/8603586.Jude_Knight

LinkedIn:
linkedin.com/in/jude-knight-465557166

Milton Keynes UK
Ingram Content Group UK Ltd.
UKHW020639230124
436534UK00016B/520